JUST
EXES

USA TODAY BESTSELLING AUTHOR
CHARITY FERRELL

To Sadie.
You were snuggled at my side, laying by my feet, or next to me on the couch since the beginning of my writing journey.
I miss you every day, and I hope you're getting plenty of treats in doggy heaven.

PROLOGUE

Gage

I JUMP out of my car, the menacing downpour coming at me sideways, and sprint into a home I frequent more than my own.

Her door is unlocked.

No shocker.

She's expecting me.

My shoes squeak against the hardwood floor as I charge down the hall and find her in the bedroom. She's parked on the edge of the bed, her frail body motionless, while a dangerous storm brews in her ice-cold blue eyes.

Eyes pointed in my direction.

"Where is he?" I scream. My voice cracks at her detached facade.

"Gage." Her tone is calm. Controlled. Not what any sane person would have in this situation. "Let me explain."

"What did you do, Missy?" My voice grows louder, angrier, more venom flowing with every sharp, nervous word spit out. "What the fuck did you do?"

"It's all your fault, you know," she fires back. "If you had loved me right, none of this would've happened!"

"You did this out of spite for me?"

I move closer at the sound of sirens in the background.

Determination thrums through me to get to her before they do, and I drop to my knees, prepared to plead if need be.

"Where is he?" I stress, tears biting at my eyes.

Her smile is wicked. "You'll never know." Those four words kill me yet satisfy her as she sings them out.

Seconds later, footsteps grow louder, and the police start filing in.

"Be prepared to rot in a cell for the rest of your life," are the final words I say before they haul her away.

CHAPTER ONE

Lauren

FOUR MONTHS **Later**

"I didn't set my apartment on fire!"

At least, I don't think I did.

My nails press into my palm, an attempt to stop myself from smacking the smirk off my asshole of a landlord's arrogant face.

Ronnie—said asshole—widens his grin. "Tell that to the police."

"The police?" I shriek. "You called the cops?"

"Sure did."

He gestures toward what's left of the burned-down complex I'd called home this morning. Thankfully, the firefighters extinguished the flames and are loading their supplies back into the truck while my neighbors watch. My apartment has been reduced to rubble and ashes, my belongings scorched, and Ronnie the Dick found it necessary to point the blame at me.

He chuckles. "Perfect timing. They've arrived."

His threat doesn't alarm me as much as it should, and I force a smile before swinging around. This will be cake. Flirting has saved me from countless speeding tickets. They'll take one look at me and know I'm not some pyromaniac.

That confidence shatters when I spot the officer stepping out of the police cruiser across the street. My breathing falters, my grin collapsing faster than panties drop after prom, and an ache plummets through my chest.

Am I dreaming?

I smack my cheeks. Squint my eyes. Pinch myself.

There's no questioning it.

It's him.

Years have passed, but his handsome face has been etched into my memory since age six. There will never be a time I won't recognize the sun-kissed, gorgeous man headed in my direction. More scruff covers his strong cheeks than when we were teens, and his chest is broader, his muscles larger.

His almond-shaped carbon-black eyes are pinned my way, attempting to outstare me, as if I'm a target he can't wait to hit. Vindication rides along with his all-business attitude. He remembers our history—how he begged me not to leave him and then told me I was dead to him when I walked away.

No amount of flirting will save me today.

I am so fucking fucked.

My father will kill me when I call for bail money.

I'm frozen in place, watching him grow closer, his partner behind him. My brain tells me to make a run for it, but my legs aren't agreeing. Instead, I use this time to take in this new man.

Everything—from the way he walks to his body—has changed. The navy uniform envelops his solidly built frame, advertising every modification on him. His jet-black hair has grown out from his boyish cut in high school. Hard lines fill his stunning face, and his strong jaw is clenched—a silent admission his life hasn't been a fairy tale since our breakup.

This familiar yet unfamiliar man no longer looks at me with love.

It's hate. Pure, unadulterated hatred.

Gage Perry—*Officer* Gage Perry—towers over my small frame like a high-rise when he reaches me.

"What … what are you doing here?" I stutter out. *Fucking A.*
I can't even form a complete sentence without failing.

Don't let him sense your nervousness.

The expression on his face switches from hateful to winning,
like a guy who hit the lottery. "Oh, little hell-raiser, you didn't
hear the news? I moved home. Disappointed you weren't my
first call?"

Oh, yeah, still hates my ass.

"Why didn't anyone tell me?" It's more of a question to
myself than him.

"Why would they?" His voice is deep, sharp, like daggers
stabbing through my chest. "What I do is none of your business,
is it, Lauren? You made that clear years ago." Our eye contact is
broken when he glances over to Ronnie and points at me. "This
your arsonist?"

Ronnie puffs out his chest. "I believe the fire started in her
apartment."

Gage's attention flashes back to me. "That true?"

I can't stop myself from rolling my eyes. "That doesn't mean
I was in there playing Boy Scout. I have no idea how it
happened." My voice rises as the reality of the trouble I could
be in hits me. *Now entering freak-out mode.* "I wasn't even home!"

"She's been harassing me for weeks to break her lease,"
Ronnie cuts in, nodding with each lying word.

"That means I thought scorching the place was a better
option?" I wave my finger in Ronnie's direction. "In case you
failed to notice, *liar,* my stuff went up in flames, too. It would've
been simpler for me to write a check for a few thousand bucks
than lose all my belongings."

Gage shoots a glance toward his high school best friend/I'm
assuming now partner, Kyle. "I think she's guilty. You?"

Kyle smiles in entertainment and narrows his green eyes at
me. He's the co-chair of my hate club. "I concur with you,
partner."

"I'll take her in for questioning," Gage tells them. "I know from personal experience that she enjoys seeing shit go up in flames." His attention turns back to me, giving me a warning that I'm in for a ride from hell. "She's an expert on obliterating shit."

Ronnie rubs his hands together. "Appreciate it, Officer."

"You've got to be kidding me," I shout when Gage pulls out the stainless steel handcuffs from the back of his belt. "Handcuffs, really?"

His amusement is gone, replaced with the look of a cold and calculated man.

He takes a step closer. "Turn around. I'll read you your rights."

I scoff, "Not a chance in hell."

He looks to Kyle in question. "Should we add failure to cooperate to her charges?"

"Damn you," I hiss, my stomach rolling while I do as I was told. The cuffs are cold when Gage slowly tightens them around my wrists. "I take it, you still hate me."

Shivers run down my spine when the solid wall of his chest brushes against my back, and he leans in to whisper in my ear, his lips sliding along the lobe, "I'll hate you until the day I die." He grips my shoulder, turns me around, and jerks me forward. "Kyle, take the landlord's statement. I'd better split, so we can get this pyro to the station before she does any more damage."

Kyle chuckles while saluting him. "Sure thing."

I throw out every curse word known to man and nearly trip over my own feet while he leads me to his car. "You sure you can handle being alone with such a criminal?"

A harsh laugh leaves his throat. "Oh, I can handle you just fine, sweetheart."

Everyone's attention stays on me during my profanity show. Gage opens the back door with one hand, pushes my head down for me to slide in without bumping it, and slams the door in my face. I scope out my audience, their phones recording my episode, and shift around in a seat that had to have been made from the same material as my childhood Barbie dream car.

"I hate you," I hiss when Gage slides into the driver's side.

He starts the car. "Good. I fucking despise you."

I slump back against the seat. "You seriously don't believe I started that fire, do you?"

"Intentionally, no. Although, knowing your crazy ass, it wouldn't surprise me."

"Then, why am I back here? At least let me ride passenger."

"Nah, it's more enjoyable, watching you throw your tantrum through the rearview mirror."

I fight with the handcuffs. "This is abuse of power! I'll be filing a complaint."

"Don't get me started on *abuse of power,* sweetheart."

I sigh and shut my mouth. An argument is what he wants. There will be no falling victim to his game.

Yeah, that'll really one-up him, Lauren. He won the jackpot in ex revenge today.

Silence takes over the ride, and my back stiffens when I notice we're heading out of town.

"Wait … where are we going?"

"Taking the scenic route."

The fuck?

"Let me out, okay? You can hate me, stick pins in the voodoo doll I'm sure you have of me, toilet-paper my new house when I'm no longer homeless. My mom will flip her shit if you turn me in. I could lose my job!" I slam the cuffs against the seat while he ignores me. "Let me out of here, Gage Perry, or so help me God, you'll regret it. Don't think I won't make it my life's mission to make yours a living hell."

I yelp, and my body slams against the steel cage in front of me when he swerves to the shoulder of the road and brakes to a hard stop.

"You want out?" He kills the engine and steps out of the car.

Seconds later, my door flies open, nearly causing me to fall out of my seat.

"Then, get out."

I scoot my butt against the seat and slowly slide out. I square my shoulders up as soon as my feet hit the pavement and shake away the loose hair from my face, blowing at the strands that aren't cooperating. The handcuffs clink when I spin around and hold my arms up behind me.

"Cuffs need to be taken off," I tell him.

Silence.

I peek over my shoulder at his failure to move. His cold stare is replaced with amusement.

"Not happening, sweetheart." He tips his head toward the street. "Enjoy your day, pyro."

"What?" My voice rises when I scan my surroundings, and he walks back to the car. "It's twenty minutes back to town *in a car*. It'll take at least an hour to get back on foot!"

He pauses, his hand clutching the door handle, and fixes his gaze on me. "I did what was asked of me—to let you out. Enjoy your walk. Maybe it'll give you time to think about your actions."

I shake my arms in a sad attempt to rid myself of the cuffs, like I'm damn Houdini. He slips into the cruiser, and the engine starts.

Screw him.

I won't allow him the pleasure of witnessing me upset. My breakdown will have to wait until he's out of sight. The car stays running in neutral while I straighten my shoulders and walk along the side of the road.

It's no easy feat, walking with your hands clasped behind your back. Pride kicks inside me when I pass the cruiser, and shock fills his face at the realization that I'm not playing his games. His not pulling away confirms his plan wasn't to leave me stranded. It was a ploy to hear me beg.

The passenger window rolls down.

"All right, fuck, I feel bad," he yells. "Get in."

I walk faster and force myself not to look back when he steers onto the street. "Fuck off."

For a brief moment, the thought that he might leave me stranded passes my mind. The old Gage would've never done something so cruel, but this isn't the man I loved in high school. This man is different, someone I recognize yet don't at the same time.

Instead of speeding off, he cruises beside me, the car not going any faster than what I'm walking. Gage might hate me, but he'd never leave me in a possibly dangerous situation. He's been that way for as long as I can remember. It's one of the reasons I fell in love with him.

"Jesus, I forgot how goddamn stubborn you are," he shouts.

"And I forgot how big of an asshole you are. Good thing I dumped your ass."

An ache rocks through my chest in regret as soon as the words leave my mouth. I look over at him, knowing they hit him harder as he goes stiff in his seat, memories and anger flashing across his face as a reminder of how much I hurt him.

It was a low blow.

Gage hadn't done anything wrong when I broke up with him. I didn't leave because I was unhappy. His begging for me to stay broke my heart as much as it did his, but my reason for walking away wasn't for me. Rather, it was for someone else. I ignored his calls for weeks and had my roommate lie when he'd show up at my dorm room to talk to me.

After three weeks of rejection, he left me a voice mail telling me to never contact him again. I listened to it on repeat, hot tears rolling down my swollen cheeks, and the severity of what I'd done clung to my heart with regret.

"Get in the fucking car, Lauren."

I don't stop. "No."

We go back and forth with our argument, and it's not until I notice the bottom of my feet are as black as the soot covering my apartment that I stop. No way in hell can I take more of this walk in my flip-flops *and* make it to the hospital in time for my shift. I also have to find a family member to let me crash with them until I get a new place to live.

"Fine," I groan. "But, before I do, I want to make it clear that I'm doing it only so I don't lose my job."

He doesn't say a word when he pulls over to stop. The door slams behind him, and he circles around the car. His touch is cold when he releases me from the cuffs, and I shake my hands out, a sigh of relief leaving my chest. *I shall never take these babies for granted again.* No conversation is made while I settle into the seat or when he drives back into town.

It's been years since I've seen him. In the past, there were no moments of silence between us. We were loud, rambunctious, lovesick teens who never shut up or got enough of each other.

"Where do I drop you off?" he finally asks.

I peek at him in confusion. "You're not taking me to the station?"

"Fuck no." A hint of a smile plays at his lips. "It'd be too much paperwork, and I hate paperwork."

I perk up in my seat in victory.

"You'd better spit out an address and calm your arrogant ass down before I change my mind," he warns at my response.

"My parents." I raise a brow when he snorts. "What?"

"I'm back in town. You're staying at your parents'. A bit of nostalgia is creeping in."

The same feeling is bursting through me. "I guess so."

I want to punch him in the face.

I want to apologize.

I want him to know I regret what I did and that my heart beats only for him.

But it wouldn't change anything.

No amount of apologizing will reverse the betrayal and pain I caused.

CHAPTER TWO

Gage

I DON'T FIND enjoyment in arresting people.

That changed when it was the woman who smashed my heart with her small fists. It changed when it was the person I'd thought I'd spend the rest of my life with who bailed on me. I grew up loving Lauren Barnes, and so help me God, I'll die loving her.

I'd been careful since arriving back in our hometown, Blue Beech, Iowa, avoiding all the places Kyle said she frequented. In the back of my mind, there was the reality that, eventually, we were bound to cross paths. This town is small, and the gossip is heavy.

Although I couldn't have planned our reunion better myself. It stung, seeing her, touching her, and when I pulled out the handcuffs, I wished I could've been using them for a different reason—preferably in my bed.

She'd ruined the chance of that happening years ago. Lauren made her choice to leave me, and my life has been shit since.

I struggle with myself on what to feel about today's events. Relief clung to me when she told me to drop her off at her parents', not a boyfriend's. No diamond graced her finger. It was the first thing I'd looked for when handcuffing her. I won't lie. I feel some satisfaction in knowing she hasn't found love again either.

I rub away the knot of tension in my neck.

Why do I give a fuck?

She's not why I came home. It was for my dad ... for my fucking sanity ... so I wouldn't charge into the Department of Corrections every time I got drunk and demand Missy pay more for what she did.

My keys hit the kitchen table next to the stack of decade-old *Time* magazines. My father is seated next to them with a newspaper in his hands, and his oxygen tank is at his side.

"She knows I'm back," I say.

He folds up the paper and places it in front of him. "How'd it go?"

"I arrested her."

His sunken chestnut-colored eyes study me before he responds, "Son, I understand you're upset with her, but was that necessary?"

"Absolutely. She set a building on fire."

He rubs his chin. "I think we both know you weren't doing it for the safety of the town."

"Of course I did it for that reason." I cock my head. "I can't say it didn't give me pleasure though."

He sighs. "Forgiveness is a brave thing, son. A man becomes strongest when he bears no malice."

"I don't want your words of wisdom. I'm not ready to bury that hatchet."

———

"JESUS CHRIST, Dad, what the hell are you doing up there?"

My head is tilted back to gain a better view of him on the roof, tinkering with the satellite dish. It looks almost comical when I eye his oxygen tank following behind him while he moves the dish in different angles and directions.

He grunts and catches a deep breath before answering, "Dang satellite dish is actin' up again. I've already missed fifteen minutes of the game."

"And you thought it was a killer idea to climb on the roof with your tank?"

How he managed to pull it off is beyond me.

He shoots me a stony stare—the same one he gives when I stop him from doing physical work that is too hard on his body. "I'm a grown man who's climbed atop rooftops and buildings taller than this. I'm capable of fixing stuff myself."

Accepting his limitations on doing manual labor has been difficult for him. His health is deteriorating, and his chronic obstructive pulmonary disease is progressing. The COPD makes it harder for him to complete his daily tasks.

"You're a *sick* grown man," I correct, hating that I have to remind him and hoping he doesn't see it as an insult. I stalk over to his old, rusted ladder settled on the side of the house and wiggle it, double-checking it's at least halfway steady before I climb up. "Let me help you down, and then I'll take a look at it."

He stomps my way, wheeling his tank behind him, and stumbles in front of me when I make it to the top of the ladder. "I got this. Stop treating me as if I were a child!"

I grit my teeth. "No, you don't *got it*. Now, let me help you down."

He teeters forward at the same time I reach for him. My arms fly out in an attempt to catch him, but it only sends me down with him, taking the ladder with us.

CHAPTER THREE

Lauren

"NURSE BARNES, treatment room three, patient fell off a ladder," Natasha, the nursing director, tells me when I stroll into the ER after my brief dinner break.

The hospital has been short-staffed since I started three years ago, and I work more than I sleep. Not that I mind it, especially now, given that I'm homeless and I need all the overtime hours I can manage.

"How serious?" I ask.

Ladder falls can range from minor to pretty damn ugly. You can walk in to find a patient suffering from a broken arm or one needing facial reconstruction surgery.

Welcome to ER life. You never know what will be thrown at you each shift.

"Nothing too gory," she answers. "I'm guessing only stitches. Guy was helping his dad off a roof. Dad fell and took them both down. Melanie is treating the father." She grins and elbows me in the side, her voice changing into an annoying bubbly tone. "I stuck you with the son in case you're in need of some delicious eye candy ... or a date."

I smack her shoulder. "You know it's frowned upon to date patients." *Not that I ever would, even if it wasn't.*

She winks. "I won't tell if you don't."

"Stitches. Got it." Stitches are easy-peasy.

"Ask him if he wants to grab some drinks with those stitches!" she yells to my back when I turn around.

I shake my head, blowing off her comment, and knock on the exam room door before entering. Work has taken my mind off Gage's being back, and giving people stitches is relaxing to me, like yoga is to some people. I got certified in suturing instead of learning how to meditate.

The voice on the other side yells for me to come in, and I don't hesitate before turning the handle and walking in, my self-proclaimed perfect nurse smile on my face.

My smile falls as I shuffle back. The door slams behind me, and I steady myself against it.

You've got to be kidding me! Is the universe against me this week?

Gage's shoulders stiffen when we make eye contact. I rub my forehead, my eyes catching his, and take a calming breath. A sleeve on his white cotton tee is ripped, and blood, grass, and mud stains decorate the front of it. His hand holds bloody gauze to his cheek, and minor cuts and scrapes are spread along his face and chin.

"For someone who despises my existence, you sure are going to extreme measures to see me again," I comment before taking a deep breath and moving away from the door to grab a pair of latex gloves.

"Funny," he mutters. "Trust me, it was not in my plan to see you today … or ever if I could have it my way." A smirk hits his bloody lip. "I won't say I can complain about the view though. Sexy nurse and patient is my favorite porn. Shall we give it a go?"

I snap on the gloves and force a laugh while moving further into the room, which suddenly feels much smaller. "You know, this is your Karma for what you pulled yesterday. Don't count on any friendly bedside manner." I give him an innocent look. "It's tragic that I can't have fun and stick you with a giant needle or shove something up your ass. Would've made my day."

It looks like he's fighting pain to give me a challenging look. The dude is here for medical attention, and I'm giving him shit. *Not cool.* This is my job, and I have to do it right, no matter our history ... or the fact that I'm terrified what emotions will be drawn out when I touch him.

He winces when I carefully pull his hand away from the gauze and peel the material back. I inhale the masculine scent of him—aftershave mixed with the outdoors. Like every muscle in his body, his scent has matured. His breathing quickens while I inspect the wound.

It's small. Not a deep laceration. Natasha was right about the stitches. It'll be an easy cut to close up.

"Wishing you could stick something up my ass doesn't sound like good bedside manner, Nurse Barnes. Doubt your boss will be happy, hearing you're discriminating against patients. Public service patients to be exact," he comments as I move away to gather my supplies.

"This might hurt," I say when I'm finished and back at his side.

"Shit!" he says through clenched teeth when I start to irrigate his wound. "You could've warned a dude."

"I did."

He flinches, a slight hiss escaping his lips, while I work. I take my time, making sure the wound is meticulously irrigated, and clean the dried blood off the scruff of his cheek.

"I'm discriminating against assholes, by the way," I finally correct, my attention on his cheek. "Not patients."

He snorts. "I'd love to see your boss's face when you use that as your argument. It's not smart to get canned from work when you're homeless."

I shrug. "He won't do anything."

His brow lifts when I pull away and start throwing my trash

away. "You seem too cocky, Nurse Barnes. You sleeping with your boss?"

"Something along those lines. Fucking him. Sleeping with him after." I pat his arm. "Tattle all you want. It'll only make him want to screw me more. I wouldn't be surprised if he drags me to the supply closet and gives it to me there."

His jaw clenches.

Exactly my goal.

So what if it's not true?

"Your dad okay?" I ask.

We're in need of a subject change before he continues his interrogation and catches me in my lie.

He clears his throat before nodding. "He's in the next room. Luckily, we fell in the grass. I took the biggest hit, and even though he seemed fine, I insisted he get checked out."

The sharpness of his voice guts me. My words hit him harder than his physical wound. Our banter dissolves, and he doesn't give me another look while he lies back, and I start dragging out my supplies. A knock on the door causes us both to look at it, and I grin at the sight of Jay walking in looking handsome in his blue scrubs. Jay isn't only a great doctor. He's also great looking.

Hopefully, he doesn't catch on to who this patient is.

"Hi, Gage," Jay says, walking into the room and extending his hand. "I'm Dr. Whitman. I heard you and your father had a fall."

Gage looks at Jay with uncertainty before shaking it, and I wish I could read his mind. "Could've been worse."

Jay snaps on gloves, and I scoot out of his way to give him room to inspect Gage. I bite into my lip at the sight of Gage's jaw clenching when Jay touches his cheek.

"Cut isn't too deep, big guy," Jay says, glancing back at me. "Good job on irrigation, and thank you for having the anesthetic ready. I'll give it to him and let you fix him up."

I nod. "Sounds good."

Jay goes to his tray and grabs the needle. "This might hurt for a second, but it'll feel much better when I'm done, trust me."

Gage grits his teeth but doesn't let out a sound when the small needle hits the opening in his cheek.

Jay hands me the needle to dispose of and pats Gage's shoulder. "Nurse Barnes will do your sutures." He holds his hand up and wiggles his fingers. "She has magic fingers. I'll be sure to check up on you when she's finished and get you set to discharge. If you need anything, don't hesitate to ask Nurse Barnes or me."

Gage nods. "Thanks, Doc."

Jay's attention turns to me while he takes off his gloves and tosses them in the trash. "I'll see you tomorrow night?"

I smile. Jay is officially my favorite person. "Wouldn't miss it. Clayton's, right?"

He nods. "Seven o'clock."

"See you at seven." I run a hand over my mouth in a *zipping* motion. "And my lips are sealed, so no one finds out."

Jay snaps his fingers and points my way. "And that's why you're my favorite woman."

He shoots Gage a final look before leaving the room. Gage's breathing turns heavy when I move back to his side, and his hands are balled into fists. He seems in more pain than he was before we treated him.

"Was that not enough to numb you?" I ask, tilting my head toward the door. "I can ask the doctor to give you another shot or maybe some pain medicine."

"No need to do that," he snaps, not looking at me.

"Okay," I draw out. "Let me know if you change your mind. It's no problem."

The air seems thicker, and his anger over my supposed affair with my boss is stronger. I sigh while grabbing the needle holder and move next to him. He doesn't say anything when I help him lie on his back, and the room is quiet while I start stitching him up.

It's the first time I've treated someone I've been intimate with.

Not to mention, it's Gage.

My Gage.

Well ... used to be my Gage.

I should've walked out and told Natasha I couldn't treat him.

Conflict of interest.

It is a conflict when the patient hates you, right?

I'm almost finished when he finally speaks, "That your husband?"

"Nope," I answer.

"He was wearing a wedding ring."

I look down at him with a gentle smile. "Was he? I've never noticed."

If he could pull away from me, he would.

Disgust covers his features. "Never thought you'd go so low as to sleep with a married man."

I don't answer him as I tie the last suture. Nor do I when I inspect my work or when I clean up my mess and help him up. It doesn't come until I throw my gloves away and grab the door handle.

"I wish you a speedy recovery, Officer."

I shut the door and stalk to the restroom, controlling my tears until I hit the first stall and let them out.

CHAPTER FOUR

Gage

MY NERVES ARE SHOT to hell, and I hold myself back from busting out of this exam room and doing something stupid, like confronting the bastard doctor using Lauren as a side chick.

I tip my head back.

Dude was wearing a wedding ring.

She wasn't.

She's a mistress.

Where the fuck is the girl I fell in love with years ago?

She's gone. That much is clear.

My attention goes to the door at the sound of a knock. As bad as I don't want to, I hope it's Lauren on the other end.

My wish isn't answered.

My nostrils flare when Dr. Whitman walks back into the room.

Fucking douche bag.

Dude looks smart, rich, like he has his life in order, except for the whole cheating thing, and I bite back the urge to demand he get out of my face. Problem is, I'd look like a dumbass.

Lauren is no longer mine. She can do whatever … or whoever … she wants.

That doesn't mean I'll be happy about it, nor will I be happy for her.

He smiles like he isn't fucking the girl who owns my heart. "Nurse Barnes said she stitched you up. You got lucky, having the nurse with the best hands, although I'm surprised at how fast she was with you. She might've broken a record."

"I'm sure she's a busy woman," I grumble. I want to rip this fucker's arm off.

He inspects my stitches and removes his gloves. "That she is. We see a fair number of patients for a smaller hospital. I'll send the discharge nurse in. Hopefully, I'll have you and your father out before the game comes on."

I can't help but laugh. "He tell you he was leaving if you didn't?"

"Sure did."

I stop him when he turns around to leave. "You married, Dr. Whitman?"

He twists his ring with a smile filled with memories. "Yes."

Don't kill him. Don't kill him.

"Nurse Barnes is a lucky woman."

He flinches. "Excuse me?"

"Nurse Barnes is your wife, correct?"

He cocks his head to the side. "Mr. Perry, I'm not sure where you got the idea." His eyes widen when I crack my knuckles. "I'm confused on where you're going with this."

"How would *your wife* feel about you having an affair with a nurse? Treating Lauren as a side piece to get your rocks off while going through some midlife crisis?"

He shakes his head while processing what I said. "Lauren is not my wife, nor is she my side piece. I'm very happily married to my husband, Alec. Alec is one of Lauren's closest friends. The invite was to my husband's surprise birthday dinner. I apologize if any behavior led you to believe there was an inappropriate relationship between us."

I'm rarely lost for words. This is one of those moments.

Fuck. Lauren's lie made me look like an idiot.

Dr. Whitman stares at me for a moment, blinking. "You're *him.*"

I raise a brow.

"You're Gage. Lauren's Gage."

What? Has she talked about me?

"No. I'm just Gage."

"Not from what I've heard." He laughs. "Alcohol makes Lauren talkative."

"Can't argue with that."

Her nickname was Motor Mouth in high school.

"I wish you a speedy recovery, Mr. Perry." He lowers his voice. "If you are the Gage she talks about during our weekly happy hour, don't let her fool you. She still loves you."

My nails bite into my palms. "You don't turn your back on people you love."

He tips his head down. "All right then. The discharge nurse will be here soon with your prescriptions. Don't hesitate if you have any additional questions for me."

"Thanks."

I pull out my phone when he leaves.

Me: Do you have plans tomorrow night?

It beeps with a reply seconds later.

Phoebe: I'm free all night.

Fuck. Lauren had better not bail tomorrow night. Phoebe is a stage-five clinger. I'm risking my privacy for revenge.

Me: Dinner at Clayton's at 7:00?

Phoebe: Pick me up at 6:30. I'll bring an overnight bag.

I stop myself from telling her not to bother. She can't bail on my ass before I succeed in calling Lauren out on her lie.

I go check on my dad after I'm discharged. He's okay. No stitches or broken bones. On the way home, he will be receiving an earful from me about not doing stupid shit.

CHAPTER FIVE

Lauren

I NEED A DRINK.

Multiple drinks. Stat.

Sleep wasn't my friend last night—for an array of reasons. The first being that I was sleeping in my childhood bedroom, the second because of all the thoughts of what I'd done with Gage in said bedroom after he snuck through my window in high school, and the third was worrying about when I'd see him next.

In conclusion, the culprit of my insomnia was Gage Perry.

The hostess weaves through white-clothed tables while leading me, gift bag in tow, to Jay and Alec. Clayton's is an upscale restaurant complete with candlelit dinners, to-die-for shrimp cocktails, and expensive wine lists. The men set their drinks down when they spot me and wrap me into tight hugs before giving me cheek kisses.

Jay pulls my chair out, and I take the seat next to Alec, who's sporting a suit complete with a *Birthday Boy* pin clipped to it, his highlighted hair pulled back into a man bun. Either this wasn't a surprise dinner or Jay spilled the beans. I'm guessing the latter. It isn't easy to keep secrets from his husband.

Jay straightens out his suit before settling back in his chair and throws me a brooding look, motioning my way with his glass of red wine. "You're lucky the hospital was a madhouse yesterday. Otherwise, you would've received quite the interrogation."

"What are you talking about?" I ask, looking around for our waiter.

"Is there a reason you told the man you stitched up yesterday that you were my mistress?"

Oh shit.

Of course Gage questioned Jay about my hinting at having an affair with him.

"What?" Alec cuts in, glancing over at Jay with humor. "You switching teams again? I thought your experimenting days were over?"

I sigh. "He was hitting on me. It was the first thought that came to mind. Sorry."

Alec squeezes my shoulder. "Oh, honey, you can use my husband as an excuse anytime that happens."

"Nuh-uh. Don't you *oh, honey* her," Jay says, causing Alec's attention to flicker between his husband and me. "She's lying." His coffee-colored eyes level on me. "It's him, isn't it? He's back."

I gulp, nodding. "Unfortunately."

"Is it unfortunate?" he counters. "You don't think it could be fate? I watched him with you. I saw the lust, the love. He barely took his eyes off you, and I'm positive he wanted to murder me after you told him we were sleeping together. Why don't you explain why you did what you did, and you two could reconnect? If nothing else, be friends."

"He hates my guts," I answer. "There's nothing I can say or do that will restore what we had."

"Whoa, whoa," Alec draws out, holding his hands up. "I'mma need someone to catch me up. I'm out of the loop here, and you know it's always critical I am in the center of the loop."

I met Alec during our residency at the hospital after

graduating from nursing school. We instantly clicked. Jay was our attending doctor. He and Alec hooked up one night after a holiday party and have been inseparable since. When the news broke that they were dating, Alec was moved to geriatrics, and Jay received two weeks of my silent treatment for taking my hospital bestie from me.

Spending time with them made me trust in love again. They ignore the snide comments and dirty looks and relentlessly love each other. Jay is the sensible one. Alec is the overdramatic. They balance each other out in a world where it's necessary.

"Gage," I breathe out. "He's back in town."

"Gage?" Alec shrieks, causing a few patrons to look at us. "*The* Gage?"

"The one and only."

"Hot damn, sweetie. Things are about to turn complicated for you." He squirms in his chair, and this gossip will mean more to him than the expensive birthday present I bought. "Now, you'd better tell me every detail."

He doesn't get any details until the waitress comes and takes my lemon drop martini order.

———

"ISN'T THIS QUITE THE SURPRISE?"

The sharp, familiar, and masculine voice startles me.

Chills shoot up my back as I jerk around to confront Gage. He's only a few feet away from me in the dimly lit and narrow hallway that leads to the restrooms, yet it seems like he's looming over me.

I don't respond right away. Instead, I give him the silent treatment while roaming my eyes down his six-foot-three frame of gorgeousness. Just because I hate the man doesn't mean he doesn't make my panties wet. Gage is and always will be the most attractive man I've ever seen.

I grew up with him sporting basketball jerseys and athletic

shorts. This dressed-up version might compete with the sight of him in his police uniform. I've been pleasuring myself at night with the memory of how desirable he looked in it. Gage sporting black jeans and a sleek, tight gray button-up will sponsor tonight's self-given orgasm.

"Keep eye-fucking me, babe. It's satisfying, knowing I'm something you can no longer have."

His comment smacks me out of my eye-fucking trance, and I'm positive that this isn't a surprise to him. Gage is back, and it seems he's taken a new hobby of making my life miserable.

"What are you doing here?" I snap.

He smirks while strolling closer into my space. "Enjoying dinner. Word is, this place is the best for wining and dining. According to Yelp, the chance of getting laid after you leave makes it five-star worthy. What are *you* doing here?"

My hands go to my hips in frustration. "Are you following me?"

"Don't flatter yourself, babe. I'm on a date."

This must mean war. He brought a date here, knowing I'd see them.

I stay quiet while taking in calming breaths. His goal was to bring out the jealousy in me. That won't be happening. I'll easily drown out that jealousy with more martinis.

"Funny, you never mentioned coming here when Jay and I talked about it yesterday."

"Jay? You mean, the man you're 'fucking'?" He uses his fingers to form air quotes around the last word. "I noticed him when I walked in. Your man seemed preoccupied with someone else. Unless you're into some harem shit with mid-husbands, I say you're lying. Is that a new trait of yours now, too? You a filthy liar?"

"Uh-uh. I'm not doing this with you tonight." I've only had one drink. A conversation like this calls for more. "Enjoy your date."

I go to walk around him but am stopped when he snags my elbow and pushes my back against the wall, out of the light.

His cool, minty breath hits my lips when he presses into me. "What? You don't like getting called out on your lies? Why'd you want me to think you were sleeping with another man?" His fingers run down my sides, and he stops at the base of my hips, grinning.

I look down, shivering, and let out a light moan.

He squeezes my hips and rocks into me. "Now, answer my question honestly. You fucking anyone? Giving someone else your sweet pussy now since you no longer want my dick?"

I close my eyes, fighting myself not to move into his touch, not to thrust against his body to feel if he's as turned on as I am. The rise and fall of his chest hits mine. His hand inches up, moving along the bottom curve of my breast, and I'm using all my power not to rock against him.

"That's …" I pause to catch my breath, my voice cracking. "That's none of your business."

He torturously teases me, his finger feathering over my nipple, causing it to stand at full attention. "It's a simple question, *Dyson*. Are you fucking someone, or did you say it to make me jealous?"

Dyson.

His old nickname for me.

An inside joke he started my sophomore year as a result of me giving him a massive neck hickey. He blamed it on the vacuum when his mom questioned him.

Hearing him call me that stills my breath as a rush of memories hits me.

I don't push him away even though I should. Instead, I'm aching for his touch while silently begging for more of him as my lips lightly brush against his.

"Would you be jealous?" I ask.

He smirks. "No fucking way, baby."

An embarrassing moan of desperation runs through me when his hand moves, and he pulls away.

His smirk curves into a menacing smile. "You have your fun.

I'll have mine."

I straighten out my dress and work to control my breathing. "Don't you worry, *baby*. I have plenty of fun. Just ask Derrick."

The hell? Why am I lying again?

This is not a common trait of mine, and I have no idea where it's coming from.

"Wow." He takes another step back, bringing him more into the light, and is now looking at me in disgust, his hands in the air, as if he's pushing me away from a distance.

All I see next is his back as he walks away, shaking his head. It takes me a minute to compose myself, and when I walk back to our table, I scan the room for him. Nothing.

Did he leave?

I mindlessly pick at my dinner when it arrives and listen to Alec ramble about the Caribbean cruise they're taking to celebrate their anniversary.

It's not until dessert is dropped off that I spot him. Unlike me, he wasn't lying about having a date. Even though all I see is her bare back and long strawberry-blonde locks, I know it's Phoebe Jedson. The familiarity is a consequence of living in a small town.

I tighten my fingers across the stem of my glass and stare at him until his eyes meet mine.

I hate you, I mouth.

I'm glad, is his reply.

I throw him the dirtiest look I can when he tilts his glass my way.

The remainder of dessert is spent with our never-ending contact. His attention isn't on Phoebe, and I only nod, feeling like a shitty friend while mindlessly hearing Alec's stories from geriatrics. I stop the waitress when she passes and order another drink.

Ten minutes later, I order another as my second dessert.

Drunken Lauren will numb all thoughts of how delicious Gage looks tonight.

———

ALEC GRABS my arm and hooks his through it, keeping me stable from falling in my heels and meeting the ground while we walk out of the restaurant to the valet. "We're driving you home."

My words leave my mouth in a slur as I shake my head. "It's *waaay* out of your way, *aaand* it's your birthday. I'll call a cab, *oookaaay?*"

"Then, we'll wait with you until it arrives," Jay tells me, wrapping his arm around my shoulders.

God, what would I do without them?

"I can take her home."

I cringe, and my back goes straight at the sound of Gage's voice.

"It's on my way."

Jay's attention darts between Gage and me until he finally settles his attention on the jerk from my past. "Whoa, dude, I don't want to know why you're here." His face fills with protectiveness, giving Gage a warning not to mess with me in his and Alec's presence.

Alec steps in. "While we appreciate the offer, I won't allow my best friend to catch a ride with some stranger. I've watched way too many murder mysteries, buddy."

Gage chuckles. "Trust me, we're not strangers."

I lose Jay's hold when he slaps Alec's back and gestures to Gage.

"Oh … boy," Alec draws out. "I thought I wanted to be in the loop, but this loop seems pretty darn serious at the moment." He grabs my shoulders and brings me to him. "Is this the ex?"

"Sure is," I mutter before straightening myself up. "I'm taking a cab home." I stumble while attempting to pull my phone from my clutch.

Gage comes to my side at the same time Alec helps me. "Let

me take her home. I promise I'll take care of her."

I snort. "Last time we went for a ride, I was handcuffed, and you tried to leave me stranded."

"Did I though?" he fires back.

I open my mouth to continue our spat but slam it shut at the sight of Phoebe coming to his side.

"Sorry, my makeup was in need of a serious touch-up," she comments, sliding a compact back into her bag before running her hand over his arm. She stops midway when her eyes land on me. "Lauren … it's, uh … nice to see you."

No, it isn't.

Don't get me wrong. I have no ill will toward Phoebe. We were never close in high school. Still aren't. Gage is a single man, who most likely asked her out. Slut-shaming isn't my game.

Gage ignores Phoebe and keeps his attention on me. "It'll take a cab at least fifteen minutes to make it here and cost you a hundo in fare. As you're someone who's now homeless, I doubt you want to throw your money away like that."

"I'm not homeless," I argue.

"Oh, really? You move back into your charred apartment?"

All eyes are on me, and I suddenly feel like a giant, drunken pain in the ass.

"Fine," I say around a groan. "But I still hate you."

"And the feeling is *still* mutual." A few seconds of silence pass until Gage points to the valet jumping out of an oversized, four-door black truck. "This is me."

Gage opens the passenger door, gesturing for me to slide in, and Jay goes to help me before I stop him.

"Shouldn't your date take the front?" I ask, more dramatic than necessary. "I'm sure you showed her a terrible time."

"Doubt she'll be saying that by the end of the night," Gage answers, winking.

I snarl while opening the back door and practically face-dive into the seat. Alec and Jay tell me good-bye at the same time

Phoebe takes the passenger seat. Gage jumps in and tosses a water bottle back to me. I struggle to twist the lid off and gulp it down when I do.

We're five minutes into the ride when Phoebe clears her throat. "Before this becomes weird, is there something going on between you two? I'm not interested in some weird love-triangle shit."

"There is absolutely nothing going on between us," I blurt out, gaining control of my voice and finishing without any slurs. "You two have your fun. Hell, go ahead and jack him off up there if you want."

But, really, don't.

I'll jump into moving traffic if they even hold hands up there.

Gage snorts and turns on the radio instead of answering her or entertaining me. I collapse onto my back across the expansive rear seat and rest my head, knowing damn well, in the morning, I'll regret both drinking so much and taking this ride.

"I'm guessing you're dropping me off?" Phoebe asks when we make it into town.

"Probably the right thing to do," he answers.

"Thank you for dinner." She turns in her seat to look back at me when Gage parks in her driveway. "Have a good night, Lauren."

Since my thoughts are delayed at the moment, she's already out of the truck by the time I start to reply. Gage, like the stupid fucking gentleman he is, walks her to the door. And me, like the fucking stalker I am, rise up onto my knees to watch their exchange.

They hug.

Eh.

He kisses her cheek.

Gag me.

I wait for him to kiss her lips next, but no action takes place.

Thank God.

He doesn't walk away until she shuts the door behind her.

Meanwhile, I'm snooping around the truck before he comes back. It's clean. No evidence of anything interesting. New tan leather seats, a flat screen in the dash filled with countless music options, and a backseat equipped with enough room to keep my drunk butt comfortable. Although awkward, the ride is cozier than what a cab would've been.

Gage slams the door shut and turns down the radio before reversing out of the drive. "By the way, thanks for running my date off."

Is he serious?

I sit up in the back seat. "Are you kidding me? In case you forgot, *you're* the one who ruined my night off work *and* interrupted my friend's birthday. If you hadn't decided to be Creeper McCreeperson and show up where you knew I'd be, you would've gotten laid, and I wouldn't have had to experience a massive hangover tomorrow." I fold my arms over my chest. "And maybe *I* would've gotten laid."

"By who? The doctor married to your friend … or was there another fake boyfriend I didn't see? Perhaps he was imaginary, like the fictional others you've tried to make me jealous of."

"Screw you," I hiss.

"Been there. Done that. Won't do it again. Now, which homeless shelter would you like me to drop you off at?"

Even though he can't see me, I throw him a glare. "Take me to my parents', please and thank you, or do you plan on dropping me off in the middle of nowhere again for shits and giggles?"

"I'm not dropping you off at your parents' while you're drunk off your ass."

I pull out my phone to text my mom and ask her to keep the door unlocked. "I have nowhere else to go, so sure looks like you are. You know them. They'll file a missing persons report if I don't come home. The people at the restaurant will say I went home with you, and your coworkers will be arresting *you* this time." I smile. "If I were to turn up dead, I'd love nothing more than for you to go prison for it."

He swerves over to the side of the road, causing me to fall back against the seat, and I throw my arms up.

"Oh Jesus Christ, here we go again."

The door flies open. He jumps out and opens the back door. My phone is plucked from my hand before I open the text app. As if it's not a big deal, he hops back into the truck and pulls back onto the road like he doesn't realize what invasion of privacy means.

"Excuse me? Rude much?" I mutter, making a grab for it, but he stops me.

"What was your birthday friend's name again? Your supposed mid-husband?"

"Fuck off," I snarl.

"Interesting name. I wish my parents were that creative." He snaps his fingers. "Alec, right?"

I don't answer.

"I'll take your silence as a, *Yes, Gage, that's it.*" He starts typing on my phone. "All your parents will know about tonight is that you were too tired to drive home and are crashing at their place."

That's what I should've done in the first place. "One problem with that. Where am I supposed to sleep?"

He doesn't say anything.

"Oh no, don't you think about it, Gage."

"You can take the loft above the garage."

"Not fucking happening." A shelter is sounding pretty delightful right about now. "I'm not spending the night with you. I can't take the chance of you smothering me in my sleep."

"How do you know I won't worry about you driving a stake through my heart again?" He glances back at me. "I'll sleep in the main house."

"Why are you treating me so nice? Is this the whole *keep your friends close and your enemies closer* type crap?"

"To be honest, I have no idea."

"You have no idea why you're being nice ... or if I'm your enemy?"

"Both."

Memories knot through my thoughts when he pulls into his drive. The ranch home hasn't changed. My attention goes to the detached garage with the loft above it, which was built when Gage was in middle school. His dad gave him permission to stay in there when he turned sixteen, and it's where we spent most of our time together.

Surprisingly, I don't push him away when he helps me out of the truck, and I don't give him shit while he helps me up the stairs.

Endless questions crackle through my inebriated mind.

Why is he back? Where has he been?

We're strangers now.

I catch the scent of him when we walk in, and I look around when the light flips on. The alcohol has taken its toll on me, and I keep quiet while moving to the couch from my past. Nothing in this room has changed.

Gage moves in front of me when I collapse onto the couch and holds out his hand. "Your legs not functional enough to walk to the bed?"

I swat it away. "Under no circumstances am I sleeping in that bed." It's where I lost my virginity. "I'll sleep here."

He drops his hand and takes a step back. "The couch it is."

A blanket and pillow are tossed to me, and I close my eyes the moment my head hits the pillow. I fake sleep while hearing him move around the loft, and my breathing shudders when I sense his presence next to me.

I tense when he runs a hand over my cheek.

"Why did you hurt me?" he whispers. "Why'd you leave?"

I stay silent and hope he doesn't notice the goose bumps crawling over my skin, and a tear slips down my cheek when he steps away. The light shuts off, and I drift to sleep.

CHAPTER SIX

Gage

IF SHE WAKES UP, she'll kick my ass.

A dim light comes through the blinds. I lean back in the tattered chair that was once my mother's favorite and feel shame as I watch the woman I love and hate sleep.

She's still gorgeous, still my favorite view. Lauren is the only woman I've looked at and not seen through. I've seen her at her worst—drunk, ridiculous, breaking my heart, in tears—and there hasn't been one instance when I didn't think she was breathtakingly beautiful. She consumed me before I hit puberty. Breakup or not, you don't heal from a love that pure, that real, that deep.

The attitude, the smart-ass woman I fell in love with, still shines brightly. She's the same. I'm not. If she knew the torture I'd been through, she'd never look at me the same.

Years ago, I loved the fact that I was the only man to ever touch and kiss her. Sliding inside her was always a high. I no longer have that privilege. And, as much as I want to convince myself she has never been with another man, I know there's no way that could be true. She wanted—*needed*—sex regularly when we were together. My nails sink into the arms of the chair at the thought of it.

My thoughts are broken when she squirms, kicking off the blanket, and I gulp when her smooth, bare legs go on display as her dress piles up around her waist. Her heels are still on, her hair messier than what it was, and the sight of her black lace panties causes my dick to stir.

I lick my lips. *Damn, I should've given her something to change into.*

Not that she would've accepted it.

When I saw her walk across the restaurant in that black number, there was no way I could stay away. The dress was short and showed off her toned legs and plump, perfect ass. I finished my drink before standing and followed her into the hallway, not sure what my plan was when I reached my destination. Pushing her against the wall definitely wasn't it. Neither was my cock growing hard as a rock or bringing her home with me.

She receives one last glance, and I pray it's not the last one I'll have in a while as I pull myself up from the chair. The sky is dark, the full moon shining bright, when I walk to the main house, kicking my feet against the gravel drive.

My dad is in the living room, leaning back comfortably in his recliner, and he looks away from the TV at the sound of the door shutting. "I thought you were going out."

"I did. And, now, I'm home."

He grabs the remote and flips off the TV. "There a reason you're not sleeping in the loft?"

"Thought I'd spend some time here tonight. My childhood bedroom, complete with a Ninja Turtles comforter, is calling my name."

He nods in understanding and what looks like devastation. "She's on your mind, isn't she?" He sighs with sadness in his eyes when he realizes I'm not entertaining the conversation. "You ever think she regrets what she did?"

I gently knock my knuckles against the wall. "Doesn't matter anymore. She did what she did, and my life has been hell since.

Sure, she might be sorry, but I can't give her the same man I was in high school."

———

"CARE TO TELL me what happened with you and your arsonist sweetie?" Kyle asks when I walk into the station. "No police report was filed on your behalf."

After arresting and dropping off Lauren at her parents' the other day, I went back and picked up Kyle. He briefly took some bullshit report from the landlord, fully aware I wasn't going to stick Lauren in jail, and pressed me for details about where my prisoner was. He didn't get shit.

I called in the next day, given I had a mild concussion from my father's roof incident, and yesterday was my night off. He's had a few days to come up with his interrogation, so it's going to be a long shift.

I'm exhausted after last night. This morning, from the kitchen window, I saw an Audi SUV pull into the driveway. Lauren jumped in before I could see the driver. A car that expensive doesn't frequently roll around our small Iowa town.

Is she dating a doctor?

There are so many things I don't know about her anymore, and I hate it.

"She swore she didn't set the apartment on fire."

I pour myself another coffee before we get in the cruiser, me in the driver's side.

"I know you're blinded by your dick and all, but you need to take a step back and reflect on how long you've been in law enforcement. *I didn't do it*, is a criminal's favorite sentence," he replies.

"Not thinking with my dick. I'm thinking with my gut."

"That goes down to your dick."

Kyle has been my best friend since elementary school. We kept in touch for a few years after I moved to Chicago and then eventually lost contact. I didn't want any connection with my life in Blue Beech. All it did was remind me of her.

I came back to town, expecting Kyle to give me the middle finger when I walked into the station looking for a job. Instead, he slapped me on the back and announced I'd be his partner. He hates Lauren just as much as I do, given that he blames her for my fleeing the state.

"She didn't do it. If anyone brings her in for questioning, you tell them I'll do it, you hear me?"

"Aye, aye, Lauren lover. Although Douche-Bag Landlord isn't going to be happy."

"He can fuck off."

He points his coffee at me. "You're in trouble, man."

I raise a brow.

"Lauren Barnes was your weakness then, and there's no doubt she still is."

No fucking shit.

"That's the past."

He nods but doesn't believe me.

"So, what's on the agenda today?" I ask.

"Don't anticipate anything crazy happening. Your menacing ex's apartment going up in flames is the most exciting thing that's happened this month. This place will have nowhere near the crimes and arrests you had in Chicago."

"Less drama is what I need right now."

I moved back to clear my head, be with my father, and not have a station filled with my old coworkers giving me pity stares daily.

"You ready to tell me why you split and transferred?"

"My dad needed me."

"Got that part. Now, you ready to tell me the other reason you came back to a place you swore you'd never step foot into again? If I recall, you said your dad would be moving there when it was time he couldn't take care of himself."

"It would've been wrong for me to drag him out of the home he loves."

"Mmhmm." He grins over at me. "Some of us guys are going to Down Home tonight for some darts and beers. You game?"

I nod. "I could use a drink."

The radio calls in and tells us there's a kid stuck in a tree.

"I told you," Kyle says. "Crazy shit happenin' in this town."

There was a minimum of one shooting each shift in Chicago. I witnessed shit I'll never forget. I lost shit I'd thought I'd never lose.

The scars are there.

And I have scars here.

Two women ruined me.

One I gave my heart to.

The other who punished me for it.

CHAPTER SEVEN

Lauren

I'M STRUCK with a blast of air-conditioning when I climb into the passenger seat of Willow's luxury SUV. My head throbs, and I use my hand to shield my eyes from the sun's reminder of the idiotic choices I made last night.

"Please tell me you have a spare pair of sunglasses." My plea is wrapped around a groan, and a sigh leaves me when she tosses a pair in my lap. "You're my favorite person in the world."

Willow looks from Gage's house and then to me as I slide the glasses on. "Morning, sunshine. And whose home is this?"

The loft was empty when I woke up. The view of Gage's truck in the driveway sent my anxiety into overdrive. I had to get out of there in case he decided to make a visit and have a conversation about last night. Facing him hungover wasn't happening.

Not only was seeing him a problem, but what I felt was, too. I slept better on that old, ratty couch than I had in my own bed. That terrified me.

My phone on the coffee table reminded me that Gage had never given it back last night. When I grabbed it, I found he'd texted both my mom and Alec, letting them know I'd made it to my destination safely.

Willow was my first call, and luckily, she was available to save me.

"A friend's," I answer.

"A friend with a vagina or cock?"

I was well aware questions would be asked by whoever picked me up this morning. Everyone in my family knows my history with Gage and where he lives. Willow was my safest option. Sure, she'd ask if I had a one-night stand, but she wouldn't think it was with him.

Still, a subject change is in order.

"Thank you for the ride."

She shakes her head. "I'll let you evade that question for now since you look like you were ran over. I owe you for all the trips you made for me back and forth from the airport. Plus, your brother practically kicked me out of the house to have some me-slash-girls' time. He and Samuel are having a daddy-son day, and Maven is hanging out with your mom at some bake sale."

Willow and my oldest brother, Dallas, had a one-night stand nearly a year ago. He was having a hard time with moving on with his life after losing his wife to breast cancer. Somehow, Willow broke through his wall one night. Fast-forward a few months, and Willow was trying to hide her pregnancy from him. Her boss and best friend, Stella, is dating my other brother, Hudson, and he overheard Willow spilling the beans to her.

Now, Willow and Dallas live together and take care of Samuel, their new baby, and Dallas's daughter, Maven. Willow was a saving grace to Dallas and our family. She's cool as hell, so I scooped her up as a best friend.

"You're a kick-ass mom," I say.

Let's keep this convo on babies.

Her lips arch into a smile. "I don't know how great I'd be without your brother. He's an amazing father who doesn't mind changing diapers. I hit the baby-daddy jackpot."

Their happiness fills my heart with joy. Our family is tight-knit, and we always look out for one another. If one of us is hurting, we're all hurting.

She glances over at me. Her red hair is pulled into a messy bun, and her sunglasses cover nearly half of her pale and freckled face. "So, I have to ask, did you catch our apartment building on fire?"

"No!" I throw my hands up. "Jesus, how can people even question that?"

"You can't blame a girl for asking. If you did, I'd be one pissed chick. Some of my shit was still in there."

Willow moved into my building after my brother begged her to move from LA to Blue Beech. She refused to stay at his house until they worked their issues out. After moving in with him, she kept her apartment as a storage unit.

"Why are you getting blamed?" she asks. "They catch you with a match in your hand?"

"Ronnie is blaming me for revenge."

"Ronnie?"

"Old Man Willard's grandson. He inherited the building when Willard died a few months back."

"Hold up. Our landlord died?" she chokes out.

"Uh … yes. You didn't know?"

She frowns while shaking her head. "Damn, I feel bad for not going to the funeral."

"Don't. They had it somewhere else. He had no living family in Blue Beech, so his body got shipped to them."

"That doesn't sound morbid or anything. So, why does the grandson want revenge?"

"For turning him down when he asked me out."

"Girlfriend, you need a boyfriend … or at least some dick. Why not take him up on his offer?"

I grimace. "Gross. I'd rather hire someone to give me the business than screw him. Dude is a creep who wears expensive suits, which he tells me the price of every time we run into each other, and polished shoes daily—in *Blue Beech*. Now, I normally don't discriminate against people's fashion choices, given I sport scrubs almost daily, but a man with a big enough complex and ego who has to show off his money is a hard limit for me."

She nods in understanding. "Hurting a man's ego can be a dangerous thing."

That's no lie.

"Tell me about it. So, because I don't want to screw his pretentious, suit-wearing ass, he's trying to make me out to be some pyro." My upper lip tightens as I roll my eyes. "Trust me, I would've made sure I snagged all my cutest shoes had I caught that place on fire. Oh, and my scrubs because those things aren't cheap."

She laughs and, for the rest of the ride, she listens to me name off the endless number of items I need to replace.

"You ready to tell me why your car is here?" she asks when pulling into Clayton's empty parking lot. She parks and presses her hands together in a pleading gesture. "*Puh-leeease* tell me you had a one-night stand."

Now, I know how she felt when I was always nagging her for details about her and my brother. Not fun.

"Nope," I answer. "You ruined the idea of a one-night stand for me after you got knocked up from having one with my brother. Lord knows, my ass does not need to get pregnant."

"Eh, I see your point there." She clicks her tongue against the roof of her mouth before her lips turn into a bright smile. "Will you at least tell me who took you home?"

My hangover headache maximizes as I slump in my seat. "Gage is back in town."

She gives me a blank look. "Am I supposed to know who Gage is?"

Willow and I are so close that I forget I haven't known her my entire life and that she didn't grow up in Blue Beech. In our small town, I'm known as the lucky girl who dated Gage. And he's known as the dude who dated me. It's sad that you're labeled by your relationship, but it's the place where sixty percent of the population has married their high school sweetheart.

"He's my ex-boyfriend and the reason I haven't had a relationship in years."

Her mouth falls slightly open as a thought hits her. "I've always wondered why you don't date. You've been hung up on him."

"Negative. I've been too busy with my job to be hung up on anyone."

Her laugh echoes through her car. "Denial only makes it hotter when you have sex again. Trust me, I know from experience."

I wrinkle my nose and shove her side. "Please refrain from talking about having sex with my brother. It'll make me puke more than this stupid hangover."

Willow gives me a loaner bag of clothes before I get out of her car since mine are burned to a crisp, and I'm waiting for my online orders to be delivered to my parents' house. I kiss her cheek, thank her again, and think about Gage on my ride home.

I need to find out if he's home for good.

If he is, I'm not sure how much pain that'll put me through.

My new home search might be out of Blue Beech if that's the case.

———

I THROW my arms around the chest of my big brother, Hudson, and squeal. "Happy birthday, you old man, you!"

Yes, I'm curing my hangover by attending my brother's birthday party at the Down Home Pub. Even if I do feel like shit, I can't bail on his party. Down Home Pub is the only place to drink in Blue Beech, so if you're looking to have a good time, this is where you go. Even though it gives you a comfortable and homey atmosphere, you'll still always end up running into someone you hate.

Hudson squeezes my shoulders and narrows his eyes on me upon pulling away. "Old man? I still don't regret cutting off half of your bangs when you were six."

Hudson is the middle child between Dallas and me. He's a tough dude, a former Marine, and a part-time bodyguard to his fiancée, Stella Mendes. She happens to be TV's *it girl*.

At first, he didn't want to work for her, but he broke down and took the job after dealing with the reality that his high school sweetheart and my former best friend were screwing behind his back. The fuck-boy bestie married said cheating ho on her and Hudson's scheduled wedding day. Good thing he did take the job, considering his life is hearts and roses with a talented and independent woman.

Yes, our family is one big dating-confusion circle. It'd take hours to break down every relationship situation. It's hard for me to keep up with it at times. They all got name tags from me for Christmas.

I slap his chest. "Joke's on you, homeboy, because I'm the one who cut the heads off your G.I. Joes, which Mom didn't ground me for *or* tell you because she understood it was done in retribution."

He plops down on a barstool at the crowded table and pulls the one next to him out. "Waitress delivered our drinks before you got here, but I'll track her down to get you something."

I wave off his offer and stay standing. "I'll run up to the bar and order something from Maliki. This place is a madhouse. It'll take forever for a drink."

He picks his beer up. "Throw it on my tab."

"You're the birthday boy. I should be buying your drinks." I hold a finger up. "Nothing too expensive though. This chick is on a budget."

He takes a drink and wipes his mouth. "Exactly. You've lost everything you owned. Add it to my tab."

I shake my head. "Nope, you know us Barnes kids don't like people feeling sorry for us."

"I don't feel sorry for your evil, G.I. Joe–killing ass. I'm having a good night, and I already told everyone at our table that drinks are on me."

I tap his head while he takes another drink and then move around the table to complete my hugging and greeting duty to everyone, including Willow, Dallas, and Stella. That takes a good fifteen minutes. A crowd of people surrounds the bar, but luckily, Maliki skips over them and heads straight to me.

A smile beams on his dark-skinned face. "There's my favorite arsonist nurse. What can I get you? Fireball?"

I lean against the bar to smack his shoulder. "So hilarious, ass. There goes your tip."

Maliki and I had a thing for a few months last year. He graduated with Hudson, and neither one of us was looking for anything serious, so we didn't feel the need to tell anyone. Not an ounce of drama happened after parting ways when the flame dimmed. That's the kind of sex relationship I want.

Perhaps I should ask him to share his bed with me tonight to fuck out all the sexual thoughts I've been having about Gage.

I shake my head. *Nope.* That's a bitchy thing to do. I won't use someone to get back at my pain-in-the-ass ex.

Maliki grins, showing off his bright white teeth. "Your usual? Lemon drop martini?"

I tap my chin. "I might be in need of something stronger this evening."

"Rough week?"

"Considering I'm homeless, yes."

He goes to open his mouth, most likely about to offer up his spare bedroom, when someone wedges himself between us, stopping him.

"My tab, man."

Ugh.

Just as I said, you never fail to run into someone you hate.

And what's up with everyone offering to buy my drinks? This chick buys her own drinks. Period.

The smile I had for Maliki slips, and the headache from earlier is creeping back in.

"Really?" I grumble. I don't have to look to know who it is. Not only do I recognize his voice, but I also recognize the smell of him, the heat of his body brushing against mine. "Maliki, do not add it to his tab. I don't accept favors from douche lords."

"Can't have a homeless woman buying her drinks," Gage throws back.

I give him a glassy stare when I finally turn to look at him and blow out a series of breaths. He's wearing a blue button-up flannel and what appears to be jeans, but I can't exactly shove away the person behind me, blocking half of him from my view. A light scruff still covers his cheeks, and I wonder if that's his everyday look now. It saddens me that I'm not sure if every change in him is recent or if he's been doing it for years and it's only new to me.

Maliki holds his palms up and breaks my attention from Gage. "The nightly goal of every bartender is not dealing with patrons' drama." He snaps his fingers and points to me. "Something strong is coming your way." His focus moves to Gage. "You two work your soap-opera shit out before I come back."

"I think this proves you are stalking me," I grumble to Gage.

He rests his elbow on the bar and leans against it, facing me. "It's a small town, Dyson. Get used to seeing me around."

"Small town, my ass. You've been here for weeks without us running into each other. Now, all of a sudden, you're everywhere. I'm not about to become a star of *Dateline*. *Everyone loved Lauren ... and her ex-boyfriend loved her a little too much.*" I wisp my hand through the air. "Blah, blah, blah."

"Again, don't flatter yourself, sweetheart. I had no idea you'd be here tonight." He gestures to the door. "I can leave if it'll make you more comfortable." He lowers his gaze on me. "Or we can leave and fuck our hate toward each other away."

Whoa.

Maliki slid some blue concoction in front of me at the same time Gage said those words. His eyes wide, Maliki holds his hands up while retreating backward and walking away.

I shyly look away and catch my breath before managing to give Gage a cold stare while hating myself for the excitement rushing through me at the idea of *hate fucking*. I rub my legs together to ease the sudden tension.

Sex with Gage was incredible when we were younger. I can only imagine what it's like with him now that he's older and more experienced.

Damn. The mood is ruined now that I've thought about him with other women.

I turn around and lean back against the bar, my drink in my hand. "Screw you. You can stay. I don't want to be blamed for your lack of getting laid *again*."

He raises a brow. "That an offer?"

"Absolutely not. That's a kind way of saying, *Stay out of my way, and I'll stay out of yours*. You're right. We're going to see each other. Let's not make a big deal about it during every encounter, okay?"

"I heard you were back in town, brother."

I freeze at the sound and sight of Derrick Howard, the man I lied about sleeping with. He slaps Gage on the back while smiling at him.

"Let me buy you a drink," he goes on.

Uh-oh.

Gage pulls away from him in disgust. "I'd recommend not touching me, *brother*."

"What?" Derrick asks around a confused laugh before slapping his leg. "Come on, man. It's been nearly a decade. Let's bury that high school rivalry shit."

Gage tilts his beer toward me with what sounds like a growl coming from his throat. "It's not done when you're fucking her. When it comes to Lauren, it'll never be done."

Derrick looks at me in confusion. "What is he talking about? We barely speak."

"Nothing," I answer, and I grab Gage's arm. "We need to talk in private."

Derrick might be a dick, but that doesn't mean he deserves to get his ass kicked.

Gage slips out of my hold. "No, we don't."

"My sex life is none of your business," I snap.

"You're right. Just answer me this one question, and I'll stop. I won't talk to you anymore. I'll let you and Derrick fuck yourselves happy." His voice breaks. "*Please.*"

"Gage, I'm not fucking Lauren," Derrick says. "You two figure your shit out and leave me out of it." He turns around and walks away without waiting for a response.

"All I needed to know," Gage yells to his back and glances at me. "This a new hobby of yours? Lying about whom you're sleeping with?"

I bite into my lip, answering honestly, "Sort of."

"Why? Is your mission in life to piss me off?"

"To be honest, yes. It's revenge for arresting me."

"Let me get this straight. You left me. You walked away for some bullshit reason after I begged you not to. Then, you tell me you're sleeping with the dude I fought numerous times for attempting to fuck around with you. If anyone should hate anyone's guts, it's me who should hate yours."

He turns around and walks away before I can answer him. I stare at his back while he maneuvers around the crowd and heads to Hudson's table. Hudson slaps him on the back, and they start what looks like a comfortable conversation. Hudson doesn't seem surprised to see him.

Not fucking cool.

I grab my drink and stomp over to Hudson as Gage moves around the table to talk to Dallas.

"You didn't think it'd be cool to give me a heads-up that he was back in town?" I ask Hudson, pulling out the stool next to him with added force and falling down on it.

He and I are close and spent a lot of time together growing up. Gage and I double-dated with him and his ex all the time in high school.

"It's a sore subject for you," he answers. "Anytime his name was mentioned after you broke up, you would leave the room."

"You know what was also a sore subject? When I found out my best friend was cheating on you and I told her to never come near me again." I press my drink to my lips. "Apparently, you've forgotten what loyalty means."

He shakes his head while slowly running a finger through his short beard. "The situation is different. Gage didn't fuck around on you with someone else. Otherwise, he wouldn't be walking. I didn't tell you because I didn't want to hurt you. Something sour went down between the two of you, and I know you have so much going on. You didn't need any more stress."

I glance over at Gage at the same time he moves around the table to my side.

He leans down, his elbows resting on the wood, and lowers his voice. "You staying at your parents'?" he asks.

I clear my throat to gain some time to get myself together. The feelings I have when he's this close are embarrassing. "Kind of have no other option."

There's a hint of mint and beer on his breath. "You can stay in the loft if you want."

I scoff, "You're joking."

He shakes his head. "My dad is listing it for rent in the paper this week for extra money."

"Where would you stay?"

"In the house with him."

I look around to see if people's eyes are on us, and about a dozen are staring. Both of my brothers have all their attention on their girls, and a few women have their gaze on Gage, assessing the situation to see if we're back together.

"Don't you think that'd be a little weird?"

More along the lines of extremely weird.

"Think on it and get back with me." He grabs his beer and tilts it my way. "Enjoy your night. If you need a ride again, let me know."

I watch his back as he walks away, and he joins a group of men at a table in the corner of the room. I finish my drink and depart for another one.

More alcohol equals fewer feelings.

"I have to say, I'm pissed you're not in jail."

I turn around at the gravelly voice to find Ronnie standing behind me. He takes my frown as an invitation to move to my side. He's, of course, wearing a suit in this hole-in-the-wall pub. His blond hair is gelled to perfection, like he's still a frat boy bonging beers in loafers, and his arrogance reeks from here.

"Word is, your little friend over there never took you in," he goes on.

"File a report, Ronnie," I answer. "I didn't set the building on fire."

The strong scent of him hits me as he comes in closer.

"I'll leave this alone if you give me one date. *One.* That's all I'm asking."

"No. I've made it clear that I'm not dating at the moment."

I look around the bar for my brothers. If they see this jackass talking to me, they'll no doubt put him in his place. I don't see either one of them.

Ronnie inherited the building but didn't grow up in Blue Beech. He grew up in some big city, attended a prestigious school, and came into town thinking he'd impress people with his money and expensive cars.

"Come on. I have to be better than these small-town chumps around here." He flashes me a smile. "You work nonstop. I own *several* buildings and will take care of you."

I grimace and pull away when he runs his hand down my arm.

"And I can promise, it won't only be financially. I do magical things with my tongue. Come home with me tonight."

I've seen enough rape victims come into the ER to know this man is a threat. Pissing him off, turning him down, will only make him more persistent.

I order a water instead of an alcoholic drink from Maliki and fake a laugh when I look back at Ronnie. "I have an early shift tomorrow and am staying with my parents. They're giving me the same curfew I had in high school."

Please buy it. Buy it.

CHAPTER EIGHT

Gage

AM I FUCKING CRAZY?

Why in the living hell would I offer Lauren the loft? My loft?

Not only did I do that, but I also lied about it being available for rent.

It's not—again, because it's *my* motherfucking loft.

The *keeping my distance* plan with Lauren is deteriorating fast. That woman has been my weakness from day one, and that weakness fucked up my life in so many ways.

I straighten in my stool when I notice Douche-Bag Landlord meeting her at the bar. He runs his sleazy hand down her arm, and she pulls away from his touch with revulsion on her face.

I slide off my stool at the same time she steps away from him, grabbing the glass of water Maliki slid over to her.

Good girl.

I flinch when a hand hits my arm.

"Gage, man, don't do anything stupid that'll cost you your job," Kyle warns. "You might've gotten away with roughing dudes up in Chicago, but that shit won't fly here. You put your hands on that guy, and he'll demand you lose your badge. I had the displeasure of hanging out with him while you ran off to do who knows what with your girl of destruction. He went on and on about how much money he has, how many cars he owns, and the endless parade of chicks he bangs. Dude will press charges in a heartbeat and demand you lose your badge." He tips his beer to his lips and takes a drink. "Not to mention, Lauren's ass won't fall for his bullshit. That girl is fucking evil."

As much as I want to, I can't bring myself to sit back down. If he touches her again, fuck my badge, fuck my job. I rub a sweaty hand over my forehead.

She's not yours to protect any longer.

I have to pound that through my thick skull and broken heart.

My attention stays pinned on her as she maneuvers through the crowd, holding her water in the air, and goes back to her table. I sit back down and make myself comfortable, knowing she's surrounded by a layer of her brothers' protection.

She circles the table, hugging everyone, and finishes off her water before heading to the door. I start to relax—until she goes outside, and the landlord does the same minutes later.

This time, I ignore Kyle's protests as I stalk out of the bar and into the parking lot. It's close to empty, which surprises me. Patrons are usually gathered out here, smoking and shooting the shit.

I follow the sound of his voice.

"Come on, baby. One night. You won't regret it. Trust me."

"I told you, my parents are expecting me," she answers. "I already called and told them I was on my way home."

I round the corner to find Lauren standing in front of her pink Mustang with Douche-Bag standing in front of her, blocking her from opening the door.

He snags her around the waist, and she pushes him away. "Then we can go to my car and mess around. A quick fuck then I'll take you to dinner tomorrow."

"You couldn't pay me to touch you, asshole."

He grabs her arms and pins them above her. "Baby, don't tempt me. Money talks. It always does."

He turns her head to the side as he grows closer, and I yell at the top of my lungs while running toward them.

"How much will it take? A few hundred? I'm willing to pay thousands to get between your legs. Now that I think about it, you need a place to stay. My bed is always open."

The idiot is practically screaming out his assault.

"You'd better step the fuck away from her before I bash your skull in," I yell, finally catching his attention.

He releases her and holds his hands up. "No need to interfere. My girl and I are having a little spat. We'll be on our way."

"I'm not your girl, sicko," Lauren yells.

She pushes him, and he stumbles backward.

He stares at me, blinking, while I clench my fist in hopes that I can control it from hitting his face.

"You're the officer who arrested her," he says.

"No shit, and she wasn't your girl when you demanded I do that," I reply.

"I now see why I haven't been updated on any charges." He lets out a gravelly laugh. "Looks like I'm not the only man who wants a piece of her. It's always more tempting when you have to work for it."

Anger spirals through my veins, and I hold my clenched fists up. "I'm giving you five seconds to split before I bust your jaw open."

Pretty boy doesn't take it as an idle threat.

He swiftly glances at Lauren. "You have my card. Let me know when you're ready for some quality dick."

There goes my patience and trying to lay low.

I charge forward, and he grunts when I slam him against the car. "The fuck did I say? Walk away, shut your fucking mouth, and don't you come near her again. You hear me?"

He repeatedly nods until I release him. He slides against the car, away from me, and then arrogantly runs his hands down to smooth out the wrinkles of his suit, which is nowhere appropriate to wear at a run-down pub like this. "Let me know if you change your mind, sweetie."

"That'll be never," Lauren blurts out. "Some words of advice: go buy a sex doll because that's the only way you're getting laid."

He sprints away to the other side of the parking lot, and I erase the distance between Lauren and me.

"You okay?" I ask, running my hand down her face, checking for any marks.

"Just peachy." She slaps my hand away. "Don't touch me."

I step away at her request, and she takes a deep breath before letting it out.

"Sorry for snapping," she says, her voice level. "He had me all hyped up."

"No need to apologize." I tip my head toward my truck a few spaces away. "Come on. I'll give you a ride home."

"I'm fine. I only had one drink."

"I'm not concerned about you being drunk. I'm worried about your safety."

"I'll be okay." She fishes through her purse for her keys with shaking hands. "I'll be fine. You scared him away."

"I'll follow you home then."

I do a once-over of the parking lot before lowering my voice and dipping down to Lauren's level. "Landlord didn't go back into the bar. He walked to his car and hasn't left. My guess is, he's waiting for you to leave, so he can do something stupid. I'll be damned if I let that happen."

Understanding dawns on her face.

"You don't think …" she mutters, stopping mid-sentence.

"Who knows how big his balls are? Regardless, I won't risk it." I hold two fingers up. "That gives you two options. One is I'll follow you home. Then tomorrow, we'll file a restraining order against the punk." I put down a finger. "The second option is you let me give you a ride, and we'll still file a restraining order."

It's her turn to do a nervous scan of the parking lot. "I'll ride with you."

I keep my hand on her back as we walk to my truck, and I help her in.

She slides her sandals off and rests her feet on the dash as soon as we pull out of the parking lot. "God, I remember these days. Your truck was older back then. Ripped seats. Smelled like your dad's old cologne."

"Ah, yes, his rusted beater," I say with a laugh, happy she's no longer shaking. "That front seat saw plenty of action."

"Plenty of awkward, first-time action."

"I won't deny that." I tap my hand against the steering wheel and curse myself for what I'm about to do. It'll ruin the comfortableness of our ride, but the question has been haunting me for years. "Why'd you do it?"

Her feet drop from the dash. "Huh?"

"Why'd you leave me?"

"Gage … I told you why."

"No, you gave me a bullshit excuse."

"And you'll receive the same one tonight. It was for the best."

I scoff, "Maybe it was for you, but it sure as fuck wasn't for me. You were my fucking life, Lauren. The reason I bled. Hell, I loved you more than my own life, my own breath, and you knew that. We had plans, and then one day, you changed your mind, out of nowhere."

She scrubs her hands over her face. "That was the problem, Gage. You can't make someone your entire life. We didn't know anything, except for each other. We never had the chance to find ourselves."

"I knew myself. Knew I wanted you. Knew who I loved."

It isn't until we pull into her parents' drive that I realize why she's kept her hands over her face. It's to mask the tears falling down her cheeks. The urge to reach out and comfort her rips through me, but I can't.

"Can we not do this? It's in the past. Let it be." Her voice breaks.

She's had a rough night, and my actions have only made it worse.

"You're right. You're over it. It's time I do the same."

She clears her throat. "Let's be friends, okay?"

"I can't be your friend."

"I understand."

She gives me a quick nod before opening the door, ending our conversation. She's gone, rushing up the sidewalk to the front porch before I have the chance to say her name. I stay parked until she disappears into the house, and my phone rings before I shift my truck into reverse. My stomach churns when I see the number, and I accept the call, though I know it's a terrible idea.

I've already hashed it out with one woman who ruined me tonight, so might as well do it with the other.

"You have a collect call from … Missy from the Cook County Department of Corrections."

My fingers fist around the phone at the sound of her voice.

"Do you accept the call and any charges that can occur?"

"I accept," I grit out.

I don't wait for her to mutter a hello when the call is processed. She doesn't deserve that. Hell, she doesn't deserve a second of my time.

"I told you to quit fucking call me."

"Gage!" she yells on the line. "Please! Please listen to me for one minute! I want you to hear me out for once."

"Nothing you say will ever make me forgive you. Don't call again."

Click.

The phone rings again. Same number.

Decline.

I whisper to the darkness, "I fucking hate you, Missy."

CHAPTER NINE

Lauren

"SOMEONE CAME HOME LATE." My mom slides me a glass of orange juice across the kitchen table before placing two Advils next to it. "You look like you had a little too much fun at your brother's party last night." Her hands rest on her hips. "I know you like to keep up with the boys, honey, but you're much smaller than them. Alcohol hits you harder."

I wave away her warning. "Psh, I can drink them under the table."

"That's my girl."

I grin at the sound of Dad's voice as he comes strolling into the kitchen.

"Where's your car, Laur-Bear?" he asks. "I planned on changing the oil today."

"At the pub," I answer. "I didn't feel like driving last night."

"The pub?" my mom repeats. "Who took you home?" The expression on her face tells me she already knows the answer.

My mother is the gossip queen of Blue Beech, and I have a love-hate relationship with that hobby of hers. It's all fun and games until the gossip spread is about you.

"I see you still excel at spying on your children," I mutter into my glass before taking a sip and popping the pills. "Even when they're grown." An omelet is placed in front of me next.

She sits down across from me. "It was Gage, wasn't it?"

I stop mid-bite. "Now, why in the world would you think that? Gage left Blue Beech years ago and hasn't come back, right?"

Her taking a sip of coffee hides her enthusiasm terribly. "Nancy just so happened to mention that he's back in town, working at the station."

My fork clashes against my plate when I drop it. "Are you saying you've known Gage has been home for who knows how long and didn't think it would be a stellar idea to drop that bomb on me, so I wasn't taken by surprise when we ran into each other?"

"From what it looked like, your relationship with him didn't end on good terms. You've been busy at the hospital, so I didn't want to stress you more. You want to talk about what happened between you two?"

"Nope."

Disappointment flashes across her face.

My mother is a fixer. There's a solution to every problem in her book.

"You're older, more mature and, sometimes, people need a break from each other to be smacked in the face with the truth. It could be a second chance at love. You and Gage were inseparable for years. You loved that boy, and he loved you."

"Don't you dare try this on me. If you and your little knitting club start plotting some scheme to force us to reconcile, I will not be in attendance for Christmas."

"No Christmas means no gifts."

I frown. "Fine then. I won't be showing up on Thanksgiving."

My dad laughs. "Unless you plan on having a Marie Callendar's frozen dinner, you'll be here."

I'VE NEVER UNDERSTOOD the phrase, Desperate times call for desperate measures, until I find myself walking into the police station.

And I'm lucky enough to come face-to-face with Kyle. I'm not sure whose look is dirtier toward the other—mine or his. He stares me down, waiting for my conversation starter, because he won't be the one to initiate it.

"Is, um …" I glance around to see if there's anyone else I can talk to who doesn't think I'm the devil. "Is Gage around?"

Kyle looks like he'd rather arrest me than let me near his best friend. "Sure, I'll go grab him, and I'm only doing this because it's my job. I'm not allowed to tell people to kick rocks here."

"How courteous of you."

"Nice is my middle name. Maybe you should give it a try."

He gives me his back before I can reply, and Gage looks surprised when he walks out. Kyle must not have given him a heads-up it was me asking for him. I lick my lips and a tingle rolls up my spine at the view of Gage in his uniform again.

Shit. Control your hormones, girl.

I ignore all the stares around us. "Can I talk to you real quick?"

"Sure." Gage motions for me to follow him and takes me into an office, shutting the door behind us.

"You have your own office?" I ask, turning around and looking at the door when I sit down. "Aren't you a newbie around here?"

"I held a high position in the force in Chicago."

"Wait," I interrupt, holding my hand up. "You lived in Chicago?"

"Yes." He scratches his cheeks and goes on before I have the chance to question him more. "There was an open position after Monroe retired, and I took it."

Any Chicago talk is definitely off the table for him. His demeanor changed when I repeated that city. It moved from hate to hurt to understanding and now indifference. Last night, Gage said he was over our past, and now he's going to prove that to me.

I'm not sure which Gage is worse.

The pissed off one or the sad one.

He sits down behind the desk. "You here to file that report against the land-dick?"

I shake my head. "Is the loft above your garage still available?"

His face is emotionless. "I believe so."

"Will you temporarily lease it to me?"

He looks as shocked as I am at my question.

I laugh. "Trust me, I wouldn't ask if I weren't desperate. I've called nearly every rental available in this godforsaken town. No one will rent to me in fear that I'll burn the place to the ground. My parents are too nosy, and both of my brothers are in the puke-inducing honeymoon phase with their girlfriends. No, thank you to intruding on their love-fests."

He opens up a drawer and pulls out a key. "Move your stuff in whenever."

"Thank you. I'll be out of your hair as soon as I find another place."

He tips his head my way. "Sounds like a plan."

I rise up to leave, but the sound of his whistling stops me.

"About that report."

"He was drunk."

"Has he hit on you before?"

I nod. "A few times, yes."

"If you're not going to file a report, let me know if he keeps coming around." His gaze lowers on me. "And no more walking through dark parking lots alone, okay?"

"I don't need protecting." I cross my arms. "Plus, you hate me, so why do you care?"

"My hate toward you won't stop me from making sure you're safe." He slides the key across the desk. "Loft is all yours. I have to get back to work."

CHAPTER TEN

Gage

"CARE TO EXPLAIN what the fuck that was about?" Kyle asks when I step out of my office an hour after Lauren left.

She came to me. That meant something.

Sure, she made it seem like she had no other options, but she did. Her parents would love for her to move back in, her brothers would always open their doors for her, and her mid-husband friends would no doubt give her a room at their place.

"Nothing of your concern," I mutter.

"You can't bullshit a bullshitter." He trails behind me as I walk through the station, out the door, and straight to the car. This conversation isn't happening for all of Blue Beech's ears. "The girl you love but wish you hated strutted her evil ass into your office. She leaves, and when you finally come out, it looks like she told you she was knocked up with another dude's baby. What gives, bro?"

His saying I look pissed doesn't surprise me. I'd set myself up for failure by inviting her to move in.

"She's crashing in the loft for a few weeks," I answer, unlocking the car door.

He would've found out sooner or later. Might as well have him call me a stupid shit now.

He spits his coffee out on the sidewalk, more dramatic than necessary. "You shitting me? She's moving in with you? As a roommate or fuckmate?"

I get in the car, slam the door behind me, and wait until he's sliding in the passenger seat before answering, "I'll sleep in my old bedroom in the house."

"You sure are being nice to someone you supposedly can't stand." He whistles. "I wish my enemies were as considerate as you. Is Miss She-Devil moving in with you when you buy your new house, too?"

I've been on the hunt for a new place since moving back, but the market sucks. Most residents stay in their houses until they die, and then their kids inherit them, repeating history. My dad has tried to sign over the house to me countless times, but I won't allow it. He built his life, his family, and memories there. I won't take that away from him. He deserves to have that happiness for as long as he can.

"It's only temporary until she finds a new place," I say. "No one will rent to her."

"Can you blame them? The chick is a walking Firestarter, à la Stephen King."

I start the engine and settle my cup in the holder. "Shut up."

He puts his cup in next. "You're too damn soft for her, man. Pussy is a weakness for some men, and there's no doubt, Lauren's pussy is yours."

I shove his shoulder. "Watch your mouth. She needs somewhere to stay. That's it."

"The chick has family. She can rent another apartment out of town. There are plenty of options for Blue Beech's golden girl that don't involve shacking up with you."

"My dad can use the extra income."

"Bullshit," he coughs into his hand. "You won't take a penny from her."

"What's up with you in my business? You been watching

Hallmark movies with your mom again? I don't question you about your women troubles."

His lips tilt into a grin. "Oh, so she's your woman now?"

"I still hate her."

"Perfect. I have a date tonight, and she's bringing a friend. Your uptight ass needs to get laid." He smacks my back. "Time to fuck that she-devil out of your mind."

———

LAUREN'S UGLY-ASS pink Mustang is parked in the driveway when I pull in.

It doesn't surprise me that she's still driving her first car. In order to buy it, she worked at the town diner for years to save up money. Her parents agreed to match whatever she came up with. I thought the car was hideous then, and I detest it even more now. The dudes on the basketball team loved giving me hell when she forced me to ride passenger while she drove around town.

I contemplate whether to head up to the loft and check on her but don't. Kyle was right about me needing to pull my head out of my ass and remember the pain she caused me. I can't let her step back into my life with her gorgeous smile, those beautiful brown eyes, and that contagious laugh and break down my walls.

It fucking killed me last time.

I wasn't as weak then.

It'd be worse the second go-around.

I snatch my phone up from the passenger seat when it beeps.

Kyle: You driving or want me to pick you up?

Me: Driving. Be there in 30.

Kyle: Bring an overnight bag. Bringing a date home to a loft you share with your ex most likely won't be a turn on for her.

Me: Fuck off.

Kyle: See you soon, assface.

I make it my mission not to look toward the loft when I head into the house. I shower and throw on jeans and a simple white tee. It takes a minute to find my duffel bag in the back of my closet. I lay it on the bed and stare down at it.

Should I?

It's been nearly five months since I've had sex. Pussy hasn't been on my mind since Missy did what she did. Maybe it's what I need. They say sex helps with stress. Let's test that theory.

I pack the bag, throw it over my shoulder, and say good-bye to my dad on my way out.

Lauren is skipping down the stairs with her keys in her hand while I head to my truck. She's sporting tight-ass yoga pants and a tank top that shows off her generous cleavage. Her tits have grown since high school, just like my hands—although they'd still cup them perfectly.

How many other ways has her body changed?

Is her pussy still as tight?

Are her weak spots still the same?

She stops and looks at me before I make it to my truck. "Your stuff is still in the closet."

I drag a hand through my hair. "I haven't had the chance to clear it out yet. It'll be gone by the weekend."

She crosses her arms, emphasizing her cleavage, and leans back against her car. "The loft was never going up for rent, was it?"

"Does it matter?"

A smile tilts at her lips. "I guess not, considering it's now my place of residence." She points to my bag. "Going somewhere?"

I hold it up. "I have a date."

What are your plans for tonight? is the question I want to ask her, but I don't.

"A date." She clears her throat, her face expressionless. "Well, you, uh … have fun with that."

"Don't worry. I'll have a blast," I say with a wink.

No, I won't.

———

"SO, YOU'RE KYLE'S PARTNER?" my date asks.

Her name is Susie ... Sandy ... something along those lines. I feel like an asshole for not paying attention to a word she's said all night. I'm comparing everything she does to Lauren, something I haven't done in years.

After we broke up, it was all I did with every woman I attempted to move on with. I compared the way they ate, how they talked, how they sucked my dick, the taste of their pussy. No one ever came close to her. Eventually, I stopped myself ... until now.

Kyle was right, goddamn it.

Letting her move in was a dumbass idea, but I can't ask her to leave now.

"A man in uniform has always been a turn-on for me," she goes on, her dark purple lips curving into a flirty smile. "Your place or mine for a nightcap?" she asks after I pay the bill.

"Yours."

Kyle grins and slaps my shoulder in celebration. "Attaboy."

My best friend was pro-Lauren years ago. He might hate her more than I do now. He blames her for my leaving, for his losing his best friend, for our falling out of touch. I've tried talking sense into him. She didn't force me to bail on everyone and everything I ever knew.

I was a big boy.

I made that decision.

And, now, I'm deciding to fuck Lauren Barnes out of my system.

———

I SHOULD'VE DRUNK MORE.

Shouldn't have stopped after two beers to make sure I was okay to drive home … just in case.

Maybe then, I'd be more turned on, my dick would be harder, and I'd be into S … something. Fuck, I feel like an asshole for not remembering her name.

I'm on her couch, wearing only jeans, and trying to focus on her grinding against my dick and doing her best to get me hard, and she eventually does even though neither my mind nor my dick is thinking about her.

My dick is hard because it's imagining someone else is on my lap.

A woman with a smart-ass mouth who could do amazing things with it.

I cringe, hoping she hasn't been honing in on those sex skills with someone else. *Did she find someone who could fuck her better than I did?*

I shut my eyes and let my imagination take over. If I can't have her, at least I can envision her, which makes me an asshole, I'm well aware.

"Fuck, Lauren, baby, slow down," I hiss, grabbing her hips and digging my nails into her dress that's pulled up around her waist.

The chick grinding on me stops. "Did you just call me Lauren?"

I grunt when she climbs off my lap and I go to grab my shirt, preparing to get kicked out of her apartment, but she drops to her knees instead.

"You want to forget about her?" she asks, licking her lips.

"Like no other."

"I'll fuck every thought of her out of you. You won't remember her name." She grabs my belt and unbuckles it. "You won't even be able to say your own name when I'm done with you."

CHAPTER ELEVEN

Lauren

I OPEN the blinds to peek out the window for what seems like the hundredth time.

"I'm officially a stalker," I say to Willow over the phone.

Does this mean I still have feelings for Gage?

That shouldn't even be a question I ask myself.

I'll always have unresolved feelings for him.

Jealousy ate at me when I caught him leaving for his date. He wasn't as dressed up as he had been for his Operation Make Lauren Jealous and Crash Her Dinner Party date, but he still put in an effort to look good for her.

Was it Phoebe again?

Ugh. Quit thinking about his date.

The worst part was the overnight bag. I stopped myself from asking him to hang out with me instead. To get my mind off him, I went to dinner with my parents, Hudson, and Stella and hoped Gage's truck would be here when I got back.

It wasn't.

I've been in freak-out mode since.

"I won't dispute that," she answers around a laugh. We've been on the phone for nearly an hour while I updated her on the whole Gage situation. "Although I do like seeing you like this."

"Like what?" I tiptoe from the window and fall back against the couch. I've done this dance all night. "A freaking creep?"

"All worked up over a man. You always seem so in charge of your feelings. It's a nice surprise."

I sit up. "Whoa, whoa. I'm not all worked up over Gage. Call it curiosity."

"Curiosity, huh? Curious if he's balls deep in another chick's vajayjay."

"You're making it sound like I'd rather he be balls deep in me."

"Hey, you're the one who said that, not me. Plus, I don't believe your lying ass."

"Looks like you don't know me as well as you think you do."

"Then, explain this to me. Why'd you move in with homeboy then? Rooming with your enemy isn't a common practice for most people. I'd never do it, for fear of getting shanked in my sleep or whatnot. So, why'd you do it?"

I groan. "For the millionth time, I needed somewhere to stay."

"Hmm … I recall offering you a room here. I have cable, a man who knows how to throw down in the kitchen—aka *free* meals—and a stepdaughter who enjoys giving free pedicures. Not saying they're good pedis, but they'll save you some dollars."

"Your house is too crowded. I need personal space."

"Personal space, my ass. You would've turned me down even if I'd offered you the house all to yourself. You're there because you want to be around him."

Am I that transparent?

I snort. "You're so wrong."

"The girl looking out the window, hoping he comes home and doesn't spend the night with his date—whom he's most likely banging at the moment—is telling me I'm wrong."

"Gee, way to make me feel better. Why am I friends with you again?"

"I told you befriending me was a terrible idea and that I was a disastrous mess, yet you kept showing up, uninvited, at my apartment, poking and prodding for details about my life."

"You were knocked up with my big bro's baby. It was imperative I made sure you weren't some weirdo. Although that's still yet to be determined."

"*I'm* the weirdo? You eat pickles on your peanut butter sandwiches."

"That's a delicacy in some places, you know."

"Where? Prison?"

"Dorm rooms for poor nursing students."

"Now, let's save the pickle-slash-friendship talk for another occasion because my time is almost up and I need a story more interesting about why you left him that's better than the Winnie the Pooh book I'm about to read to Maven."

"Don't get your hopes up on that happening."

"Did you run over his cat or something and can't look at him without feeling guilty?"

"No. What's wrong with you? I've never killed an animal."

"My ex killed my gerbil. Accidentally, but that should've been the first sign that dating him was a bad idea. Now, spill. I only have a few minutes to spare before the bedtime festivities begin."

"There's no story. It was for the best. We needed to find ourselves."

"Bullshit," she coughs into the phone.

"I was leaving for college. His only plan after leaving high school was to follow me and figure out his life from there. He needed to find out what he wanted in life without it revolving around me. I made the choice for him."

Crying erupts in the background. "That's not the truth, but I'll take it for now, considering my baby requires attention. Hold on a sec."

I yawn. "Attend to my niece and nephew and call me tomorrow. I have to wake up at the ass crack of dawn."

She says good-bye and hangs up, and I lean back against the couch, doing a once-over of the loft. It was a mistake, staying here.

I run my hand over the couch cushion and smile as a memory hits me.

Gage begged his parents for years to move into the loft, and they always said no. They planned on renting it out. That decision changed when his mother died. When he asked six months later, his dad Amos finally agreed even though I could see on his face that he wanted to say no. Amos feared to be alone, and only agreed because his heart broke for his son losing his mother too soon.

This loft is where we spent most of our time together. The bed is the one I lost my virginity in. This is the same couch where I gave him a blow job for the first time.

Memories surround me.

Yes, most definitely a mistake.

To put my mind on something else, I hop off the couch, open a cabinet, and unpack the bag of groceries sitting on the counter. I start making the only thing I know how to concoct from scratch. The asshole on a date with another woman is on my mind while I cut the chicken breasts. I wonder where he took her for dinner—hell, if they even had dinner—when I dice the peppers, and I curse them both while pulling out the Dutch oven.

———

I HATE myself for the relief I get when the headlights of Gage's truck shine through the window. No night cuddling and breakfast the next morning for his date. I inch forward and slowly peel the curtains back, hoping he doesn't notice me in stalker mode.

He looks up, meets my eyes, and grins.

Of freaking course.

I run away from the window, pause the TV, and shut the lamp off. Maybe he'll think I'm going to bed. The faint sound of a knock on the door echoes through the room, and I debate on whether to answer it. A groan leaves my throat while I pull myself up and check the peephole before answering, just in case his date is with him and he wants to rub it in my face.

"Can I come in?" he asks when I open the door.

I peek out, checking that he's alone, while he waits for me to invite him in like a vampire from a horror movie.

All clear.

No date.

No sex mate.

Unfortunately, he looks like sex. Smells like sex, too.

I should shut the door in his face, but dude is letting me stay in his loft, so I take a step back, a silent yes. I won't admit that the urge to hang out and question him about his date tonight is biting at me.

"You settling in okay?" he asks.

Yes, if you don't count my anxiety-induced cooking to punch out the thoughts of you with another woman.

He still looks good, but his shirt is wrinkled at the bottom, evidence that there was a hand pulling at it. His hair is rustled, the messy look maybe brought on by another woman.

"For the most part," I say, turning on the light and stepping into the kitchen. "Not that I have much to settle in. The insurance company is giving me a hard time since Ronnie is accusing me of arson. No money for me until the investigation is complete."

"I'll have a look and try to speed up the process." He looks across the kitchen, his head tilting up. "Is that gumbo?"

Crap.

"Yep."

Don't remember. Don't remember.

"You know that's my favorite."

Busted and mistrusted.

"Is it? I had no idea."

He raises a disbelieving eyebrow.

I didn't make it for him. Maybe, subconsciously, I did. Gumbo isn't my favorite dish. Hell, it's not even in my top ten. So, why is it the only dish I can make successfully without burning? It's the single meal I know how to make because it was the favorite of my boyfriend.

I shrug. "There's extra if you want a bowl."

He does, and I go back to my spot on the sofa and turn the TV back on. He plops down on the other side of the couch with a full bowl.

"This still the only thing you know how to cook?" he asks.

"Yes. For some reason, I haven't been able to master anything else without burning it."

He chuckles. "Perhaps you shouldn't admit to burning shit to anyone else for a while."

I smile. "Good idea."

He takes a bite and groans while pointing to the bowl with his spoon. "I appreciate you making sure your landlord is fed … with his favorite meal."

I roll my eyes with a laugh. "Oh, shut up. I made it for myself. I'm sure you had plenty of food *on your date.*"

"Food sucked. This is better. Everything you made was always better than anything I could pick up at a restaurant."

"Yeah, right. You do know every *good luck* cupcake I made before your games was burned or tasted like shit."

"Yet I still ate them, didn't I?"

"To be nice and not make me feel bad."

"Yes, to be nice, but also because I loved that you took the time to do something special for me. You didn't give up. You kept trying to make them better with each game, and I loved that. I missed those bitter-ass, burned cupcakes after you left."

"I'm sure you've met someone who doesn't burn everything she touches."

"I haven't met anyone who doesn't burn shit as well as you." He leans in. "And, honestly, I haven't been looking either."

My lips pull up, ready to smile, but the air drifts my way as he goes to take another bite.

"J'adore," I whisper. "Dior."

His spoon drops into his bowl. "Huh?"

"You smell like her."

At least he screwed someone with decent perfume taste.

The reminder of him with another woman ruins the moment, ruins the memories that were rushing into me like waves. He's questioned me about whom I've been sleeping with since he moved back, but he thinks it's okay for him to do whatever he wants.

I shake my head. "How's that for a double standard? Don't you dare question me about my sex life anymore." I want to snatch the gumbo from him and pour it over his head. "I'm going to have sex with whomever I want to have sex with, too. If I didn't have to work tomorrow morning, I'd have a collection of men here, an orgy, getting screwed in every position possible while hanging from the ceiling."

A hard laugh interrupts my rant. "Keep lying if it makes you feel better."

"I'm not lying. I've had experiences, *plenty* of experiences, with other men."

He leans forward to settle his bowl on the table and slumps down in his seat, looking defeated. "Well, that ruins a man's appetite. I'd appreciate your not going into details, please."

"Why are you here?" I question.

His arm stretches along the back of the couch, settling behind me. "I have no fucking idea."

He needs to leave. He needs to stay.

Jesus, what do I want him to do?

"So, you hit it and quit it?" I ask. His bringing up the fact that he was with another woman tonight might lead me away from wanting his company.

An exasperated sigh leaves his lips. "I didn't fuck anyone tonight, Lauren."

"Yeah, right," I snort.

"I tried to."

"Tried to? Is your cock broken now?" I'm silently calling *bullshit* with the dirty look on my face.

"I couldn't get … into it. I was thinking about someone else. I *called* her by someone else's name. She gave me a free pass and dropped to her knees to suck my cock. A trooper who was ready to rid me of my thoughts of the woman who didn't deserve them."

God, I don't want to hear this, but I have to.

I can't stop myself from interrupting him. "If a man said another woman's name while I was grinding on him, I most likely would've poured battery acid on his junk."

"Are you sure you should be in the medical field?" He kicks my foot with his. "Better yet, are you sure you should be around anyone's junk? I'm suggesting you change professions and seek employment at a convent."

I roll my eyes. "Go on. So, chick gave you a blow job to rid your thoughts of a woman you shouldn't be thinking of—aka, most likely me. How is that any different from me talking about my sex life?" *It's weird, sitting on the couch where I did the same thing with him.*

"I shouldn't be having this conversation with you."

"Nuh-uh. You started it. You come in, smelling like the perfume of an expensive hooker, and start this story. You'd better finish it." My tone changes from friendly to annoyed. "You fucked her, didn't you?"

"She stroked me twice, and I stopped her."

"Whatever," I mutter, rolling my eyes. "You don't have to lie."

"Trust me, Dyson, you have no idea how much I'd love to go into detail about fucking another woman to hurt you."

"Then, why didn't you have sex with her?"

"Because, every time I tried to go through with it, I would stop because I didn't want to fucking hurt you. I couldn't think about her lips wrapped around my cock while you sat in this apartment, alone. It would've been wrong for me to have her suck my cock when I wished she were you."

What the hell do I say back to that?

"I, uh ... appreciate it, but don't think our situation has to stop you from having ... sexual encounters. I'm looking for a new place, and I will be out of your hair as soon as I can." *That's a lie.* "Then, you'll be free to go back to screwing women in here again."

His brows scrunch together. "You're the only woman I've had in here. Never felt the urge to have anyone else." He lets out a stressed breath. "I'd appreciate it if you extended the same courtesy. Go to their place. Screw them in their car. Let's have a mutual understanding that this is a no-fucking zone."

"What about the bedroom at your dad's you're crashing in? Is that in the no-fucking zone?"

"Do you want it to be?"

Yes! Yes!

"You can do whatever you want, Gage."

My breath catches in my throat when his gaze locks on mine, and he goes quiet until our eye contact is strong. I want to close my eyes, cut off our connection, but I can't pull away. I feel this affinity in my core, and that's exactly what he wants.

"Do you want it to be?" he repeats, enunciating each word.

I shrug and play with my hands without looking away. "I mean, it'd be weird, knowing my ex-boyfriend is only feet away, screwing another woman, but that's what they make Xanax and headphones for."

"Then, my bedroom is also a no-fucking zone."

"Glad we could come up with an agreement of where the

no-fucking areas are." I pause. "Have you ... slept with an ungodly number of women since me?"

What girl wouldn't want to scoop him up and throw him into her bed?

"A few here and there. You?" He shakes his head. "I don't know if I want to know the answer."

"A few here and there," I say in the same tone as his.

"Were they as great as I was?"

I slap his shoulder. "Really?"

So not going there. If I share stories, he might do the same.

"I had to crack a joke. Otherwise, I'd want to kill any other man who'd touched you." He picks up the bowl and goes back to eating. "You know, back then, I thought I'd be the only man who ever touched you like that. The only man you ever made love to."

"I haven't made love to anyone else." I sigh, and my answer stops him mid-bite.

He keeps our eye contact, his spoon half in the air, and waits for me to keep going.

"I mean, I've had sex, but it's never been anything serious. What about you? You ever *made love* to anyone?" I don't bother asking if he's had sex. No way he's been celibate since our breakup.

"Made love? Only you."

Those are the same words he said the first time he slid inside me. The same words he repeated every time we had sex.

"Only you," he mutters again.

The bowl goes to the table again, and he turns, so he's facing me. I lick my lips, and the mood in the room drifts into something dangerous.

No, I can't get turned on right now.

The need to straddle him and see if he's still as good as he was then tears at me.

Does he still know every weak spot on my body?

No. Don't go there.

This crazy thinking must be a side effect of the lack of sex in my life. It's been months since I've gotten laid.

He moves in closer.

One time.

Maybe we can do it one more time and get that frustration out. I've heard hate sex is all the rage.

I close my eyes, waiting for him to make the first move, and open them at the sound of the bowl moving. He's up on his feet, gumbo in hand, and walking to the kitchen.

"Are you leaving?" I ask while he sets his bowl in the sink.

"I have to before I push you down on that couch and fuck you."

Wait! I want to say. *Please do.*

I don't have time to state an argument before he's gone, the door slamming shut behind him.

I told myself that Gage would never come back to Blue Beech after what I did.

That a second chance was never in the cards for us.

Maybe I was wrong.

CHAPTER TWELVE

Gage

AS SOON AS I walk into my bedroom, I rip out of my jeans and head straight to the shower, desperate to tend to my hard-as-a-rock cock. The water rains down on me while I settle one hand against the tiled wall and stroke myself using the other, the same way I have done for years while thinking about her.

Rough and hard and fast.

Anger and frustration mingled with lust.

Lauren was as turned on as I was.

She wanted to fuck, and so help me God, I wanted to fuck her more than anything. More than when I had been a horny teen, sticking my dick into her for the first time.

I pump my hips, imagining it's her hand instead of mine, her lips sucking my tip. Even if she had wanted it, there was no way I wouldn't be disgusted with myself for letting her touch my dick after Susie the Grinder had her hands on me.

"Fuck, Lauren," I grunt out. "Fuck yes."

My cum shoots down the drain as I catch my breath.

Letting her move in was a bad idea.

Letting her back into my head was a terrible idea.

This time, it'll be tougher getting her out.

———

MY HAND CLENCHES around my phone when I read the text my friend—slash—once partner from Chicago sent me this morning.

Luke: Missy applied for an appeal.

Motherfucker. That won't be happening on my watch. My hands shake as I type out my response.

Me: I'll die before I allow that to happen.

I have to stop myself from throwing my phone across the room.

Luke: I'm with you, bro. I'll ask around and collect as much info as I can.

Me: Appreciate it.

Luke: You doing okay?

Me: As good as I can be.

Luke: Take care of yourself. You have my number if you need anything.

Me: Thanks, man.

A text comes in with the link to Missy's appeal paperwork. My teeth grit, my shoulders turning tense, while I slowly read it, taking in word by word. I nearly drop my phone at the sound of a knock at the front door. I shove it into my pocket and kick my feet against the hardwood floor on my way to answer it.

My interest piques when I eye Lauren through the glass. She's moving from one foot to the other, and the sight of her wearing one of my high school tees helps ease some of the anger from Luke's revelation. I hope like hell our conversation will stop me from boarding the first flight to Chicago to raise hell.

"Hey," she greets when I step out onto the porch and shut the door behind me.

Her short blue pajama shorts, which stop mid-thigh and show off her toned legs, are an extension to one of my old T-shirts. Traces of her nipples cut through the fabric of the white tee.

Shit, don't stare.

Is she trying to kill me?

Her gaze shoots down my body the same way I did hers, but I was more discreet about it. She's either clueless to how transparent she is or she doesn't care. My cock twitches in my shorts. She needs to quit looking at me like she wants me for breakfast before I have her pussy as mine.

I tip my chin up in response. "Morning."

She bites into her lip and looks past me, into the house. "Sorry if I woke anyone up, but something is wrong with the water. I can't get any decent water pressure in the shower. Hudson said he'd stop by sometime today to look at it, so I wanted to give you a heads-up he was coming."

"I'll take a look at it."

There's sleep in her eyes, exhaustion on her face, and her thick hair is pulled into a ponytail, loose strands moving with the morning wind. "You sure?"

"If there's a problem, it's my responsibility." I cock my head toward the loft. "Come on, let's take a look at it."

The sun is rising as I lead her to the loft, and I don't realize I'm not wearing a shirt until we make it into the bathroom. She's sans bra. We're both somewhat bare to each other. A bra is on the floor. Red. Lace.

So fucking sexy.

She kicks at it with her feet. "Sorry. I was planning on cleaning up before I left for work."

"I don't mind the new decor." I step into the tub and quickly figure out the solution. "Looks like the showerhead is clogged. I'll get a new one and fix it after work."

"Should've been the first thing I checked. I'm working a double today, so I won't be back until late. There's no rush."

"You can use the shower in the house if you want."

She shakes her head. "Dallas said he'd lend me his shower in exchange for me bringing diapers."

"I heard you were a second-time auntie."

"It's a big responsibility, you know." She leans against the counter and crosses her arms. "Giving them candy and sending them home on a sugar high. I'm the best aunt ever." She sighs. "In all seriousness, it did bring my brother out of the darkness. Samuel is one of the best things to happen to our family lately."

"Glad to hear that. Dallas is a good dude. Good things happen to good people." I step out of the tub. "I'll try to have it fixed by the time you're home tonight, so you won't be on diaper duty again."

"Thank you." She pauses. "We, uh … never discussed rent."

"Let me talk with my dad and get back with you." *Not happening.*

Kyle was right when he said I wouldn't take a penny from her.

"Cool." She picks up her bra, tosses it into the hamper, and closes the lid before grabbing her bag.

I stop her before she leaves. "As your landlord, it's probably smart I give you my number—you know, in case anything else like this happens again."

"Fair point."

I rattle off my number, and she punches it into her phone. I'm tempted to ask for hers but don't. I can't go there … can't risk texting her when I'm desperate.

I'm about to leave the bathroom when she stands on her tiptoes, grabs my chin, and pulls it to the side, examining my cheek. "How are your stitches? Any pain or irritation?"

"No pain, no irritation. They haven't been bothering me at all."

She keeps inspecting them. "They're healing nicely."

I smile. "Because they were done by the best, right?"

"Duh." She follows me out of the bathroom. "I'll see you, uh … later. Thank you for fixing the shower."

"It's no problem." I clear my throat when she turns around. "And nice shirt."

She pulls at the bottom while hiding a smile. "My wardrobe is limited right now."

"Wear my clothes as much as you like. The sight makes my dick hard."

A blush fills her cheeks when I take one last glimpse at her before leaving.

———

"WHO TOOK the report on Lauren's landlord situation?" I ask. "It was reported to her insurance company that she might've started the fire, so they're trying to fuck her over on cutting a check."

"Oh, you mean, after you were supposed to bring her in and never did?" Kyle replies.

Pretty much.

"I questioned her. She didn't do it."

"You're believing criminal exes now?"

"The dude is pissed she turned him down for a date. He followed her out of Down Home the other night and gave her shit for not going home with him. Lauren hadn't started that fire. His dick is the one blaming her."

"Damn, does she have a golden vagina? All you men falling for her."

"You might want to shut your mouth if you don't want to be eating through a straw for the next six months."

"Yeah, yeah. She's your first love, your one and only, the other half of your heart."

"You need me to mention the straw part again?"

He opens the dashboard and pulls a straw out, opens his coffee cup, tosses the lid, and drops the straw in. He annoyingly slurps from it while taking a drink of his coffee. "Straw or not, I'll still drink like a motherfucker."

"I hate your ass, you know that?"

"Love you, too, brother. I'll have Sanders look into your arsonist sweetie's case."

"Appreciate it."

"You sleep with her yet?"

"Who?" I know whom he's referring to.

"Who the fuck do you think I'm talking about? Kim Kardashian? Have you slept with *Lauren* yet? The date who you not only bailed on but also called the wrong name called *my* date and told her about it after you left, interrupting us during sex. I love you, dude. I loved y'all together, but I don't like seeing you get fucked over—again."

"We're not screwing. That ship has sailed, and we both know it."

"Not yet."

I shoot him a dirty look.

"If that's the case, Tamra has another friend she can hook you up with. Quit pining over your live-in ex-girlfriend."

"She doesn't fucking live with me," I cut in.

"As I was saying, you two are only feet away from each other, and I'm sure you're dying to have her. Might as well let a hot chick help with that frustration."

"I'm too busy to worry about women at the moment."

CHAPTER THIRTEEN

Lauren

JAY SLAMS his tray down on the table and takes the seat across from me in the hospital cafeteria. "FYI, my husband is pissed at you."

I drop my fork in my salad. "What? Why?"

"He has yet to receive an update on the ex situation. It's imperative he knows if you've had sex with him yet."

"No," I answer around a groan. "There will be no us having sex. In case you've failed to remember, he had his date in the car with us!"

"And he couldn't have given a shit about her. He was at Clayton's *for you*. He took you home *for him*. For his own peace of mind that you'd be safe. I'll bet he dropped his date off and went home alone."

Not exactly alone. But I won't be divulging that information.

"Behind all of that pissed-off, hard facade, Gage is a caring man who'll always think about my safety. That's who he is. He's a police officer. It's his duty."

"True, but he also does it because he loves you." He sighs. "You loved him at one point. Those feelings were there, and from what it looked like at dinner, they still are."

"That's not true."

"When's the last time you went on a date?"

"My job is my boyfriend. Saving people's lives is my orgasm. This is where I spend all of my time. You know that."

"So, why not date someone who works here? The doctors talk. I know how many people in this building have asked you out."

"I'm not interested in dating, and FYI, I've slept with someone I work with, so I'm not depriving myself of orgasms," I lie. I've never even gone on a date with someone from the hospital.

"Who was it?" He stares at me. "Tell me it wasn't Pete from ortho."

I draw a line over my lips and fake zip.

It wasn't Pete from ortho.

It was Victor, my vibrator, courtesy of Amazon Prime.

————

I CANNOT WAIT to shower and sleep this shift away.

The lights are on at the loft when I pull into the drive.

Gage must've forgotten to turn them off after he fixed the shower. Unless I left them on, which wouldn't surprise me, given I'm supposedly a lousy tenant and all. If this place goes up in flames, I'm for sure getting locked up.

There's no sign of life in the main house, but Gage's truck is here, so he must be in bed. I walk through the front door and start stripping out of my scrubs. I didn't check myself in the mirror before leaving work, but I know my eyes are puffy, and hints of mascara are running down my cheeks.

I'm rubbing my eyes and yawning as I make my way into the bathroom and then let out a full-on dramatic scream.

Gage is standing in front of me with a smile on his face, wiping his wet hands off on a towel. I'm in my bra and panties. I repeat, I'm in my bra and panties in front of my ex-boyfriend, and they're suddenly more soaked than what I'll be when I get in the shower. He's shirtless, and remnants of water are running down his fit chest.

"What are you doing here?" I ask, catching my breath.

"Fixing your shower," he says, pointing to the tub. "Sorry, I didn't mean to scare you. I should've given you a heads-up that I'd be here, but I don't have your number. I had a long day, and this was the first free minute I had."

"It's no problem."

He hands me a towel. "Trust me, babe, there's nothing on you I haven't seen before. To be more specific, I've seen *much more*." He chuckles and licks his lips. "I also know what you taste like."

"I can say the same for you," I whisper.

He wipes the side of his mouth. "Kyle is convinced we're going to have sex."

"Kyle must have turned mental since we last talked." I give him a frustrated glare. "You know he hasn't talked to me since we broke up? I know bro code is real and all, but homeboy hates my guts."

"That's my boy."

"Gee, thanks. I don't remember forming a hate club against you."

"Never told him to hate you. He formed that opinion on his own, and I'm not sure how anyone could be pissed at me for your ending our relationship." He leans against the wall. "You know I would've never done that to you, especially the way you did it."

"Can we go back to joking about sex now? I'm too exhausted to talk about blame and people being mad at me."

He blinks at me a few times. "You're upset."

I nod, trying to stop myself from bursting into tears.

"Long day?"

"You have no idea." I slump down the wall and settle on the floor.

"What happened?"

A tear slides down my cheek. "We had a baby come in this evening who'd gotten into his mother's coke stash while she was passed out. He overdosed, and instead of calling for help or bringing him to the hospital, she called her mother. His grandmother brought him in because his mother was afraid she'd be arrested for possession. By the time he got to us, he was having seizures, and we knew it was too late."

"Fuck," he hisses.

"I was his nurse. Jay, his doctor." Another tear falls down my face. "We tried everything but we weren't able to save him. Two years old and no longer alive, thanks to his selfish mother. I had no choice but to let her see him when she finally got the balls to come to the hospital. God, I wanted to snap when she screamed at us to save her baby like it was our fault, and then she dared to say we didn't do enough to keep her baby alive." I sigh, the memory jerking through me, and clench my jaw. "They prep us for situations like these. I've watched patients of all ages die, witnessed people lose limbs and go through severe trauma. It's hard, but for some reason, this woman infuriated me. Her son died because she was irresponsible and negligent."

His face pales when he sits next to me and drags me into his arms. "There's nothing worse than a mom who purposely endangers her child. Any parent who does that is a self-centered piece of shit." It doesn't feel weird when he tilts his head down and kisses the top of my hair. Surprisingly, it feels comfortable and comforting. "What you do is extraordinary, Lauren. Hard on the heart but extraordinary."

"You do the same," I whisper, snuggling into his side. "You're just as upset as I am."

He squeezes me. "I'm not someone who likes people hurting others. Trust me, there are times I've had to hold myself back from snapping, too."

I want him to tell me more, but I also don't.

Police officers are a constant in the hospital, and some of their stories make my skin crawl.

I wipe my eyes and slowly pull away, sniffling. "Thank you for listening to me." I nod toward his tear-and mascara-stained tee. "And for letting me ruin your clothes."

"Anytime. You either ruin them or steal them. Nothing has changed there."

"For some reason, when you steal a guy's shirt, it makes it a hundred times more comfortable."

"You're welcome to them anytime." He stands up and helps me to my feet. "Shower is fixed and all yours. Is there anything else you need while I'm here?"

Pull me back into your arms.

Stay here with me.

I shake my head. "You're probably just as tired as I am."

He rubs my back. "Get your shower. It'll help you relax."

I undress, and the water pressure is perfect when I step underneath the hot water. My tears fall down the drain, and I wish it'd take the memory of today with it. These are the days I don't love my job, when I question if I went into the right field, and when I wonder if I should take another career route.

I made the decision to set my feelings aside when I decided to become a nurse. Caring for my patients is priority number one. At times, it is the hardest part of the job.

Not having emotions would be beautiful because pain is so ugly. Watching neglect and not having the freedom to scream about it at the top of your lungs is painful. It's hard, having a heart when people come in without one.

And that's what I feel like happened today.

My sobs grow stronger.

I fought for that baby.

At least, in the short time he was with us, he had people fighting for his life, for his safety, for his happiness.

The hard part was that we failed him.

His mother failed him.

The system failed him.

And those are the cases that are the hardest to fight at work.

I wash my hair while releasing all my frustrations and scrub my skin harsher than necessary when cleaning it. I shiver as I dry off and throw on my pajamas.

Gage is sitting on the perfectly made, untouched bed when I get out, and a glass of water is sitting on the nightstand next to it.

"You haven't slept in the bed yet?" he asks.

I shake my head. "I crash on the couch."

"Why?"

I shrug. "The memories. The sheets still smell like you."

"Do me a favor and make them smell like you, so I have something to look forward to when I move back in."

"What? You said the place was for rent."

I had been right. He never intended to rent it out. Gage loved this place, loved his space, and would never let anyone take it over. Even when he moved. Neither would his father.

Amos had numerous offers to rent it when Gage left and turned them all down, hoping his son would one day return.

"My dad was thinking about it but changed his mind. You're more than welcome to stay until you find a place though. He enjoys my company in the house."

I narrow my eyes his way. "I don't understand. Why would you give it up and let me stay here?"

"It's late. You've had a hard day." He kisses my forehead. "Catch some sleep. Let me know if the shower gives you any more problems, if you need someone to talk to, anything, okay?"

CHAPTER FOURTEEN

Gage

I GRAB my phone from the nightstand when it beeps.

Unknown: You up?

I start to text back, *Who's this?*, when another text comes through.

Unknown: It's Lauren.

Fuck. I was afraid of having her number.

Me: Wide awake. What's up?

Lauren: Care to give a girl some company?

Me: Can't sleep?

Lauren: No.

Me either.

Me: On my way.

I jump out of bed, fully aware it's a bad idea. I step into a pair of gym shorts and throw on a shirt before quietly slipping out of the house and into the warm summer night. Grasshoppers chirp as I stroll down the walkway and then up the stairs.

The door is unlocked, and she's on the couch, her legs brought up to her chest. Hair wet. Eyes swollen.

"You know," I say, walking into the room, "the chances of

you falling asleep are higher in a bed than on the couch. I can almost guarantee that."

She pats the cushion next to her. "Hey, I find this couch comfy. I can't believe you haven't changed anything in here."

"I have yet to find the time to hone in on my interior design skills." And I want to keep the memories. Even though they haunt me like a motherfucker, I want them all. "I had nothing in Chicago that reminded me of home, so the recollection is nice sometimes."

Curiosity crosses her face, curiosity of what my life was like in Chicago, but she stops herself from asking those questions.

Not that I blame her for her interest. It's what every Blue Beech resident has wanted since I came home. Answers. A report of what I was up to. Questions of why their golden boy got dumped, moved thousands of miles away, and then never came back for years—not for holidays, not for reunions, not even for my father's retirement party from the electrical company. Instead of celebrating that with him here, I flew him to me. I kept in touch with no one, didn't join any social networks, and became a stranger to the place that had raised me.

She clears her throat. "You want to watch a show or movie?"

I'll do anything to get her mind off of her horror of a day. I collapse on the other side of the couch and keep my eyes on her while making myself comfortable. "True crime still your jam?"

"My jam. My peanut butter."

"Your pickles on your peanut butter, you mean?"

A flicker of a smile comes my way. "My pickles on my peanut butter."

Lauren is the only person I know who enjoys PPB & Js— pickles, peanut butter, and jelly. She's most likely the *only* person on the planet who does, considering I have yet to meet someone else with that indulgence.

"True crime it is then," I say. I dramatically shake my head. "You and your serial killers."

She snags the remote off the coffee table. "Blame yourself. You're the one who got me obsessed with all those documentaries. My nickname at work is Nurse Paranoid because I assume everyone is a serial killer."

"Those shows are what made me decide to go into law enforcement."

My mom was the ringleader in our true-crime obsession. I grew up watching them and, as Lauren and I grew closer and older, we shared our loves of different interests with each other.

I got her hooked on true crime, and she got me hooked on strawberry-banana milkshakes.

She messes with the remote and scrolls through the guide on TV. "See, something good did come out of our documentary binges. Do you have any new favorites?"

What I want to tell her is no, I don't because I stopped watching any shows involving true crime years ago. Not because it reminded me of her, but because it became my life. I've seen it firsthand—the murders, the bribery, all of it. I don't though because she needs this. Her mind deserves to venture into somewhere else, and if it means I have to sit through something that might give me flashbacks, so be it.

"The choice is all yours," I answer.

Her feet drop as she lies back on the couch and brings herself to the fetal position after making her selection. A thin blanket is wrapped around her shoulders, her head rests on a pillow, and her attention goes to the TV.

I stay in my corner, my feet crossed at my ankles, and I surprisingly stay calm. Maybe it's her presence. Maybe my attempt to soothe her has done the same for me.

Two documentaries later, she's snoring. We made no light conversation. It was all solitude as we sat in the dimly lit room. I quietly slide off the couch and tiptoe out of the loft even though all I want to do is stay there, drag her into my arms, and create more memories on that couch.

I don't bother turning on the lights when I make it into my room and fall on the bed. My heart feels lighter tonight, and a smile is twitching at my lips as I think about how great it is to be around Lauren again. It doesn't take long for me to fall asleep, which is out of the ordinary.

Too bad my nightmares still come back to haunt me, sucking away all the calmness she gave me.

It's the same conversation.

The same scene that plays over and over again.

"WHAT DID YOU DO, MISSY?" My voice grows louder, angrier, more venom flowing with every sharp, nervous word spit out. "What the fuck did you do?"

"It's all your fault, you know," she fires back. "If you had loved me right, none of this would've happened!"

"You did this out of spite for me?"

I move closer at the sound of sirens in the background. Determination thrums through me to get to her before they do, and I drop to my knees, prepared to plead if need be.

"Where is he?" I stress, tears biting at my eyes.

Her smile is wicked. "You'll never know." Those four words kill me yet satisfy her as she sings them out.

I'M COVERED in sweat when I wake up. I jump out of bed and throw my soaking shirt off. Then, I go to the kitchen for water and decide I'm in need of fresh air.

CHAPTER FIFTEEN

Lauren

"OH, COME ON," I mutter during attempt number five of starting my car.

Can anything else go wrong this week?

My apartment catching on fire.

Check.

Ex back in town.

Check.

Having one of the hardest shifts in my career last night that emotionally drained me.

Check.

My car playing the game of not wanting to start.

Check.

The sun beams down on me. It's the butt crack of dawn, which means it'll be an inconvenience to wake anyone up and ask for a ride. I grab my bag from the passenger seat and start to rifle through it, searching for my phone. I hope it's not too complicated for them to find a replacement for me at the last minute.

I unlock my screen at the same time I hear the sound of a door slamming. I look through the windshield to see Gage stepping off the porch, a coffee cup in his hand, and sweat trickling down his chest.

The TV was still on and Gage was gone when I woke up on the couch this morning. I don't know how much longer he stayed after I fell asleep, but if it weren't for him being there with me, I wouldn't have slept at all last night. He was there for me as I broke down and cried in his arms, and the memories of when he'd done that in the past haunted me while I got ready for work.

I drop my phone back into my lap as he hops down the steps and meets me.

"Car trouble?" he asks.

I cringe as I attempt to start my car again, and it fails. I dramatically grip the steering wheel. "Yep."

"You know what the problem is, don't you?"

"If I did, I would already be gone."

"It won't start as a result of its ugliness. It's decided that it's finally time to go to car heaven."

"Shove it," I grumble. "It's too early to hear you passing judgment on my car."

"You have to work?"

"Supposed to, but I was about to call off. I can't expect anyone to make an hour round-trip to take me back and forth to work."

"I can. My shift at the station doesn't start for another two hours and will most likely end before yours does."

I think back to what happened last night. The way he held me as I cried, how the memories of when we'd hung out crept back into my soul. Getting attached to Gage will only ruin me later. It's dangerous for us to get close again. He hates me. And what if he wants to know why I broke up with him? It'll kill him that I have to keep my secret.

Everything is moving too fast. We went years without speaking, and now, all of a sudden, we're talking daily.

"Thank you for the offer, but I can call off."

"Lauren, I don't have cooties."

"You have much more than that."

My heart. A cock I can't stop thinking about.

"In my truck now."

I lose sight of him as he moves and taps the hood of my car.

"Let me change real quick."

I jump out of my car. "You don't have to do this."

He turns around and starts walking backward. "It's no big deal."

"Why are you being so nice to me?"

"As I told you before, I've been asking myself the same question since I arrested you."

His truck is unlocked, and I throw my bag onto the floorboard. Gage comes back, dressed in jeans and a tee. Two coffee cups are in his hand.

"In case you want one for the ride," he says, handing it to me.

I take a drink and groan. "This is delicious."

"My dad likes that sweet shit, which I can't stand. I think the creamer is cinnamon roll flavor or some shit."

I sip the coffee and straighten my legs out while he pulls out of the drive. He hasn't turned on the radio or initiated any other conversation after the sweet-coffee talk. I can't stand silence. I'd rather face an awkward conversation than awkward silence.

"What have you been up to since … you know?"

He glances over at me. "Since you dumped my ass?"

Well, shit. Maybe the silence would've been a better option.

"Since we broke up," I correct.

"I moved to Chicago, worked a job in law enforcement, and then decided it was time to come home."

"That's it? Anything else happen in all those years?"

"Nothing I want to talk about." He focuses on the road. "What about you?"

"After graduating from nursing school, I snagged a job in the ER at the hospital, moved back home, and my apartment caught on fire, which lead me to crashing at my ex's place."

"That's it?" he asks, throwing my words in my face. "Nothing else happened in all those years?"

"Hudson got engaged to Stella Mendes," I add, moving the attention from me to my family.

There's been nothing too exciting in my life. During college, I immersed myself in my studies, and now, all I do is work to keep myself busy, so I don't think about my high school sweetheart. I've been disciplined enough not to look him up, though the urge has hit me so many times.

Admission time. I did look him up twice when I drank too much. The first time was the day after I graduated from college. God, I wanted to share the news with him. He had known it was my dream. The second was a year ago when my sister-in-law passed away from breast cancer. She'd died young, in her early thirties, and regret hit me that day. I wanted to apologize for what I'd done.

I couldn't find anything on him. He had no social media accounts, nothing. Gage was a ghost to everyone I knew since we broke up.

"I heard about their engagement," he says. "News travels fast when a Hollywood celebrity gets engaged to a Blue Beech local."

"Lucy died," I go on, my voice lowering as my chest aches.

"I heard about that as well. My heart broke for your family when my dad told me."

"Dallas had another baby with Stella's friend and personal assistant."

"Damn, I have missed some shit."

"Care to share anything else personal about *you*?"

"Not much to me, Dyson. I've never been engaged to a celebrity or knocked anyone up."

I wait for him to elaborate, wishing on anything that he'll give me more, but he doesn't.

"One-sided conversations are so fun," I comment.

"The hell do you want me to tell you, Lauren? What do I owe you?"

This is not a conversation I want to have first thing in the morning before working a double.

I cross my arms and shift in my seat to look out the window. "I wish I had never told you anything. I should've moved on, gotten married, had fifteen kids, so I could prove to myself and everyone else that I could be happy without you."

"Yeah, well, I wish I could say the same shit, but my love for you, my fucking *obsession* for you, has never allowed that. My love for you has ruined my entire fucking life."

The hell?

"What did I ruin for you? You could've easily gotten married and started a family. Don't blame that on me. It was your stubbornness."

"I was married."

I suddenly feel like I'm suffocating. "Say what?"

"I got married."

"You're married?" I shriek like I misheard him.

"No, I got married and am now divorced."

"You're lying." The words sound like whimpers leaving my lips.

He shakes his head. "I'm not."

"You said you'd never made love to anyone else," I whisper.

"Never loved her."

My brain is scrambling. "Why would you marry someone you didn't love?"

"It's complicated."

"Good thing we have plenty of time."

"That doesn't mean I'm talking about it."

"You were married."

"Yes." The topic seems to frustrate him.

I play with the fabric of my scrubs. "Where is she now? Do you guys still talk?"

Is she prettier than I am? Skinnier? Smarter?

I'm jealous of a woman I've never met.

"In prison."

Okay, maybe not so jealous now.

"What?" I wait for him to tell me he's kidding, that it's some sick joke, but he doesn't. "Care to elaborate on that truth bomb?"

"No. We married for a stupid reason, she lost her goddamn mind, and I divorced her."

"Just to clarify real quick. Does the wifey work in a prison, or is she an *inmate* in prison?"

"She's incarcerated."

That doesn't tell me anything.

"What did she do to earn her trip to the pen?"

"She was fucking selfish."

"Okay," I draw out. "With your work in law enforcement, I'm sure it's no secret that you can't be given a cellmate for simply being selfish. You have to commit a crime to do the time."

"Cool. Thanks for the education. Still not talking about it."

This morning conversation has taken a wrong turn. A turn I don't like.

"My stuff will be out of the loft by the end of the week. Hopefully, before that, considering I don't have much. Don't worry about picking me up tonight. I'll find a ride."

He points to himself in amazement. "You're pissed at me?"

I throw my hands up. "Yes!"

"Lauren, you have no right to be angry with me."

"You married another woman!"

"And you left me, giving me the opportunity to marry her. Had we never broken up, you would've been the only woman I ever said *I do* to."

"It doesn't matter or change how I feel about it. You've been harboring this grudge, this resentment toward me, for breaking your heart, yet you married another woman." I snort. "Then, you lied straight to my face about never falling in love again."

"Never loved her. We were friends, and I married her as a favor."

A favor? Who marries someone as a favor? Not sane people, that's for sure.

"Bull-fucking-shit. Maybe you need to be locked up with her —for *selfish* reasons, of course."

"Lauren," he says in warning.

"Screw you, *Gage*. If you didn't love her, why did you feel the need to marry her, like it's a common courtesy or some shit?"

"Not going there, nor will I ever." He shakes his head. "I should've never told you. Forget I said anything."

"*Whoa*, pump those brakes, buddy. You can't throw that truth bomb and then expect me to *forget it*."

I have so many questions.

"That's where you're wrong. Just like you don't owe me an explanation of why you broke up with me, I don't owe you one about what I've been doing since then."

I stomp my feet against the floorboard when he turns into the entrance of the hospital. I need more time to drag admissions out of him. Although I doubt he'll be confiding in me about anything else.

"What time does your shift end?" he asks, shifting his truck into park.

"Don't worry about it. I'll find a ride. Go call your wife." I'm acting petty, I know, but I'm dizzy while processing that he moved on with someone else. I shouldn't be, given I'd pushed him into her arms, but it's the only reaction I can give at the moment.

"We're too old to play fucking games," he says, annoyance running through his words. "What time, Lauren?"

"Eight," I huff out.

"I'll be here."

I step out and slam the door.

He got married.

Said *I do* to another woman.

Gage Perry has no right to be angry with me.

CHAPTER SIXTEEN

Gage

TELLING Lauren about Missy was a mistake.

Her too-many-questions road-trip game defrosted my defenses. My admission clipped out before I knew I'd even been thawed. Lauren is notorious for bringing my every thought out into the light, but she'll never know *everything*.

That shit is going with me to the grave.

No one in Blue Beech but my father will ever know. That nightmare will stay in Chicago.

The story made local headlines but never went national. Missy grew up in a family with politicians hitting every branch in the tree. Their pockets were full of old money, and they were experts in writing checks to fix any blemishes on their reputations. They could erase any word in an article with the click of a pen, forming the dollar sign.

That was the first and only time I was grateful for their pocketbooks. The thought of *his* picture being dissected and on display for the world to see would've ruined me. From the first time I found him outside the station, I made it my job to protect him but failed miserably.

I sink my fingers into the leather of my steering wheel.

Moving here was my solution to take me away from the memories of hell.

Chicago was nothing but a reminder of what I'd lost.

———

"DUDE, WHAT'S UP YOUR ASS?" Kyle asks, sliding into the passenger seat of our cruiser. "I told you this would happen. You bring the devil into your home; it'll turn into hell. You know, that's why her last building went up in flames ... because she's an evil demon."

"It's too early to listen to your shit," I mutter.

The thirty-minute drive back into town had given me time to clear my head before going to work. I went home, showered, and skipped breakfast with my dad. He would've known something was wrong.

Swear to God, he and Lauren are better at reading me than I am myself.

Kyle takes a sip of coffee and sets it in the cupholder. "Dinner at Mom's tonight. Be there at seven."

"Can't," I answer.

"You *can*, and you *will*. You know how I feel about people bailing on my mother."

Not a lie. Kyle will throw down with anyone to defend her.

"I have to pick Lauren up from the hospital after her shift."

No doubt he'll find amusement in that.

"You her chauffeur now, too? Driving Miss Demon?"

"Her car broke down this morning. She needed a ride."

His green eyes light up in amusement. "Bring her with you."

I glance over at him before pulling out of his driveway, seconds passing, to verify he's the one in the car with me.

I snort when I realize he's not kidding. "That's a big fuck no."

"It's my mom's birthday dinner, bro, and she's been asking about you nonstop since you moved back. You've been blowing off every invitation since you've been home. Not cool."

Damn, I feel like an asshole.

He's not lying. I haven't done much of anything, except work and hang out with my dad.

"I'll drop Lauren off and then be there. That cool?"

"Not so fast. You opened up the can of worms. Bring her with you. I want to see with my own two eyes that you're over her. Prove it to me."

"And I want to kick your ass sometimes, but it doesn't mean it'll happen." I narrow my eyes at him. "I take that back. You keep talking shit about Lauren and me getting back together, and I'mma end up kicking your ass."

"Yeah, yeah," Kyle mutters, fishing his phone from his pocket before hitting a name and pressing it to his ear. "Hey, Ma. I'm with Gage." He pauses. "Yes, I invited him, but he declined." Another pause, and he shoves the phone into my chest.

"Gage, honey," Nancy says over the phone when I grab it. "Please come. Growing up, you were like another son to me, and I'd love to see you."

"Trust me," I say around a sigh, "I'd love to see you, but I wouldn't be able to make it until after eight. That's a long holdup for dinner."

"No holdup whatsoever," she replies in her sweet Southern voice. "I've been a night owl since retiring. I eat late."

"All right then. I have to pick up a friend from work, and then I'll be there."

"The friend is Lauren!" Kyle yells in the background and grunts when I press my fist into his stomach.

"Lauren Barnes?" Nancy asks. "I haven't spent time with that nice girl since my son shunned me from talking to her. I'd love to catch up with the both of you. See you tonight!"

The line goes dead.

I throw the phone into Kyle's lap.

"I can't wait for this shit," he says, rubbing his hands together. "It'll be the best excitement I've had—aside from your arresting her."

"Remind me to file a request for a new partner," I mutter.

Lauren is going to flip her shit when she finds out about this.

CHAPTER SEVENTEEN

Lauren

JAY WALKS in and leans against the break-room door, arms crossed, while I grab my bag from a locker. "Alec requests a full report on tonight's festivities with your ex-lover boy."

During our lunch break, I spilled the dilemma with my new roommate situation, and it's no surprise that he went and tattled to his hubby. Not that I can blame him. I would've done the same thing ... if I had a husband.

I let down my ponytail and brush my fingers through the strands. "There will be no story."

He grins, his bright white teeth on display. "You're rooming with your ex. There will never be a lack of a story."

"We're not *rooming* together. It's more like neighbors. I'm going home *alone*, eating canned soup, showering, and then hopping my tired butt into bed. Nothing exciting about that."

He steps away from the door and pats my arm. "Keep telling yourself that, love."

Trust me, I do.

"Have a good night, Jay," I sing out, throwing my bag over my shoulder.

He laughs. "And you have an even better one. Get laid! You deserve it for all your hard work!"

There's a text from Gage when I power my phone on that says he's in the parking lot and to let him know when I'm walking out. I reply, and he pulls up to the automatic doors as soon as I make it out.

In the back of my mind, I had wondered if he'd bail on picking me up. During every break, I checked my phone, waiting for him to tell me to call a cab, considering our ride this morning had been cringe-worthy. Tonight's goal is to make it bearable.

No ex-wife talk.

No past talk.

No breakup talk.

The weather and why NSYNC broke up will be the only conversations happening tonight, ladies and gents.

The masculine smell of aftershave and peppermint hits me when I slide into the truck.

"Long day?" he asks as I settle myself into the leather seat.

His midnight-dark hair is covered with a blue baseball cap, cloaking his forehead and showing me only a sliver of his hooded eyes. The thin white V-neck tee he's wearing shows off the tan and muscular arms that wrapped around me like a security blanket last night. Guys in V-necks are right there underneath guys with huge cocks in the What I Lust For list. He also looks as tired as I feel.

"You have no idea," I answer, strapping my seat belt on as he exits the parking lot. I thought I'd seen everything until I worked in the ER. "I appreciate the ride. Hudson said he'd have my car towed to the shop tomorrow to take a look at it."

My grandfather started Barnes Machinery and Equipment decades ago. When he retired, my father took it over, and now, my brothers are in charge. They specialize in fixing large machinery and typically don't take on pink Mustangs, but they're making an exception for their sister.

"I'll do it," Gage answers. "I hoped I'd have a second to look at it today but got caught up in some shit."

We are not friends. We cannot try to be friends.

Our trying to be friends would only produce more scars when he asks for what I can't give him.

"Don't worry about it," I say. "It's my problem, not yours." My words burst out more harshly than I intended.

"I take it, you're still pissed at me?"

No. Yes.

"I'd be lying if I said I wasn't, though I have no right to be."

Today's shift was spent working and digesting the truth bomb Gage had thrown on my breakfast plate this morning. My rationality finally returned three hours ago. I'm not too proud to admit when I'm wrong, and it wasn't fair for me to be angry … or jealous.

I gave him the opportunity to fall in love with another woman, the green light to *marry* another woman, and I have no one to blame for my anger besides myself. I've dated and slept with other men since we've been apart, and my fear of commitment with someone else doesn't mean he had to do the same.

"I appreciate the honesty," he answers, tapping his fingers against the steering wheel.

Silence passes, and the only noise cutting through the awkwardness is the faint sound of the radio. I stare out the window but steal glances at him every few seconds, hoping he doesn't notice my taking in the way he bites into his lower lip when he's holding himself back from saying something he shouldn't.

He's done that for years. I've read him and picked up on his quirks, and I consider myself a specialist in body language. At this moment, I'm sure his lack of sharing whatever he's thinking is for the best.

I'm wondering how to move this conversation to my love of Justin Timberlake when he interrupts my thoughts by clearing his throat.

"By the way, you won't be thanking me for the ride when we make it back to town."

"Why's that? You planning on killing me and throwing my body in the woods?"

"Nancy invited me to dinner tonight," he answers. He presses his teeth to his lips again.

"Cool. Word on the street is, she makes a killer roast."

"You're about to find out for yourself."

"Such a sweet man to bring me leftovers."

"Let me correct myself. Nancy invited *us* to dinner. My mistake for the miscommunication, Dyson."

"Did you tell Nancy there was no *us* to invite?" My stomach growls, like it's fighting for its right to be pro-dinner at Nancy's. It wants something better than SpaghettiOs. I pout out my lip. "Leftovers will be both accepted and appreciated though."

"Have you eaten?"

"I managed to chow down a sandwich and an apple during one break. The other breaks were filled with chugging down coffee, so I wouldn't give a patient Viagra instead of antibiotics."

He cocks his head to the side. "That happened before?"

I shake my head. "Nope, thanks in large part to coffee."

"Doubt that's why. You know how to do your job. You've wanted to be a nurse for as long as I can remember."

His mother is the reason I became a nurse. Melody worked in the same ER years ago, and I'd sit at their kitchen table for hours, listening to her tell story after story while I threw millions of questions her way. Her passing away from congestive heart failure at forty only strengthened my passion. I wanted to pursue this career path in her memory.

He grabs his phone from the console when it rings and answers the call. "Yes, I picked her up, and we're on our way. I don't have to reply to your ungodly number of text messages for check-ins." He chuckles and sneaks a look my way. "I'll be sure to divulge that you can't wait to see your favorite person."

Oh, hell. He wasn't joking about dinner.

"Not happening," I tell him when he hangs up. "Call your pain-in-my-ass partner back and tell him I won't be in attendance." I squish my face together in a smug smile. "I wish y'all a happy dinner though."

He's still chuckling, and though it's directed at me, it feels good to hear laughter coming from someone who regularly looks like he has a stick up his ass. "I promise I did my best to stop it."

"You're a grown-ass man, and the last time I saw you naked, you had balls. Tell them no."

He smirks. "Balls are still intact, FYI. I can show you, if it helps."

"Nice to know. No need for evidence."

"I can't bail on Nancy," he says, blowing out a long breath. "It's her birthday, and she's excited we're coming. And Kyle obviously is, as well." He smirks again, unable to hide it at the mention of his best friend and Blue Beech's biggest asshole to me.

Kyle will taunt me all night. His invite isn't genuine. It is an excuse to drag me through hell.

"The last time I talked to Kyle, he gave me a ticket for a broken taillight and said he'd hate me until he took his last breath for running you out of town. I don't trust the fool around my food. He'll be topping off my drink with antifreeze."

"Chill, Dyson. He won't poison your roast." He shakes his head as I give him my best death stare. "How about this? You come, and I won't make you pay rent this month."

"Your way of convincing me to hang out with you is free rent? What am I? Vivian in *Pretty Woman*?"

"Don't say it like that."

"Is there a better way to say it?"

"It's different. Dude got laid in that movie. Doubt our night will end up with me screwing you on an expensive-ass piano."

"Don't hold your breath on that happening. You're a *married* man." Yep, my selfish ass still can't let that go.

"I'm a *divorced* man, sweetheart. We were married for five years, three of which were hell."

Five years?

His marriage wasn't a temporary thing or a favor. You can't be with someone for half of a decade and not have feelings for them. It just doesn't happen.

"Doesn't matter if it was for a day. You can't keep throwing the *I ruined your life* bullshit in my face. You found love. You had a wife." I throw my arms up. "Hell, you might have kids. Any Gage Juniors running around that I should know about?"

The mood in the truck shifts, as if a surprise storm suddenly rolled over us with the clench of his jaw. Instead of his fingers tapping to the beat, they're now biting into the steering wheel.

"Nope, no kids," he grits out.

I'd hand him water if I didn't think he'd throw it out the window with enough force to split the street. My question cut out a grim memory lodged inside him.

Were he and his wife unsuccessful in having a baby?

"What did I just open up there?" I ask, the words falling from my mouth slowly and carefully—a skill I mastered in nursing school for better communication with patients.

"Nothing," he snaps. His attention is on the road, as if he were waiting for something to run out in front of us.

"Okay," I draw out.

Don't push him. Don't try to get back in.

I went into nursing because I wanted to heal and help people.

The problem is, Gage is a lost cause because he doesn't want either from me.

"I don't have to go to dinner," I say. "Tell Nancy I'll visit her sometime this week."

"We're both going."

"Why? You look like you'd rather have your toenails ripped off than have dinner with me."

"It's not you, I fucking swear it." He pauses to take in a few breaths and calms himself. "If anything, you'll be the only person capable of pulling me out of this funk, so I don't walk into that dinner and act like a miserable dick."

"All right."

There's a new level of pain powering through this gorgeous, tattered man. That teenage boy I fell in love with years ago has been replaced by someone darker. I'll take responsibility for some of that pain, but something else had ripped him apart harder than I had.

Whatever it is, it's something he doesn't want to have come out because it'll bring him to his knees. He needs someone to keep him standing, and I was thrown into his space just in time. No matter how shattered our relationship is, I'll never let him hurt alone.

Everything happens for a reason.

People can redeem themselves.

My redemption for breaking his heart will be helping him get through this dark time.

I shift around in my seat. "I am pretty hungry."

He tips his head down. "Thank you."

His fingers go back to tapping against the beat, and the rest of the car ride is limited to the sound of the radio. It's quiet yet comfortable, like we've thrown out and taken too much for one night.

———

NANCY IS happy to see me when we walk in.

Kyle, not so much.

I'm shocked he's allowed me to step foot into his parents' home. The shit-eating grin on his face confirms his invite is for research purposes only. He wants to study Gage and me together.

Nancy's warm arms wrap around me in a tight hug. The last time I saw her was when she brought in Kyle's younger sister with a broken leg from a cheerleading stunt gone wrong.

Her attention goes to Gage, his hug tighter, sadder, filled with more relief. She moved into the second-mom role after his mother's death, and I'm sure it hurt her just as much as it did Amos when he left town.

Did they still talk after he left?

"Lauren, honey, it's been so long," Nancy finally says after her hugging spree. She pokes Gage in the chest. "I'm not happy with you, young man. You haven't visited me once since you've been home."

Gage wraps his arm around her shoulders. "Sorry. It's been a busy month, but I promise I'll make it up to you. You can make me roasts anytime you like."

I'm the only one who notices the forced excitement in his voice. It's not that he's unhappy being here, but our truck conversation had stirred something hard inside him that won't be let out anytime tonight. I feel guilty that it will interfere with Nancy's time.

'Tis why I need to keep my mouth shut.

"Your father must be thrilled to have you back," she goes on, looping her arm through his. "Dinner is ready."

Kyle comes to my side before I move out of the foyer, arrogance splashed on his face, and I know this conversation is going to be a fun one.

"Satan," he clips.

"Asshole," I mutter.

"I see we're still fond of each other." He moves in closer, his voice falling to a whisper. "Don't fuck him over, you hear me? This is a new Gage, a darker man, and I won't let you hurt him again. I'll be running *you* out of town next time."

A long sigh leaves me. "Gage and I are only friends. There's nothing wrong with that."

He scratches his cheek. "Wrong. Gage will never see you as just a friend. He cares about you more than his own life. He'll never choose anyone over you, and he will sure as fuck never move on from you for some goddamn weird reason. You were his life then, and you're still his life, no matter how much he denies or fights it." He shakes his head. "I only hope to God the feeling is mutual."

My stomach twists like a coil. "We've grown up. You have no idea what you're talking about."

"Figure out what you want with him. If you plan to only be *friends*, you're doing nothing but hurting the dude. If there's a chance you can make shit right again, then I'll be Team Reconcile. He needs love, not heartbreak." He glances over to Gage in the kitchen, talking to his mom. "I don't know what's going on, but it's something deep."

We're huddled in the corner, and I'm surprised no one has called us out for looking sketchy. It helps that everyone's eyes are on Gage. Kyle's two younger sisters and brother are staring at him as if he owned the world, and Nancy keeps insisting he taste-test different desserts. Kyle's dad is nowhere to be found, which doesn't surprise me, given he's the mayor of Blue Beech.

"You don't know why he moved back to town?" I ask, watching over my shoulder, just in case Gage wants to come through and eavesdrop.

"No idea. Been trying to drag it out of him for weeks."

"Was it the wife?"

"Wife?" He scrunches his brows. "He was married?"

"You didn't know that?"

"Nope. Never mentioned a wife to me." He shakes his head in pain. "I promised myself I'd give him time to tell me what was going on before I went looking around for it. He can't lose trust in someone else."

"Good luck. Whatever it is, it's not leaving his mouth."

"You have a much stronger pull. If anyone can do it, it's you." He leans in. "You make him happy, and maybe I'll stop hating your selfish ass."

I give him the brightest smile I can manage. "Cool. I'll never stop hating you."

His hand goes to his chest, faking offense. "Me? The fuck did I do to you?"

"Pissed me off when you called me Satan and for pulling me over for stupid shit over the years."

"Prove to me you're not."

———

"WHAT MADE you come back to this boring-ass town?" Rex, Kyle's younger brother, asks.

We're at the dining room table with a spread of food in front of us. I can't believe I'm eating so many carbs this late.

"Language," Nancy warns. "Just because you graduated doesn't mean you can talk like a grown-up."

"I technically *am* a grown-up," he fires back.

"Not in this house. Here, you're still my child. So, keep your profanities to when you're hanging out with your friends."

Rex groans while putting his attention back on Gage. "Let me rephrase. Why'd you move away from Chicago? There's nothing to do round here."

That's the mystery of the year.

I grab my water, hoping Gage will give him a better answer than he gave me. Doubt that will happen. Gage has loosened up since our heated talk in the car, but there's still a wall built up in there.

"My dad needed me," is all he says, taking a sip of water.

"We're happy to have you back, and I'm thrilled you and Kyle are partners," Nancy cuts in, most likely to stop her nineteen-year-old son from blurting out personal questions. "I had no idea you were in law enforcement."

Gage wipes his mouth. "After I moved to Chicago, I went to school for a few years and did some security work, and that's when I decided that I for sure wanted to be a police officer."

"It's what we said we'd always do," Kyle chimes in.

Gage nods. "I guess the both of us still felt that calling."

"I bet you saw some traumatic shit around Chicago, huh?" Rex asks. "I've heard at least one person gets shot a night."

"Rex," Kyle says in warning.

Instead of joking like he did when Nancy reprimanded him, Rex shuts his mouth and leans back in his chair.

"It's a high-crime area for sure," Gage answers. "It could be hard at times."

"What …" Sierra, Kyle's sister, hesitates before going on, "What is the worst thing you've ever seen?"

I don't blame them for their curiosity. Blue Beech has one of the lowest crime rates in the country. Robberies are rare, let alone a homicide. Had I not worked in a hospital outside of town, where I saw more than they did, I would've been full of questions, too.

"I saw a woman kill her child," Gage answers. "The worst thing I've ever seen is a mother who murdered her son."

The table goes quiet. I drop my fork. A whimper falls from Nancy's lips.

None of us expected that answer. Sierra and Rex were anticipating some high-speed chase, something exciting, not this appetite-killing reveal.

And, with the click of a question, Gage's wall has returned, now stronger than ever.

His back is stiff against the chair, his fingers clenched around his fork, and from years of Gage experience, I know when he's close to losing it. Someone needs to take this conversation down a different path. Everyone is thinking the same thing yet not saying anything.

I take it upon myself to do it, racking my brain for a good

conversation turner. "So, uh … I get puked on all the time at work."

Probably isn't the best dinner conversation either.

"That's gross," Sierra says, her face scrunching together.

She made it a point to tell Gage she was *all grown up* when she sat next to him at dinner. There's no doubt she's *all grown up*. She'd been in her early teens when Gage left and always crushed on him. Gage called it cute, but the way she's looking at him now is anything but *cute*. She recently turned twenty-one, and there's nothing not grown-up about her. To be honest, she's gorgeous.

And she's staring at him as if he's more appetizing than dinner.

Not that I can blame her.

I see a hint of a thank-you in Gage's eyes when he looks over at me, and Sierra and Rex start questioning me about hospital horror stories. I give them short ones that involve vomit and dealing with objects in places where no sane person would stick in certain areas. My job talk puts everyone at ease, and we enjoy Nancy's roast.

———

"SOOO …" Sierra draws out. "Are you and Gage back together?"

Jesus. Can we be in the same room without that question popping up?

She followed me into the kitchen after dinner while the others went outside. I can't stop myself from looking down at the sloppy outfit that I threw on after work, considering I'd planned on showering and throwing my ass into bed, and then look at hers. I've never been jealous of the chick, but she's dressed to impress tonight.

I shake my head. "We're trying the whole friendship thing."

She grins. "Perfect."

"What do you mean, *perfect?*"

She shrugs one shoulder. "Perfect as in he's single and you have no interest, which means it's okay for me to ask him out."

Am I okay with this?

I have to be. Might as well get used to seeing Gage with someone else now before we start enjoying each other's company and get hooked again.

"You can do whatever you want," I say, grabbing a water bottle from the fridge. "He can do whatever he wants."

She nods and walks out of the room, as if I've given her permission.

I've never wanted to tackle someone so hard in my life.

CHAPTER EIGHTEEN

Gage

SURPRISINGLY, I managed to keep my cool at dinner.

No breakdown happened when Rex asked me about the bad shit I had seen in Chicago.

As much as I enjoyed seeing Nancy, anxiety crawled through me with the need to leave so that I could clear my head. It's the same reason I've been avoiding people. Questions don't surprise me, and their curiosity can't be blamed. I was gone for years without a word. I'm a stranger to them now. A stranger they want to pick apart for entertainment.

On top of that, too much shit happened today.

Lauren knows about Missy, people wanted too many details about my life away from here, and Lauren's stepping in with the vomit talk helped buy me time to regain some of my composure. Her saving my ass doesn't do anything but drag out all the feelings for her I've tried to keep stored away. They're coming back harder and faster, hitting me while I'm weak.

The short ride back from Nancy's is filled with small talk about how delicious Nancy's meal was, and Lauren jumps out of the truck as soon as I park in the driveway. Her door slams, and she doesn't look back at me while going up the stairs to the loft, her bag thrown over her shoulder.

I step out and watch her when she makes it to the top stair.

"You're coming up," is all she says.

It's a demand, not an offer.

And I stupidly obey.

I toss my keys on the counter as she turns on the light.

"There's something you're not telling me," she says.

My hands slide into my pockets. "Don't know what you're talking about." It was a mistake, following her. I should've said good night and gone to bed.

"Don't lie to me, Gage Perry. I know you better than anyone. You're hurting. Something happened while you were gone."

No shit.

I steady myself and lean back against the wall. "Whatever you think you know, it's wrong. I'm tired. Fucking sue me for it."

She stomps her foot and drops her bag. "I know you, Gage!"

"No!" The word leaves my mouth louder than I intended. "You used to know me. You used to course through my motherfucking veins." I push off the wall and stand straight. "You left me. You left me, and I ran and got hurt worse than any girl breaking my heart could ever cause. It's not about you." I throw my arm out and gesture to the room. "Nothing going on in my life is about you anymore."

I expected my response to anger her, but it does the opposite.

"What happened there?" Her voice cracks in her question.

A rush of adrenaline flushes my cheeks. "It doesn't matter."

"What happened?" The words come out more confident this time.

And mine are harsher. "It doesn't fucking matter."

I stiffen when she takes a step into my space. "You're hurting."

I snort. "Since when do you give a shit about my feelings?"

She doesn't come any closer, but stops only a few inches

from me. "Can we please move on from the past? My God, it was years ago! We were freaking kids."

"*Kids?* We were eighteen. Eighteen and making adult decisions!"

Sadness passes over her dark features. "What happened, happened. Yes, we have a past, but that doesn't mean we can't be friends now. And, from the looks of it, you need someone to confide in."

I don't want her pity. "I have plenty of friends. Don't need another."

This is the moment she closes me in, not giving me an escape as she stands in front of me, and if I back away, I'll hit the wall.

"Then, what do you need?" she asks.

My answer leaves my mouth as if it's been waiting there on autopilot, ready for when the time came.

"You." I take my hat off and toss it to the side. Not another second passes before my hand curls around the back of her head, my fingers digging into her silky hair, and my lips crash into hers. "I need the girl I fell in love with. Fuck, I need her now more than ever."

The thought of rejection and her pulling away doesn't faze me. I'm lost in the moment of touching the girl who got away. Her mouth falls open, and our tongues dance together so easily when she slides hers into my mouth, like our years of separation never happened. My body reacts to the memory of her. Hers does the same.

When she steps closer, I don't stop her. I wrap my hands around her waist. Her chest hits mine, and I'm pushed back against the wall. A groan leaves her mouth into mine, and that's what pulls me away. My hands fall, and I use them to brush her fingers from my chest. A whimper leaves her when I slide along the wall to move away.

"Fuck," I breathe out, wiping my mouth. "I'm sorry. This isn't a good idea."

"Gage," she says in an attempt to stop me from reaching the door.

I turn around to show her who I am now, so she can see the evidence of a broken man. "Lauren, I'm not who I used to be. You don't want me. I'm destructive, dark, and unhappy. You're smiles and sunshine. We no longer go together, and I refuse to release my darkness onto you."

She repeats my name as I walk out and jog down the stairs.

————

AS IF MY timing can't be any worse, I walk into the house to find my dad in the living room. I give him a head nod as a silent good night, but he stops me.

He moves back and forth in his old recliner while keeping his eyes on me. "Everything okay?"

I scrub my hands over my face. "Peachy. Just need to hit the sheets."

His wrinkles become more prominent, the longer he stares at me. "Have you told her?"

That question only fuels the uncontrolled fire burning inside me tonight. "Nope, and I'm not planning on it, so keep it to yourself, okay?"

"Maybe she can …" He stops to take in a breath of oxygen from his tank. "Maybe she can help you get through it."

"No one can."

He only gives me a slow nod, and I leave the room. I don't bother turning on my light, changing my clothes, or taking off my shoes as I fall onto my old twin-size bed. Endless thoughts on an array of topics rush through me. I consider asking Lauren to move out, consider running back to Chicago until justice happens, consider telling her everything.

As much as it pains me to admit, Lauren might be the only person capable of bringing me in a few steps from the darkness, but I can't do that to her. I won't. It's not only for my protection from getting hurt again, but it's also to protect her from getting involved with someone so fucked up. I moved home, hoping to go back to the chill guy I had been before, and I'm waiting for that to happen.

Not sure if it ever will though.

My phone goes off, and I fight myself on whether to look at it.

I regret it as soon as I do.

Unknown Number: Hey, it's Sierra. I got your number from my brother's phone. Let's get together sometime this week and catch up. ☺

My phone beeps again with a picture.

It's her in lingerie.

Shit.

I quickly delete it.

The last thing I need is Kyle being mad at me for fucking around with his baby sister.

Fuck this day.

CHAPTER NINETEEN

Lauren

HIS MOUTH FELT SO FAMILIAR.

Comfortable.

Warming.

I brush my fingers over my smiling lips. They feel different— plumper, lighter, more alive. His walking out on me shouldn't have me grinning like a cheeseball, but I can't stop myself.

Does your body remember someone's touch as intensely as your brain remembers your memories with them? Our kiss felt different from those I've had with meaningless men. My skin tingles, wanting more of him everywhere.

That cheeseball smile is still on my face when I grab my phone and flop down on the couch, fully prepared to call Willow and scream out my frustrations, but I don't. Instead, I open my texts and hit his name.

My heart races like I've been sucking down caffeine on a quick work break. Now that I've experienced grown-up Gage kisses, I want everything from him.

Is it desperate to text?

Yes, probably.

I should wait until tomorrow.

Do I care at this moment? Hell no.

His kiss lit my world on fire, and I need more. The problem is, what can I say that won't result in an eye roll ... or a possible restraining order from him?

My goal in my text will be to make him remember what we had.

Me: Your kisses are amazing. Good night.

I put my phone down and get up to make a cup of tea. My phone chimes as I'm walking back to the couch. I take a sip of tea before looking at the screen.

Gage: That kiss brought up everything I'd wanted to forget.

Cheesy smile growing.

Me: Maybe you should stop trying to forget.

Gage: Maybe you shouldn't have left me.

Cheesy smile gone.

Here we go again.

His answer has made it clear. Nothing more between us will happen from that kiss.

The more I'm around Gage, the more I want to fix him, and from the looks of it, that's the furthest thing from what he's looking for. Now, I understand why Gage stayed away for so long. The pit in my stomach is feeling the pain he must've felt from wanting someone he couldn't have. My breathing quickens, and from his response, I know I can no longer stay here.

Me: I'll be out by tomorrow. You won't have to keep fighting to forget me.

Is it an idle threat? I'm not exactly sure.

I walked away from Gage for a reason—a damn worthy one, one I saw as selfless. I gave away my happiness, so someone else could have light. Since he's been back, the urge to explain to him why has never been stronger, but I can't.

It'd ruin him.

It'd ruin someone else.

I slide out of the comfort of the couch at the sound of a

knock on the door, and my bare feet stomp against the floor. I turn on the overhead light and peek out the window before answering.

It's Gage.

He's pacing back and forth.

His gaze fixes on me as soon as I swing the door open, and my heart sinks as I take a good look at the man in front of me.

Unease lines his handsome face as he presses his fist to his lips and blows out a long breath.

"Are you trying to fucking ruin me?" he bites out.

My lungs constrict. His words chill me to the core.

It's not me Gage is fighting.

He's fighting his fears.

The fear of my hurting him.

The fear of him hurting me.

Fear that rekindling our relationship will drive him out of Blue Beech again.

That means I need to bow out of our living situation.

"No!" I blurt out. "That's why I'll leave. We're only hurting ourselves, getting close, spending time together, and dragging out old feelings that should've died with our teenage years." I step out and cup his cheek. "I'll leave, so you don't have to again, and then it'll be easier for us to get over each other."

His chin trembles under my hand. "Get over you?" he scoffs. "Is that what you think I want, Dyson? You think I want to get you out of my head and lose you again?"

I pull away and throw my arms up. "Yes! We're playing a childish game. You push me away but not enough that I'm out the door, and then you pull me back in. We've been dancing to this song since you came back to town. I've grown up. My heart has grown. I'm more mature, and in that, I know when to stop following my heart and listen to my brain." I lower my voice. "I don't want us to end on bad terms again. Consider this saying good-bye mutually, and we'll both smile and wave next time we run into each other." I take a step back when the first tear falls down my cheek. "Good night."

"Don't leave," he says, nearly a whisper, and his arm darts out to stop the door from shutting.

I freeze in place, and his eyes are glassy when we make eye contact.

"What?"

"I've lost enough people in my life. I'm fucking terrified of losing you again."

I lose a breath when his lips hit mine again, rougher, pleading. I gasp when powerful hands grip my hips, and I'm pushed back into the loft. The door slams with the kick of his heel, and my head spins as I'm picked up and set on the table.

Oh, hell yes.

CHAPTER TWENTY

Gage

MY HEAD IS CURSING my heart, fighting with my dick, and screaming what an idiot I am.

This.

Her.

Us.

Has the ability to ruin me.

My dick throbs when she wraps her legs around my waist to pull me closer. I pause and force us to make eye contact before this goes any further.

"You're so damn beautiful," I whisper, skimming my fingers over her jawline.

She bites into her bottom lip after I brush a single finger over it and then smiles. "I don't want to sound like a cheeseball, but damn, you're beautiful, too."

I respond by tilting my head down and kissing her again.

Passionately. Brutally. Carnally.

A kiss that makes up for the millions we'd lost.

The sweet taste of her mixed with cinnamon hits me when she slides her tongue in my mouth, stroking it against mine, and I hiss when she rocks her hips, brushing her heat along my jeans-covered erection.

"It's been too long," she says, pulling away. "Please, Gage, I need you inside me *now*."

Desire pumps through my veins, but I force myself to shake my head. "We haven't had enough fun yet." For years, I've imagined the thrill of tasting and touching every inch of her body before sliding into her sweet warmth. A quick fuck isn't how I want this to go down.

"You inside me will be plenty of fun," she snaps. Her demanding tone only turns me on more. "Let's save the extracurricular activities for another time. I need this, Gage. *We* need this. Right now. It's been too long."

How the fuck can I say no to that?

She curls her hand around the bottom of my shirt and drags it over my head. It gets tossed on the ground at the same time I go for hers. My mouth watered when I noticed the faint tips of her nipples through my tee the other day. I've been salivating to taste them.

Her back arches when her chest and dark pink nipples are exposed to me. I tip my head forward and circle my tongue around the tight bud. She inhales a deep breath when I capture one between my lips and suck hard.

My knees feel weak when she goes to work on lowering my pants. My dick springs free, fully erect and aching for her. There's no missing her annoyance when I step back at the same time she reaches for my dick. I grip her ankles and run my hands up the soft skin of her tan legs.

"I've been waiting to see all of you again," I whisper.

"Gage," she gasps when I pull her ass to the end of the table and slide her shorts off. "Don't make this some dramatic, soap-opera shit. Screw me, and then we'll do the whole foreplay thing on another occasion."

Another occasion.

Is that a guarantee of another night together?

Excitement burns through me at this happening again.

Her petite body is on full display. A beautiful exhibit I'd

forever pay anything to see. I'd give my money, my heart, and my sanity for just a glimpse of this every damn time.

She licks her lips and rubs her thighs together before I spread her legs.

"One lick, and then I promise you'll have all of me," I say, maneuvering between her hips and sinking my nails into her skin. I ignore her protests of disapproval while lowering myself and resting her thighs on my shoulders.

Her heels sink into my back at my first taste.

Well … my first taste in years.

"Holy shit," she breathes out.

She tastes divine, sweet, like perfection, all wrapped in one. I plunge my tongue inside her while my finger goes to work on her clit. My one-lick plan has shattered.

Okay, maybe three licks.

Her frustration turns into pleas, begging for more of my mouth while she wiggles beneath me. I give her that and more by thrusting a finger inside her while still sucking on her pussy. She moans when I add another finger and reach up to play with her nipple again.

I don't stop until I feel her falling apart as her body shakes, and her pussy clenches against my fingers.

Her chest heaves in and out as she comes down, and determination sets on her face. "Inside me *right fucking now.*"

No more fighting this.

No more delays.

We've been holding out for too long.

I wipe my mouth and claim hers when I stand up, allowing her to taste herself before situating myself between her legs. I stroke my shaft, wrapping my hand around the head, and just as I'm about to give us what we both want, it hits me.

"No condom," I say with a groan.

"I'm on the pill. I'm clean." She slams her hips forward, her wet opening sliding against my dick, causing me to grunt.

"Me, too." I pause and chuckle. "Clean, I mean. Not on the pill."

She laughs. "I've already suggested the doctors start looking into that for men."

I arch a brow, my hold on my dick tighter. "I thought you needed me inside you?"

"I do."

I drop my hold. "Then, take me."

My head falls back when she grabs my dick in her hand, and I take a deep breath while staring at it, not wanting to miss a glance of her carefully placing my cock at her entrance.

"Slide into me," she says, tilting her hips up.

I tighten my fingers around her waist, and with one hard motion, I am inside her.

Hot damn.

She feels amazing.

She takes all of me in one thrust.

And, just like our kiss, we give in to each other and make love.

Passionately. Brutally. Carnally.

She feels like paradise, and her juices slip down my thighs as I pound into her.

"God, I missed you," I bite out, watching her tits bounce as she meets each thrust. "Missed this."

She runs her hand across my six-pack. "Me, too, baby. Me, too."

Surprisingly, I don't stop when she finds the mark on my side and runs her fingers along the scar tissue.

My response is to continue our game of giving and taking.

We fuck like we can't get enough of the other, and I get swept away, inside her. Inside us. I'm at the top of the world when I know she's close.

I have her on the brink again.

She's going to cum around my hard cock.

And I'll be doing the same inside her pussy.

Bare. Raw. Nothing between us, whether it be latex or problems.

Nothing matters, except our love and lust for each other.

Fuck. Did I say love?

All my thoughts shatter when her legs shake around my waist, and she lets out a long moan before screaming out my name. Perspiration covers my chest as I fuck her until my back goes straight, and I let myself go inside her.

It takes us a moment to catch our breaths.

Even longer for me to calm my heart.

She presses a kiss to my chest, and every muscle in my body tenses when she reaches down and brushes her hand along my scar.

"This," she says, her breathing still catching. "What's it from?"

I gulp and rest my forehead against hers. "Work accident."

She nods, and the room goes eerily silent.

"Everything okay?" I ask, tapping her temple.

"That was … impulsive." She blows out a breath. "I'm trying to figure out if we made a mistake."

She thinks this was a spur-of-the-moment, lapse-in-judgment fuck?

"You decide and let me know," I say against her hair before kissing it.

"That's your answer?"

"Dyson, anytime I'm with you is never a mistake. That's how I feel, but you have to make that decision on your own."

"You don't … you don't regret this? You hate me."

I pull away and rest my hands on her still-shaking legs. "I've *wanted* to hate you for years, but I can't. My heart won't allow it."

She grins, which causes me to grin back.

"And don't fucking smile like that."

She doesn't stop. "What?"

"You know what." I lightly tickle her side. "You always liked it when I was wrapped around your little finger."

"You were never wrapped around my finger. You were a good boyfriend. Nothing like my friends' boyfriends who would brag about every base they hit with them, and then the girls would get slut-shamed while the guys would get high fives. You kept everything we did between you and me. You respected me."

Yet she didn't respect me enough to be honest.

I hold my response in, and her legs are wobbly as I help her down from the table. Nearly every piece of furniture in here has been sex-broken in by us when we were teens, except this one until now.

I make sure she's stable and grip her hips when she leans back against the table. "You ready to sleep in my bed now?"

She reaches down to link our hands. "Only if you join me."

I allow her to lead me to the bed and watch as she rips the blankets down. She flips the light off, and we quietly slide into bed. It feels comfortable when I pull her into my side, like she's always belonged there and a missing piece of myself has been put back in place.

"That better than expensive-ass piano sex?" I ask, squeezing her side.

She laughs and snuggles in closer. "Much better."

CHAPTER TWENTY-ONE

Lauren

WAKING up next to Gage is a high I never want to come down from.

Sex might complicate our situation, but I don't regret it.

Sex with teenage Gage was amazing.

Sex with grown-up Gage is nothing like I've ever experienced.

That doesn't mean I'm not scared.

Sometimes, history shouldn't be dug up.

One thing is for sure; history repeated itself in the sex department.

Never have I felt something so intense and intimate as what I feel with him—*every single damn time.*

I turn on my stomach and rest my palm on his chest, looking up at him. "Good morning, landlord."

He chuckles and sleepily looks down at me. "Morning, beautiful."

"I have to say, I didn't think this would ever happen again."

He reaches down and cups my ass, sending shivers down my spine. "Never has a truer statement been made."

The sight of Gage, naked and in bed with me, is breathtaking. I would be a woman on top of the world if I could do this every morning. It sounds so easy for us to go back to what we were before, and I'm ready to take that step if he is.

Ready for this to become a lifetime thing.

I reach up and trail my fingers over the stubble on his cheek before inhaling a deep breath of courage and closing my eyes. I open them and stop myself from saying what needs to be said.

Not this morning.

Expectations ruin moods, and I want this good time to last for as long as it can.

"Was this ... is this ...a one-time thing?" he whispers, taking the words from my mouth.

Shit.

"Can we not talk about expectations and just enjoy this morning?" I ask, my hand venturing under the blanket and grabbing his erect cock. "I know of a better way to spend our time."

His hand cups mine, an attempt to stop my hand from pleasuring him. "Before we do, I need my breakfast."

Even though he's cut off some of my power, I stroke him the best I can under his touch. "You're a breakfast-in-bed guy, huh? In that case, you might need to run to your house because all I have is cereal here."

He flips me on my back. "You have exactly what I need."

I yelp when the blanket is torn off, and he crawls down until his face meets my thighs. I thought a beautiful sight was him next to me in bed in the morning, but dear God, his head between my legs might compete. My hands travel to his hair, and I grip the strands as he gives me the good morning I've missed for years without him.

———

CAPTAIN CRUNCH IS in my bowl, and I'm eating my breakfast in bed.

Gage is at my side, enjoying his second breakfast.

The man has definitely improved in the oral sex department. There's been nothing but comfortableness with us this morning. We've hung out, watched TV, and had light conversation. No mentions of where this is heading or of expectations.

Hopefully, it stays that way.

I want to relish this moment where no resentment or regret exists.

"What time do you go into work?" I ask, swallowing down a bite.

"I'll head out in about an hour," he answers. "You have the day off, right?"

I nod.

"Any plans?"

Other than agonizing about what happened last night on repeat?

It's a bummer that I'm not working. The hospital is the best place to tear me away from my problems.

"I'm hanging out with Willow and the kiddos."

Knowing Willow, I'll be answering questions about him all day.

"Sounds like fun."

Goose bumps run along my leg when he runs his hand down it.

He smacks a kiss on my cheek before sliding out of bed and grabbing our bowls. "Want to do dinner tonight?"

I bite into the edge of my lip. "It's our mandatory monthly dinner at my parents' house." I pause to take a deep breath. "If you're hungry, you can tag along."

He grins. "You asking me to meet the parents, Dyson?" The bowls clank when they hit the sink. He cleans them and starts tracking down his clothes around the loft.

I narrow my eyes at him. "Oh, shove it. Pretty sure you've met the parents."

He sits on the side of the bed, next to me. "So, are we going to do this? Try again?"

That's the question of the damn year.

"I mean ... I don't know." I wipe the sleep from my eyes. "What happened last night terrifies me but in a good way, if that makes sense?"

"As much as it doesn't, I understand because I feel the same way." His face softens. "But, what I said last night about being a different man, I wasn't lying. It wasn't a ploy to keep you away from me. I am, Lauren."

"I know you have ... history, what with having an ex-wife locked up and all." *And secrets. You have secrets. A shit ton of secrets.* I'll save that conversation for another day. "And, uh ... more."

He stands and starts to get dressed. "Yes, more."

I break our eye contact and start playing with the blanket, hoping my words sound comforting. "Do you think you'll eventually tell me sooner or later?"

His gaze is downcast.

"I'm not asking you to spill out your past right now, but I'd like to understand what you're going through. Maybe I can help."

"We'll see." He kisses the top of my head. "Let's take things slowly, okay? You might come to the conclusion that you can't stand my ass anymore."

"And you might conclude that you actually *can* stand me."

"Already figuring that one out, babe."

My phone beeps with a message, and I snag it from the nightstand to see Willow's alert that they're about to pull into the driveway. I jump out of bed as if it suddenly caught fire and start throwing clothes on.

Gage follows me into the bathroom and leans against the wall, hands sliding into the pockets of his pants, while I start brushing my teeth. "About dinner tonight."

I spit out my toothpaste and rinse my mouth before answering—with an inner fear of rejection—"You know what? Don't worry about it. It's too early for something that serious."

He takes a step forward and wraps his arms around my

waist, lightly pushing into me. "Ask Mama Barnes if there's anything I need to bring." His lips go to my cheek, causing me to blush as he kisses it. "I'll be there."

My cheeseball grin has returned as I look at him in the mirror. "Really?"

"Really." He whips me around and clasps my hands in his, holding them between us. "Let's see where this goes."

"I like that plan."

My phone fires off again, and I pull away to grab it.

Willow: Coming up! Any exes in the building I should know about?

"Oh shit," I hiss.

"Oh shit what?" Gage questions.

"Dallas and Willow are here."

He scratches his stubble-covered cheek. "That a problem? I thought you had plans with them."

"They're coming *up* here. As in right this second."

A triple series of knocks interrupts our conversation, and Gage goes to answer the door. I'm behind him, my chest hitting his back, when he opens it.

A bright smile pops on Willow's cherry-colored lips. "Well, well, look at what we have here." She points to Gage. "Bet me five hundred bucks I know your name."

"Willow, stop messing with him," I say with a groan.

She smiles. "And who exactly is *him*? He your milkman, your landlord, your *ex*?"

Gage holds out his hand. "I'm Gage, definitely not the milkman, kind of the landlord, and yes, the ex ... *for now*."

"I vote for you to keep him," Willow says to me.

We move to the side to let Willow in. Maven is next to her, their hands entwined, and Dallas is behind them with Samuel in his arms.

"Gage, man, good seeing you," Dallas says.

Gage nods toward Samuel. "Congratulations on the addition to your family."

"The little one is my daughter, Maven, and the loudmouth to her side is my baby mama, Willow," Dallas says, jerking his head toward them. "A heads-up, she wasn't born with a filter."

Gage laughs. "The good ones never are. I'd love to catch up, but I'm due for work soon." He kisses the top of my head. "See you soon."

"Gage, huh?" Dallas asks when Gage shuts the door behind him. "Can't say I'm surprised once I heard he was back in town."

Willow sighs, her shoulders slumping. "Man, this is one of those times I wish I had grown up here. I need some juicy dating history."

Dallas hands Samuel over to me at my request and gives his good-byes. He drove the tow truck to take my car into their shop. Even though Gage offered to look at it, I can't put that on him.

I sit down with Samuel in my arms and rock back and forth while Maven roams around the loft, loaded with curiosity. The girl might be only seven, but she's a nosy one. She must've inherited that gene from my family.

Willow points to my clothes. "This a new style of yours?"

I glance down at myself. I'm sporting a pair of Gage's shorts and a scrub shirt. "Thought I'd try something new."

She snorts. "Yeah, whatever. I can't wait to get you alone."

CHAPTER TWENTY-TWO

Gage

"AND GOOD MORNING to my best friend who finally got laid," Kyle calls out, slapping me on the back when I walk into the station. "Was it an exorcism with the ex?"

All eyes of my coworkers go to me, and I don't answer him as I take long strides to my office, him trailing behind me. I've already been a subject of gossip since I got home, and now, Kyle has sparked the curiosity in their heads even more. They'll be keeping their ears open for any information they can gather and spill out to their friends and family.

I expected him to give me shit eventually, but damn, am I that transparent when it comes to Lauren? Maybe it's easier for people to read us than it is for us to read ourselves.

I read Lauren this morning, and I saw the confusion and panic in her. It was a familiar feeling.

"How about you quit worrying about my relationship?" I respond when we reach my office, and he plops down in the chair in front of my desk.

Kyle has his own office, which he hardly frequents because he hates being alone. Blame it on growing up in a large family where there was always noise in the background.

His eyes crinkle at the corners. "Ah ... so it's a relationship now?"

I rub at my tired eyes. "Why are you asking me these questions?"

"You look the happiest you've been since you moved back, which is a giant motherfucking dis to my ass, considering you haven't ever been that happy to see my smiling face."

"Shit, my bad. I wasn't aware you wanted a make-out session to celebrate our reunion."

He flips me off. "You could've at least brought a guy some flowers."

"Noted. Next time we have a spat, roses and champagne will come your way. Are we finished with this whole bro-bonding talk?"

"Hell no. I'm only getting started."

"Doesn't surprise me," I mutter.

"So what? You two back on?"

"We didn't talk about anything. It's fresh, and bringing up the future isn't a good idea yet."

I don't want what we had last night and this morning to be a one-time thing. If I could have it my way, I'd have her before we shut our eyes at night and the second we woke.

The problem is, between those times, it's more complicated.

"You two are a hot-ass mess," Kyle goes on.

"It only happened last night. Dragging up old memories and expectations is a dumb idea."

"I'm sure you didn't think it was a dumb idea when your head was between her legs this morning."

I grin. "I'd never think that's a dumb idea."

CHAPTER TWENTY-THREE

Lauren

MY DAY CONSISTED of strolling around downtown with a strawberry smoothie in my hand and then running around the park with Willow and her kiddos. The chaos of keeping up with them has distracted me from my thoughts of Gage and what happens from here with our relationship.

We had straddled the line and played games since our first run-ins, and it doesn't surprise me that we finally crossed it.

We had sex, although I'm not sure how we got there in that moment.

Maybe it was the hurt on his face that drew me closer to helping him.

Maybe it was the way he looked at me.

Maybe it was the fact that I'm still in love with him.

I'm back in the loft. Maven is sleeping off her exhaustion from the day on the couch, and Willow is feeding Samuel while we sit at the kitchen table. She's been waiting to get me away from Maven's ears to grill me about Gage.

"Dude is hot, especially with the after-sex glow. It's about time you got laid," she says. "Are you back together?"

As much as I don't want to partake in this conversation, I

need to. Willow might be overdramatic at times, but she's logical and levelheaded when it comes to relationships.

"We talked briefly, but I don't know where his head is. The last thing I want to do is get my hopes up, and then it falls apart."

Gage made it clear weeks ago that he wanted nothing to do with me and that he hated my guts. Sure, I said the same, but I was lying.

So, what changed his mind?

"Why would it fall apart?" she asks. "It's obvious that he still has feelings for you. You love him. Maybe it'll work out this time."

"He was married." *Is this my way of talking myself out of giving us another shot?*

"But he's divorced now, right?"

I nod. "Yes, but he *got* married. That's a big step for someone. He gave another woman a ring, said I do, and was with her for years. And get this; no one knew about her, not even his best friend."

"Divorces aren't that uncommon. Maybe he thought marrying her was the right thing to do. Did he knock her up maybe?"

I shake my head. "He said he doesn't have any kids. He might've divorced her because she went to prison."

"Prison? Chick is in prison? Like murder prison or fancy *I didn't pay my taxes* prison? I need details, pronto."

"Trust me, I want details as much as you, but he won't give me anything."

She sets Samuel's empty bottle on the table and starts burping him. "You didn't check the internet? Hello? Google is the new private investigator. It'll save you time and money."

I shrug. "I thought about it, but it doesn't feel right to go behind his back. I want him to trust me enough to tell me himself."

"You are a patient soul. I would've already had the prison wife's entire family tree looked up, seen her middle school yearbook pictures, and known her blood type."

"I just"—I sigh—"don't want to break his trust."

"I understand, but let me know if you change your mind and need assistance in the stalking department. I excel at it."

I laugh. "Why doesn't that surprise me?"

"Are you inviting him to dinner tonight?"

I can't stop myself from grinning like a teenager who just scored her first prom date. "Already did, and he said he'd come."

As if his ears were burning, my phone beeps with a text from Gage.

Gage: Just pulled in. You up for some company?

His offering to hang out is a good sign.

Me: If you don't mind a baby, a napping kid, and a nosy future sister-in-law, come right up.

Gage: Sounds like a blast to me. I'll stay quiet.

I set my phone down and attempt to give Willow a serious look. "He's coming up, so please don't interrogate him."

She frowns. "You're no fun anymore."

Gage doesn't bother knocking before walking into the loft, and I can't stop myself from licking my lips at the sight of him in his uniform again. He could sport that every night when he comes home, and I'd still never tire of it.

Willow swoons when he kisses my cheek and pulls out the chair next to mine. I can feel my cheeks blushing. This is the first time we've touched like this in front of someone.

He tilts his head toward a cooing Samuel. "You've got a cute little man there."

Willow peeks down at Samuel and plays with the fat roll on his arm. She scoots her chair out, situates my nephew on her side, and stares at Gage. "Thank you. You want to hold him while I use the bathroom real quick?"

At first, Gage seems taken aback by her question, but he eventually nods. "Yeah, sure."

"I can take him," I blurt out, sliding my chair out from the table.

Willow glances away from him to me. "Was that too intrusive?"

Gage holds his arms out. "No, not at all. Hand the little guy over."

Willow carefully places Samuel in Gage's hold and makes sure he's steady before heading to the bathroom. I'm tempted to kick my foot out and trip her. Her question was a test of his character.

My mom always says, "You don't know someone's patience until you see how they act with a child."

"You sure you don't want me to take him?" I question.

He shakes his head. "I've got this, Dyson."

My heart tightens as I watch him stare down at Samuel with an expression I know all too well. I see it regularly at the hospital. It's emptiness. Pain. Disappointment.

What happened to him?

Whom did he lose?

My thoughts jump back to when I asked if he had kids. He said he didn't, but there's a longing there.

Did he and his wife have fertility problems, and that's what broke them apart?

Did he want children, but she didn't?

Did she miscarry?

Samuel relaxes as Gage rocks him in his arms. My stomach flutters, and I wish I could record them together. Everything in Gage changed in that small moment—his demeanor, his skin bunching up around his sorrow-filled eyes —and his face confessed I was missing something significant about his past.

"Wow," Willow says, causing me to jump at the sound of her voice. She moves back into the room with a smile on her face.

"He takes to you, Gage. Lucky for Lauren, it looks like you'll make a great father one day."

Her last words are like an electric bolt smacking into a power line, shutting Gage off from me. His shoulders still, his body going tight, and the lost expression on his face fires through harder.

He holds Samuel out to Willow, and his voice turns cautionary. "It was a pleasure meeting you and your family. I have to go."

His hands shake as Willow takes Samuel from him, and as soon as their exchange finishes, he jumps up from the chair and rushes to the door. I'm on his trail, reaching him at the stairs, and I grab the back of his shirt to stop him.

"Hey," I say, unable to get him to turn around. "What's wrong?"

"Forgot I needed to shower," he clips before sniffing his armpit. "I had a long shift."

Liar.

Alarm rings through my mind. There's something wrong. This isn't the right time to question him. Even though I don't know why he's upset, his slumped shoulders and emotion-choked voice tell me the pain is deep. Trying to draw out the reasoning from him with Willow here is selfish.

"Are we still on for dinner?" It's not a serious question, but it feels like a thousand bricks hit me when I ask.

He moves down a step, and I expect him to walk away, but instead, he turns around to look at me. "Shit, I forgot I promised my dad we'd do pizza, beer, and the game tonight."

Liar.

He's a pro at faking; I have to credit him for that. He's absorbing the pain deeper, hiding it from me, with each passing second.

"Want to stop by when the game ends?" I ask.

He rubs his eyes. "Sure. Have fun."

With that, he turns around.

I don't head back into the loft until he disappears into the house.

"Okay, what just happened?" Willow asks when I walk back in. Her face is filled with guilt as she stands with Samuel on her hip. "Did I cross a line, asking him to hold Samuel? Does he not like kids?"

I shuffle back to my chair and sit down. "He needed to shower."

"Is he still coming to dinner?"

"I'm not sure that's a good idea."

"Maybe he thought he really did smell." She laughs while lifting Samuel up, smelling his diaper. "Maybe my little guy here had a dirty diaper, and he thought it was himself."

"Does he have a dirty diaper?"

She frowns. "Negative."

I blow out a long breath. "He just randomly shut down. I don't know what happened."

She plops back down in her seat. "Did you ask if he wanted a shower mate?"

A snort leaves me. "Really?"

"What? Sometimes, sex helps to figure out problems. He also might feel more open to discussing personal stuff post-orgasm."

I scrunch up my nose. "You want me to sex-manipulate him into sharing secrets?"

"Wouldn't hurt to try. Plus, shower sex is the best sex."

"Shut up," I whisper, standing up and snagging Samuel from her. I lower my voice and cover his ears. "There are baby ears in here, and ew, I'd rather not listen to you divulge anything sex-related about my big bro."

She points to Samuel and laughs. "That little nugget heard sex talk hotter than that when he was hanging out in my womb."

"Ugh, you've now been demoted to my second favorite brother-dater." I rock Samuel back and forth as an attempt not to assume the worst why Gage bailed on me. "Do you think this was his plan all along? For us to have sex, for him to draw my feelings for him back out, and then dump me like I did him?"

"I'm not the best person to answer that question, considering I don't know your history and all. Maybe talk to your brothers and get an opinion from a male mindset." Her tone is now soothing, like she's trying to put Samuel to sleep, but instead, I know it's an attempt to make me feel better after Gage's rejection.

"Yeah, not talking to my brothers about my sex life."

"It's worth a try. They went through a tough time that forced them to push the people they loved away from them. Maybe they can provide insight into what could be going through Gage's head."

———

DURING MY RIDE with Willow to my parents' house, I had to stop myself from pulling out my phone and reaching out to Gage countless times. The fear of coming off too needy is what stopped me. Call it pride, but I can't be the woman who fights for a man who doesn't want her.

Good thing I didn't give my mom a heads-up that Gage was coming. Otherwise, I would've been answering questions while I watched her work around the kitchen as she waved away all my requests to help her. The only job she gives me is setting the table and laying out the food in her perfect spread. Every dish has the same place it's had for years.

"Lauren, honey," my mom says next to me, mid-dinner, "you've been so busy. I feel like I haven't had the time to talk to you about where you're staying."

"Correction: you haven't had the time to interrogate her," my dad chimes in, resulting in a death glare from her.

"Did you find another rental?" she continues.

Dallas snorts. "Sure, if you count Gage's being her landlord."

I throw a dinner roll across the table at him. "Shut up, big mouth!"

My mother is weakly attempting to hold back her grin. "Have you two gotten back together?"

I take a long drink of lemonade before answering her while all eyes are on me, even Maven's. "Nope. Amos had the loft up for rent, and it was my only option until I find something else."

"You're roommates then?" my dad asks, his face unreadable.

"No, he's staying in the main house with his dad."

My mom straightens out the napkin on her lap and isn't camouflaging her smile any longer. "I think it's just wonderful that you two are spending time together again. His coming home was a great surprise to all of us."

Now is the time to take advantage of my mom's gossiping ways. If I can't pull it out of Gage, maybe she can give me even a crumb. Anything will do at the moment because, right now, I feel like I'm fighting against the unknown.

"Mom," I say, setting my fork down, "do you know why he moved back, by chance?"

"The word around town is, he was worried about Amos being sick," she answers.

"Amos is ill?" Dallas asks.

"COPD," my mom replies with a soft, concerned tone. "And an array of other problems, I assume, even though Amos is too proud to tell anyone what's going on with him."

Gage's dad is a prideful soul who isn't one to accept handouts. Even when his wife died, he never asked for help. He worked two jobs, was present at every game of Gage's, and did all the grocery shopping and cooking. The man lived for family, and it doesn't surprise me that he's still the same.

"Is that *all* you know?" I push.

What's the plus of having your mom be in the gossip crew if she doesn't give you anything juicy?

"Sorry, honey. I wish I had more. He's cloak-and-dagger about what happened in his life when he was gone, and so is Amos. Give him time. If you push, he'll only pull."

I nod, and luckily, Hudson changes the subject. He has the best intuition on when to cut a conversation short and move on to something new.

"HEY THERE, BIG BROTHER," I say, sitting next to Dallas on the porch swing after dinner.

"Hey there, my mischievous little sister," he replies.

The sun is setting. My dad is in the yard, playing with Maven, Willow is taking care of Samuel and his dinner business, and my mom is deep into final wedding arrangements with Stella and Hudson.

They're having the ceremony at my parents' house, which was a surprise to me. The fact that she'd trade out some big Hollywood nuptials for something small here made my heart warm.

"Can I ask you a question?" I ask.

"Asking permission has never stopped you before."

"It's not exactly a question, I guess. More like advice."

He chuckles. "I might be the wrong person to go to for advice. I'm the dude who has to get that from others."

"You give good guidance," I say, elbowing him. "Sure, you're not the best at taking it when it's your own life decisions, but you've helped both me and Hudson with our problems I don't know how many times. If it wasn't for you, Hudson and Stella wouldn't be together."

He nods. "I won't take all the credit for that one, but thank you for coming to me. So, what's up?"

I hesitate before answering for two reasons. The first being I'm not sure if I'm making a bigger deal than what it is, and the second being it might bring up painful memories for my brother.

"Gage …" I pause. "He was married before he moved back."

"And?"

"That's a big commitment."

Other than my parents, Dallas is the only one in our family who's been married. He also is no longer with his wife. The circumstances are different since he had no say in his marriage ending. He became a widower too young.

He nods in understanding. "Committing to someone in the past can't stop you from loving another, nor does it mean you have to keep the person in your heart forever. Not that I can say from experience, but people divorce for different reasons. But one thing to remember is, your heart is big enough to give people pieces of it. You can scatter your love along as you proceed through life. Maybe Gage was married, maybe he did love another woman, but that doesn't mean he can't love you, too."

"He's a different man from who he was when we were younger." Something else Dallas can relate to.

"Yes, most people change as they get older."

I shove his side and laugh. "Shut up, big head. You know what I mean. It's like he's carrying something on his shoulders that he can't let go of."

"You think it was a bad marriage?"

"I have no idea what to think. It's so confusing. He said he didn't love her, and whenever I bring her up, there's nothing but hatred on his face. Maybe she did him dirty, and he can't accept it?"

"Could've been a messy divorce."

I stop myself from telling him about her being locked up. I'll save that for another time. "There's something I'm missing. He shuts down anytime I bring it up, and he does the same with Kyle." I gulp and stop to determine if he can handle my next question. "How did you heal ... you know ... when you were broken?"

"I fell in love again."

He tips his beer toward Willow. She's in the yard with my dad now.

"She's who healed me." He goes on after taking a drink, "If Gage is broken, be his Willow. Don't push him, because admitting you're hurting takes time and courage."

CHAPTER TWENTY-FOUR

Gage

"YOU'LL MAKE a great father one day."

I tried.

I fucking tried.

And failed.

I don't deserve to be a father.

Had that chance.

Fucked it up.

I stomp through the front door, chug down a glass of water, and rest my forehead against the cool countertop.

The five words that haunt me daily drift through my mind.

"What did you do, Missy?"

I throw my glass across the kitchen, hearing it shatter against the wall, hoping it does the same to those words crammed into my mind forever. I stare at the wall as if I'm stuck in a daze, wondering when the pain, the memories, the guilt will finally end.

Never.

My failure to protect *him* will haunt me forever.

I don't move until I hear voices outside. I creep to the window that overlooks the driveway. Lauren is strapping Maven into the backseat of the SUV while Willow concentrates on getting Samuel into his car seat. Lauren slides into the passenger seat and slams the door shut.

It's not until the car pulls away that I start to pick up the broken glass from the floor. Lauren has every right to be angry with me. I should tell her about *him*, but I can't.

Can't open those wounds.

She'd understand. She'd comfort me. She'd also look at me differently. I have yet to come to terms with what happened, so bringing someone else into it would only cause more damage. She doesn't deserve that in her life.

Doesn't deserve being around a broken son of a bitch.

―――

"HEY, PA, HOW ARE YOU FEELIN'?"

I drop the box of pizza I carried out on the table and start dragging out plates.

I haven't talked to Lauren since I sped out of the loft as if I were on fire. There's no way my behavior didn't embarrass her. I'd finally gotten my girl back, had her in my arms, my bed, and I ruined it. I tried to handle my shit, but it was impossible.

Holding Samuel and hearing Willow say he was drawn to me was too hard on my heart. She was wrong. So fucking wrong.

"As happy as a tick on a big, fat dog," he answers, falling into a chair. He snags a piece from the box and takes a bite without worrying about a plate. He speaks as he swallows down his food, "You moving back into the loft with Lauren yet?"

I stay standing while grabbing a piece and throwing it on my plate. It won't get touched. I have no appetite, but if I don't eat, he won't either. "You getting tired of me already?"

He shakes his head. "Not even close." The room quiets while he takes a long draw of Coke before he shrugs his shoulders. "Just want to see you happy, is all."

Instead of grabbing a Coke from the fridge, I choose a beer.

Hopefully, it'll help calm these nerves. "Doubt that will be happening anytime soon … or ever."

He drops his pizza and looks at me with pain in his eyes. "You know you can talk to me, right?"

"I know, and you'll be the first person I see if it comes to that."

Luke is the only person I've talked to about what happened. He was my best friend in Chicago and stood by me through my fight. He saw the highs and the lows, and he understood. Luke joined the fight against Missy and has been as hell-bent on her paying for her crime as I have.

"She'd understand, too," he adds, slipping the words through in a low tone.

"Don't do this."

"Don't do what? Think about your future? I want to see my son happy. She'll make you happy. She's always been what makes you happy."

"A woman is not the basis of my happiness. Maybe in high school, yes, but shit changes when you grow up. Priorities change."

"She can help you heal."

I shake my head. "I need to get out of here."

———

I'VE BEEN NURSING my second beer for the past hour.

It'll be lukewarm and taste like piss if I take another sip, but I'd put money down on that not happening. Even though I walked into Down Home Pub with every intention to get ass-face wasted, I can't.

There's a massive fear embedded in me that always stops me from finishing my second drink. There's unease in the back of my mind of something bad happening. My phone could ring at any second with tragic news—at least, that's what I tell myself.

I wonder if I'll always have that uneasiness or if, eventually, it will fade away.

Will he fade away?

I shake my head and force myself to take another drink.

Yep, tastes fucking terrible.

"There's a handsome man I didn't expect to see tonight."

I peek over my shoulder to find Sierra pulling out the barstool next to mine with one hand while gripping a drink in the other.

Fuck.

Dealing with Kyle's kid sister isn't what I need tonight.

"Why do you say that?" I ask when she sets her drink down on the bar and makes herself comfortable.

"You never replied to my texts."

She doesn't appear to be pissed. It's more along the lines of annoyed. It's not a lie that Sierra has grown up and found her sexuality. She's attractive, fun, and most likely isn't looking for a commitment.

I move my neck from side to side, hoping to release the tension shooting up it but fail. "Not exactly a good idea to sext your best friend's little sister."

She flips her blonde hair over her shoulder. "Your best friend's *very legal* little sister." She holds up her beer. "Looky here, I'm even old enough to drink."

"Fair point."

Doesn't mean I'll be putting my hands on her. I've always seen Sierra as a little sister, nothing more. Even if I didn't, I'd never betray Kyle. That's a line you don't cross.

She swings to the side, so she's facing me, and she rests her elbow on the bar. "Care to be honest about why you ignored me? If you're not interested, I totally get it. Just be up-front with a girl."

"Don't think there's an easy way to say it without pissing you off." I'm not a dick. I don't want to hurt the chick's feelings.

"I'm not easily offended," she answers around a laugh, "but

this little exchange answers my question." She turns to face the bar and bumps my shoulder with hers. "Don't worry, Gage man; I don't take it personally."

I nod. "Appreciate that."

"So ... what girl don't you ignore?"

"Huh?" I'm halfway in this conversation with her. Half of me is listening while the other half is thinking about someone else.

"You're drinking in the corner of a bar, looking like someone ran over your dog. There's a story, and most of the time, this type of behavior is caused by someone's relationship problems." The happiness in her face falls, unmasking that Sierra isn't as playful as she puts on. "Trust me, I've been there."

"Not a specific problem. *Problems*," I correct.

"One of those problems Lauren?"

I shrug. Not about to seek relationship guidance from the youngin'.

She holds up her hand when Maliki looks our way. "Get my friend and me another drink."

Maliki nods and slides two beers in front of us while shaking his head at Sierra. "It's weird, serving your young ass here."

She grins. "I'm legally allowed to drink now, so no more kicking me out of this place and confiscating my fake IDs."

He laughs. "I'm sure going to miss that weekly occurrence."

She hands Maliki her credit card and glances over at me when he leaves to help another customer. "You want to talk about it? I'm a woman, so I like to think I'm good at giving advice about women."

I move my piss-warm beer to the side and grab the fresh one. *Here goes nothing.* "It's hard to ... rekindle with the woman who fucked you over before."

She nods. "Understandable. I know what it feels like to love someone and not have him ... or her, in your case."

I ignore her comment, hoping it wasn't directed at me.

She laughs. "I'm not talking about you. Even though I've

had a crush on you since you and my brother have been friends, there are other men in this godforsaken town who like to play games. Not to say I wouldn't forget about them had you come to your senses and hung out with me."

"I'm the brother's best friend. Off-limits crush, huh?"

A playful smile hits her lips. "I'm so basic."

"It sucks that we can't help who we like."

"Or, in your case, it sucks that you can't help who you *love*."

"Little one, I came here to forget my problems." I gesture to Maliki for another round while finishing off my beer. *Fuck it.* I deserve to forget for a night. "So, if you want to keep a man company, let's chat about football, random shit, what you were up to while I was gone."

She salutes me. "Aye, aye, captain."

Our drinks arrive, and I sit back in my chair, drowning my thoughts, while she takes over the conversation.

CHAPTER TWENTY-FIVE

Lauren

THE PASTEL COLORS of the sunset are dissolving into the night when my dad drops me off at the loft.

Gage hasn't called or texted, the driveway is void of his truck, and he's not in the loft when I walk in.

What happened?

Does he regret having sex with me?

My thoughts go to the worst-case scenario.

Gage made it clear that he hated me when I got arrested, and though I thought we'd moved past that, maybe he hasn't.

Maybe it was for revenge, to make me fall for him, so he could then give me the big fuck you for leaving him.

No, he's not that spiteful.

Correction: the old Gage wasn't that spiteful.

This new Gage is different—a rougher version on the exterior yet more vulnerable inside.

I check my phone again in case I missed something and collapse onto the couch. I reach for the remote at the same time I hear a car door slam in the background. Lucky for me, the blinds are open, so I don't have to creepily peek through them.

The floodlights beam down on an unrecognizable four-door

sedan, spotlighting the young blonde getting out of the driver's side and circling around to the passenger.

Sierra's skinny frame leans down, nearly on her knees, to wrap Gage's arm around her shoulders, and surprisingly, she takes his weight.

He is wasted.

Can barely stand straight.

With another woman.

A combination of fear and confusion seeps through me, drowning out any thoughts that we could reconcile. Now I know our time together was nothing but a game to him.

He went to her. Drank with her. No doubt shared his problems with her.

She'd asked if he was single, and I'd stupidly told her to go for it.

I don't bother hiding my stalking while watching their every move.

I'm silently begging for him to see the disappointment and disgust on my face.

His head is tipped down, his view locked to the ground, his feet dragging against the ground on their way to the front door.

Look up. Look up. Look the fuck up.

My heart sinks when he finally does.

It's a fast look, brief, and it only lasts a glimpse of a second as his eyes catch mine, and they're void of emotion, shut out, out of order.

He lowers his head in shame, and I stay there, looking pathetic, while Amos lets them in.

It isn't until they disappear into the house that I throw my hands up and snatch a blanket to sleep on the couch.

Joke's on me.

———

NOW THAT I'VE spent time in the bed, Gage was right; the couch is nowhere as comfortable as the bed is. Not that I got much sleep. I tossed, turned, and contemplated marching into that house and kicking his ass.

Problem is, it's not smart to kick a police officer's ass even if he did break your heart. Jail time isn't how I want to spend the rest of my summer.

Instead, I'm going to choose which brother I'm moving in with, find a rental, and steer clear of Gage for the rest of my life ... or until we awkwardly run into each other in a public setting.

I have my coffee in one hand, my bag on my shoulder, and my scrubs on when I hear my front door being unlocked. Gage comes through the doorway, big and broad and looking like shit, complete with red-rimmed eyes, arms hanging loosely at his sides.

He clears his throat and scratches his neck when he sees me. "You ready to go?"

I clutch my cup, silently staring, waiting for him to clarify what last night was about.

"Look, I'm sorry about yesterday." His apology is rushed, panicky, and regret is evident on his face—along with signs of dehydration and lack of sleep. If Sierra did spend the night, he must not have been a decent lay. "It was a bad day."

My bag slips off my shoulder, and I don't stop it from falling on the floor. "What are you doing here?"

"Apologizing for my bullshit behavior."

I assess him, the need to figure out what I'm missing rushing through me, but there's nothing there. All I see is a hungover man who doesn't care about anything right now. The same empty man from last night.

Broken people make for regretful actions.

Gage came home with Sierra and is asking me for forgiveness.

I can easily give him what he wants.

But I can't play games with someone who freezes me out and isn't interested in giving me his all.

"Don't you think it's rude not to take your one-night stand to breakfast?" I ask before scoffing. "Or wait, is that what you had for breakfast, considering that's your *favorite meal* and all? Looks like you have no preference of whom you get it from."

He slowly blinks at me. "What?"

"Sierra. Did you already kick her out of your bed this morning?"

"Sierra? She helped my dad put my drunken ass to bed last night and then went home."

I shake my head and snatch my bag up from the floor. Getting myself worked up before my shift isn't a good idea. "It doesn't matter. I have to go."

He stops me from moving around him to get to the front door. "I said I'm sorry. I had a rough day. Just hear me out."

I cross my arms. "Want to talk about it?"

"Nothing to talk about. It was a stressful day at work." His voice turns into a fake playfulness. "You know how those are. You've had them."

My smartwatch pings with a text message that was sent to my phone. "My dad is here. I have to go."

I'm grateful that my parents answer their phones at any time throughout the night. Two in the morning, my dad answered, no sleep in his voice, and didn't ask any questions when I asked for a ride.

"Tell your dad to go home. I'll take you to work. I already committed to it."

Commitment. Ha.

"Things change, Gage. I will no longer be needing any rides from you."

"*Lauren.*" His false playfulness is gone. Since he walked through that door, Gage's mood has gone from regret to forced jest and now to desperation.

My heart breaks as I look at him, and I see this as an

opportunity to fix him, to fix us. "I'll share a ride with you if you tell me what's going on."

He violently shakes his head. "I can't. Don't ask me to do that."

"Enjoy your day, Gage."

Even though he doesn't block me from brushing past him, he's on my tracks, and he waits at the top of the stairs as I hop down them, taking two at a time. I jump into my father's truck without looking back, slam my cup into the holder, and sigh.

My dad's gaze pings from Gage to me. "Rough morning?"

"You have no idea," I mutter.

He doesn't continue the conversation until we're miles from Gage's house. "Are you and Gage attempting to reconcile?"

I peek up at my dad in surprise. Sure, he and Mom had the birds and bees talk with me when I started dating Gage, but he's never questioned or commented on my love life. Maybe he knew my mom had that department covered. My father is a man of few words, but those words always have deep meaning to them.

He's a strong man and the mentor my family needs. He's also one of the most compassionate people in the world.

"I'm not sure," I truthfully answer.

There will be no bullshitting him. He can see right through me. What I do hold back from saying is, *We had sex, and now, he's closed off.*

"Do you still love him?"

"I do," I honestly answer again, finally admitting it out loud.

"Does he still love you?"

I hesitate before answering.

"I think so."

"Then, you'll figure it out. It might be a complicated journey to get there, but love conquers all, my girl."

If only quotes were solutions to real problems.

"That's easy for you to say. You and Mom have been in love since forever and have been inseparable ever since."

"That doesn't mean there weren't hardships. Love isn't easy

for anyone. Your mother and I have had our fair share of problems, but it was *us* against those problems, not *us* against each other. Talk to him. See where his battles are, and join him in fighting those battles. Then, your love will be stronger."

I use my arm to clean the tears falling from my cheeks.

"You decide if his problems are worth the trouble. That's all you can do. If you can't, then it's better to move on. But, if you love someone, you fight those demons together and live happily ever after, as your mom and I have."

His questions about Gage end there. He moves the conversation to my work, to my apartment-hunting, to offering me my bedroom back at home. He fills the ride up with easing my mind, and it works.

"You have a good day," he says when he pulls into the parking lot. "I'll be back to pick you up, and Dallas said your car will be fixed soon."

"Thank you, Dad."

He stops me before I leave the truck. "And, Lauren?"

I peek back at him. "Yeah?"

"I'm proud of you."

"Thanks, Dad," I say around a giant smile.

Time with him is exactly what I needed. Sometimes, you need to talk to someone who lets you see from a different perspective because it's easy to get blinded by your own hurt and your own needs. I owe it to myself, to Gage, to our relationship to talk to him. Whether we end up in a relationship as friends or as nothing, at least we wouldn't have given up before finding out what the other was feeling.

I PICK MY PHONE UP.

Set it down.

Pick it up.

Set it down.

I've been playing this game since I sat down in the cafeteria for my lunch break.

Should I call or text Gage? See if he wants to talk tonight ... or give him time before I try to pull all his secrets out?

I'm shoving a bite of salad into my mouth when a voice clears in front of me. My spoon drops into the plastic container, and I have to tilt my head up to see the tall stranger's face.

I wait for him to speak, and when he does, his words come out smoothly, like a practiced politician.

"Excuse me. I'm sorry to interrupt your meal, but are you Lauren Barnes?"

I swallow down my food before answering, taking in his expensive suit and Rolex watch. "Uh ... yes."

"My name is Robert. I'm Missy Perry's father."

"Missy?"

I run the name through my mind. The hospital has been busy, but I try to remember my patients' names the best I can, and Missy isn't ringing any bells. And I would've remembered this man if he had been in the room with Missy.

"Is she one of my patients?" I ask.

He shakes his head. "No, Missy *Perry*," he stresses. "Gage Perry's wife."

Dizziness rocks through me. "Wife?" I repeat, and it's my turn to clear my throat. "I, uh ... thought they were divorced."

"My apologies, Miss Barnes." He doesn't look sorry. He said it for the shock factor. "His ex-wife."

This is a black hole I do not want to jump into.

This guy looks like he's either the head of the mafia, the president, or someone I should be terrified of.

I wipe my mouth with a napkin. "No apology necessary, *Missy's father*. Gage's business is not my business." That's a lie, considering I've done nothing but persistently ask him to open up, but I'm not going to let Missy's pompous daddy interrogate me.

He pulls out the chair across from me and sits down.

Looks like I don't have a choice.

"Do you have a minute?" he asks, clearly ignoring the fact that I'm uncomfortable.

Fuck no.

I look to each side of the cafeteria, trying to catch the eye of someone I know who can save me from this weird situation, but it's dead. Mafia politician dude was lingering around until the timing was perfect.

He doesn't wait for my response. "Missy asked that I speak with you."

"How do you know where I work?" is my first question.

"We hired a private investigator." He shows no shame in his answer, like it isn't creepy at all.

"What?" I say, fixing my glare on him. "You've had someone following me?"

"Of course not. All he did was find out where you worked and when you'd be here."

"That's disturbing and a complete invasion of privacy."

"Some might think that. I'm only here because my daughter is convinced that Gage has been in contact with you."

"I don't think that's your business or hers."

His chubby cheeks form a patronizing smile. "I see this isn't going to be easy. I understand you see this as intrusive, but please talk to Gage. Missy is filing an appeal. She was ill then and is making progress since she was diagnosed. We're expecting Gage to fight her release. My daughter made a mistake and deserves to be free. Please pass the message on."

I slowly digest his words and replay them through my head before answering, "I'm sorry, but I'm lost here. What happened?" I'm getting the sense that Missy isn't in prison for a minor infraction like receiving too many traffic tickets.

His blond brows squish together. "You don't know about Andy?"

I shake my head.

"I assumed he would've told you. Please relay the message."

He pulls two pieces of paper from his pocket and slides them across the table. "Here's my business card and an incentive in hopes that you'll convince Gage to hear us out. If you accomplish this, there will be more coming your way." He smacks the table before getting up. "I'll let you get back to your job, Miss Barnes."

"Wait," I call out, causing him to turn around and look at me. "Care to tell me who Andy is?"

His face falls—the first sign of emotion he's shown since he interrupted my meal. "Not my story to tell."

———

A HINT of relaxation hits my body when I step out of the shower and tie a towel around my wet hair. My shift was long, hard, and busy. Hell, the last twenty-four hours have been long, hard, and busy.

Luckily, it kept my mind off Gage and Missy.

Her father was gone when I looked at the papers he'd left me. The first was a business card, as he'd said. It was simple— white with only a phone number and his first name. There was no associated business. The second item he'd handed me was a check from a law firm, not him, for five thousand dollars. His visit to my job was to bribe me to convince Gage to do what they wanted.

I was tempted to tear up the card and bribe money but decided against it. Not because I wanted the money, but because I was going to show Gage when the time was right. He needed to set the man straight that it wasn't cool to have someone follow me around for their own shits and giggles.

I pad through the loft, barefoot, wearing only a towel, as I head to the kitchen for a glass of water and a snack. I snag a granola bar and am on my way back to the bedroom to get dressed, but a knock on the door stops me.

Gage is standing on the other side when I peek out. He looks as tired as he did this morning, now wearing his uniform with a five o'clock shadow covering his cheeks and chin. It's not the time to talk about Missy's scary dad. I'll save that conversation for later.

He steps in as soon as I open the door and then leans back against it, arms crossed. I wait for the roaming eyes, given I'm in a towel, and that's what's to be expected when you're half-naked in front of a guy you've had sex with, but Gage's gaze doesn't move away from my face.

"How was work?" he asks.

Got a visit from your ex-father-in-law, bribing me with money.

I shrug. "It was fine." I shrug again. "Busy."

He takes a step forward. "About this morning … and yesterday … and last night—"

I hold my hand up, stopping him from continuing. "I'm tired. Let's talk about it tomorrow, okay?"

My answer surprises him, and I'm betting he'd thought I'd tell him to kick rocks.

"Yeah, of course," he answers, running his fingers through his hair. "You still have the day off?"

I nod. "You?"

"Yes. How 'bout I bring you breakfast?"

"That'll work but not too early. I'm exhausted."

My response grants a small smile from the both of us.

He takes a step closer and hesitates, waiting for my reaction, but I slowly nod, giving him permission. His arms wrap around me, and it's exactly what I need. I relax against him, melting into his warm chest, and rest my hands at the base of his neck.

His lips go to my hair. "Soon. I promise."

I nod at his words, the top of my head brushing against his chin, and hug him tighter, closer, as a silent thank-you.

That's all I've wanted.

Another layer of insecurity peels away when he kisses my lips.

"My shirts and the bed are all yours," he says, pulling away and running his hands down my arms. "Get some rest, and I'll have deliciousness coming your way in the morning. And it won't be too early."

"Good night."

He kisses my cheek this time, and my hand reaches out, ready to stop him when he turns to leave, but I don't. We might be okay right now, but the wounds from today are still fresh. We wouldn't be able to walk into that bedroom and go to bed after what happened in the cafeteria today. I'd have too many questions, and we're too tired for it tonight.

I eye the check on the bathroom vanity after he leaves.

Why would his ex-wife's father give me money?

It doesn't make any sense. Nothing makes sense anymore.

I go to his dresser and shuffle through a drawer in search of another one of his old high school tees. I embarrassingly hold the shirt to my nose and take in the smell of fabric softener and cheap cologne. I slide it over my head and pull it down to cover my hips, the tee fitting me perfectly.

A yawn escapes me, and I can't wait to hit the sheets. As I go to shut the drawer, something catches, stopping me. I attempt to push harder. Nothing. I grab an armful of shirts out of the drawer and toss them to the floor next to me.

I find the culprit. It's an envelope. My hands shake as I pull it out. It's shredded at the top, and a return address sits on the left from the Cook County Correctional Facility with Missy's name above it.

Her name is printed at the top with bright pink cursive handwriting—*Missy Perry*, complete with an I dotted with a heart. I examine the envelope like it has the answer to all my questions, looking at the front and the back, analyzing the swoops in her name.

It'll kill Gage's trust in me if I do what I'm thinking, but I can't stop myself. After his ex-father-in-law's visit, after that man expecting me to know about someone named Andy, after Gage shut down on me yesterday, I need answers, and as much as I want to wait for him to give them to me, it's like candy sitting in front of me. There's no beating this temptation, and I only hope he doesn't hate me when I find out what he's been hiding.

I grab my phone, deciding to Google his name and Chicago, but then set it back down.

Ugh. What do I do?

I'll sleep on it. Ask him about it over breakfast tomorrow.

I go to shove the shirts back into the drawer but stop when I notice the stack of pictures and envelopes in the corner. My attention goes straight to the picture at the top of the stack. It's of Gage with a baby in his arms.

Gage looks happy as he stares down at the baby wrapped in a blue blanket and wearing a blue cap. All the blue leads me to assume it's a boy. The baby boy doesn't have Gage's olive skin tone. His is dark, and his eyes are wide and innocent. There's no familiarity in looks between them.

I might be able to hold myself back from reading bitch-face Missy's letter, but there's no stopping me from flipping through the pictures. I fall back against the dresser, and tears fall down my face. There are photos of him and the baby and photos of Gage and I assume, Missy holding the child up over a birthday cake that says *Happy Second Birthday Andy!* There's another one of them smiling while the boy, now looking a few years older, sits on Santa's lap. I look through memory after memory of their family … of Gage's family.

What happened?

The pictures only amplify my curiosity. I've already opened Pandora's box. There's no turning back now. I pick up the envelope in shame and pull the letter out before I can change my mind.

It's the same pink writing. The heart trend staying and added to the margins of the lined and wrinkled paper.

I slowly read it, digesting each word.

My dearest Gage, my husband, the man I love,

Why won't you take my calls? My father says he will pay any collect call bills. I NEED to talk to you, to hear your voice. Why can't you understand that? I love you. I'd do anything for you. I will never leave you. Please visit me. Write me back. DO SOMETHING! Let me explain myself, so I can tell you why I did what I did and how I realize now that it wasn't the answer to our problems. I loved our little boy. We can give him a sister or a brother. You know he'd want us to be happy as his mom and dad. Let us remember him as husband and wife. Let us remember the baby boy we rescued years ago. LET ME MAKE THIS RIGHT!!! I am hurting without you, and I'd rather die than not have you in my life. Is that what you want? For me to kill myself?

I love you so, so, so, so much!!!

Your wife,

Missy Perry

(I will ALWAYS be Missy Perry!!!)

There's one last picture in the envelope.

It's the three of them.

Gage is sporting a shirt that says *Andy's Dad*.

Gage has a son.

Andy.

CHAPTER TWENTY-SIX

Gage

I CALLED THREE TIMES.

Texted five.

Picked up breakfast.

It's noon, and worry is setting in.

Lauren never sleeps this late.

I call once more before unlocking the loft and walking in.

Her phone is on the counter, and I set the box of doughnuts down next to it.

The couch is empty, which means she slept in my bed. *Finally*. There might be hope for us after all. She's most likely still asleep. She had a long shift yesterday and deserves a decent night's rest.

I was up all night, going back and forth with myself on what to do today. Lauren wants me to let her in, but I'm not sure how much to give yet. The two women I trusted more than anything both hurt me.

Once I tell Lauren about Andy, our relationship will change. She'll be getting more of me than my heart. She'll be receiving my secrets, my burdens, and my trust.

Trust is a precious treasure to hand someone. You're giving

them a piece of you, unknowing of how they're going to play with it.

I stroll into the bedroom, expecting her to be passed out and snoring in my bed.

It's not what I get.

She's on the floor, curled up in a ball, wearing only my tee and panties.

My heart is ready to burst out of my chest as I take in the scene in front of me. Surrounding her are pictures, memories, all I have left of my son. The sight of Missy's letter next to his preschool picture makes me snarl. Her handwriting and her pleas only taint the memories of him.

Those pictures were not meant to be seen.

They were hidden, only making it out into daylight when I was feeling lonely or missing the only sunshine in my goddamn life.

The pictures gave both good and bad memories.

Brought both the light and dark out of me.

I take them in, one by one, while Lauren lightly snores in the background.

One of my worlds circling my other.

While I was nervous about giving her pieces of me, she went behind my back and invaded my trust.

And this, ladies and gentlemen, is why I decided never to let anyone in again.

She read Missy's letter. Saw my son. Most likely studied each picture.

It was what I prepared myself for all night. The questioning I knew was impending.

Do I walk away and tell her it's done?

No. She needs to know why I was hesitant to let her in.

"You went through my shit?" I ask through clenched teeth, regretting how harsh my voice sounds as soon as the words leave my mouth.

You can't blame her too much. You would've done the same.

She stirs, her eyes slowly opening, and she looks up at me. A brief smile passes her lips but drops when she takes me in. Recognition dawns on her when she looks around.

She probably intended to hide what she'd done.

She probably planned to put everything back in that drawer before I got here this morning.

"You went through my shit?" I repeat.

She scrambles to her feet with pity on her face. "No! I grabbed a shirt, *like you told me to*, and couldn't shut the drawer. When I tried to fix the problem"—she pauses, swinging her arm to gesture to the pile on the floor—"I found all of this."

"You went through my shit." Right now, those are the only words I'm capable of forming.

She blows out a long breath. "Was it wrong for me to snoop? Yes. But, after Missy's dad showed up at the hospital last night, I was so confused. I didn't go looking for this, Gage, I promise."

"What did you say?" My mind has jumped from the pictures to what she told me.

"You want me to repeat all of that?" She stressfully runs her hand through her hair and blows away the few strands in her way.

"Missy's father paid you a visit at the hospital?"

"Yes. He asked me to talk to you about not disputing her appeal … something along those lines." She holds up a finger and runs into the bathroom before reappearing with a paper and handing it to me, as if it's counterfeit money. "He gave me this."

I take a look at it, recognizing Missy's parents' attorney's signature. I've gone round and round with this guy, torn up checks, and told him to fuck off more times than I can recall. He's a fucking sleazebag attorney … and Missy's sleazebag-ass family loves to have him do their dirty work. He writes their checks. They keep their hands clean.

"The hell, Lauren? Why didn't you tell me about this last night?"

"I don't know! It was late, and I didn't want to fight with you." She grabs my hands, the check falling to the floor, and leads us to the edge of the bed. "Gage, please tell me what's going on. Let me help you."

Tears prick at my eyes when I sit, and memories flood me. I've never said the words out loud. Luke is the one who gave my father details. The only time I've said what little I know about what Missy did was when I gave my police report and then interrogated her for hours straight until her parents came in with the check-writing, sleazebag attorney.

"I don't want to bring you into my mess," I tell her.

"Your mess is my mess," she says softly. "They involved me, not you. They hired a PI to track me, showed up at my job, knew my schedule. I'd like to know why they're doing all of this. Let me help you. Let me know what *we're* dealing with."

"It's too much, baby," I say, unable to stop the tears now. "I won't bring you into the darkness with me."

"Who's Missy?" she asks, refusing to let me off the hook.

I shake my head.

"You don't have to answer that. I already know. She's your wife." The words sound spiteful, but her tone doesn't. She's upset, somewhat angry, but holding it together for me. She can sense my pain.

"She's my *ex-wife*," I clarify for what feels like the hundredth time.

Missy made it hell to divorce her and convinced her parents to hire the best divorce attorney by threatening to hang herself in her cell. I fought them, declined ungodly amounts of money, and eventually won in the end. I'd still be struggling had I not had a buddy who was one of the top litigators in the state.

I lose contact with Lauren when she gets up from the bed and snatches a letter I will always recognize from the floor.

"Wifey doesn't seem to realize you're divorced." Her arm falls to her side, the letter still clutched in her hand, and hurt is on her face. "You have a child with her?"

I scrub my hands over my face. *Had. I had a child with her.* "It's complicated."

"You hated me because I kept a secret from you about something as simple as breaking up, and you act like I'm Satan, but you've been hiding the fact that you have a child. Where is he? Why isn't he here with you? Do her parents have him? Gosh, I have so many questions. You think keeping a secret like this from me is okay?"

Anger is replacing her understanding as she paces in front of me.

The problem is, people don't think of the worst-case scenarios because they've only seen it on the news, seen it on true crime documentaries; most people don't know someone close to them who's lived through the hell of real-life *20/20* episodes.

I drop my head, take a few deep breaths, and then slowly look back up. "Missy was my partner in Chicago."

She stops her rambling and pacing, at my first admission. Her back is straight, and she's still. I can see her mind working, telling herself to come up with a question to get her as much information as she can.

"What do you mean, partner? Life partner ... sex partner?"

"We were both police officers ... partners."

Her eyes widen in understanding. "And then you started sleeping together? Isn't that against the code of conduct?"

"There were no rules restricting officers from having relationships with other officers. It's actually common. Partners understand each other."

"So you started sleeping with her because she understood you?" That hurt is back on her face.

"I'm not sure how it started. It wasn't planned. We were drinking at a friend's birthday party. One thing led to another, and we had sex."

"Only once?

I pat the space next to me, and she sits down.

"We had sex off and on for years."

"I'm so confused. You had sex off and on for years while you were married? Shouldn't that stay consistent?"

"It was before and during our marriage."

"You said you got married as a favor to her?" She points to the stack of pictures on the floor. "Not to be rude, but that little boy doesn't resemble either of you. Was Missy pregnant with another man's baby and you married her to help raise him?"

My story with Missy is one people wouldn't guess. It's complicated. The preacher who married us called it a kind gesture and said we were saints for what we did.

"The station was a safe haven," I say. "Someone dropped off a baby one night, and Missy and I were the ones who found him. We brought him to the hospital. He was malnourished, addicted to every drug imaginable, and filthy."

I'll remember that day for the rest of my life. We were ending a shift, walking into the station to finish up some paperwork, when we heard the loud cry ring through the chilly wind. We followed the sound to a set of steps, and as soon as he saw us, he stopped.

My voice breaks. "Three months old and an addict. We visited him in the hospital daily, and Missy fell in love with him. *I* fell in love with him. She got in touch with his social worker to adopt him. Since we'd slept together plenty of times, and we had a trustworthy relationship, she suggested we do it together and co-parent. I agreed, and we got married."

"Why couldn't you co-parent him without getting married?"

"They were giving Missy a hard time about being a single foster parent. The social worker said they'd consider placing him with a married couple over her, but he'd be in the system until then. We didn't want him put in the system, so we made the decision to become that married couple who could have him."

She nods for me to continue.

"The first few years of our arrangement ran smoothly. We lived down the block from each other and spent time together, and yes, we still did sleep together. I'd told her I wasn't looking for anything serious before we slept together the first time."

"You got married and adopted a baby with her. You can't say that's nothing serious."

"You're right. I realize that now, and I should've earlier, but it seemed so simple."

"Then, what happened? Why is she in prison?"

"I told her about you, about my life here, about why I'd left. It's easy to get personal with someone you spend so much time with. Missy said she understood and agreed we'd never be a real married couple, but she started to change as Andy got older. She grew more protective of me. Called me nonstop. Showed up at my house at all hours of the night. Started drinking more. She got suspended from the force as a result of aggression with arrestees.

"We had keys to each other's places, and I came home with Andy one evening to find her in my bedroom. She'd found a box filled with pictures of you and asked if I still loved you. I answered honestly and said yes. Her next question was if I loved her, to which I also responded that I loved her as Andy's mother, but I had no romantic feelings for her. She had known I didn't love her when we got married. We'd planned to divorce after gaining full rights to Andy and to split custody fifty-fifty. That never happened."

"Why not?"

I choke back a sob and look at the floor while shaking my head. "Because Missy murdered Andy," I whisper.

CHAPTER TWENTY-SEVEN

Lauren

GAGE'S SHOULDERS hunch in pain.

I begged him for the truth, demanded it, but now, I wish I hadn't.

His truth is too powerful to take in all at once.

Andy was his son.

Missy killed him.

His then-wife murdered their child.

Jesus.

I didn't prepare myself for a truth bomb of that magnitude.

As an ER nurse, I've witnessed death—parents losing children, children losing parents, lovers losing lovers.

Watching people hurt isn't easy.

It's harder when it's someone you love.

His shallow breaths engulf the room, and sweat lines his forehead. I swipe my tears away before doing the same to his.

Am I ready for this?

Prepared to hear the details of his tragedy?

I spent all night reading Missy's letter and repeatedly looking through the stack of photos until my eyes couldn't stay open any longer. I never meant for him to find out that I saw them. That's my karma for snooping.

"I'm positive she suffocated him," he says, his voice cracking. An empty stare covers his face, and he chokes back more tears while I gently rub his back. "Andy died because she was angry with me."

I've only seen Gage cry only one other time—when his mother died. We were in his bedroom. He was in a similar stance—head low, eyes to the floor so that he could hide his hurt—and only seconds passed before he pulled himself together.

He inhales a deep breath before continuing while I shake my head in disbelief. "We never found his body."

"Then, how ..."

"She left me a voice mail, admitting to sending Andy to heaven to be happy. Later, in the car on the way to the police station, she admitted to killing him and then dumping his body in an undisclosed location. When she was brought in and it was time for her to confess, she took it all back. Her family's high-profile attorney came in and cut off all her communication with us. In the end, she feigned innocence and took a plea."

My hand flies to my mouth. "Oh my God."

"I failed him," he cries out. "I failed him, and now, he's dead."

I violently shake my head. "No. Her selfishness took him away, not you." Guilt sweeps through me. Missy's resentment of me led to her rage. "If anything, I'm more to blame than you. Had you not been in love with me, maybe he'd still be alive."

It's his turn to shake his head. "Don't you dare put that on yourself."

I want to tell him not to place the blame on himself, either. He's suffering from the guilt of Missy's actions. This isn't what I expected. Fixing him isn't going to be as easy as I thought.

How does someone get over an experience that traumatic?

I shudder. I can't even imagine.

It's easy, blaming yourself in situations like his. People go back to what they might've done wrong, what they didn't do, and what they could've done.

"I'm sorry," I whisper. I might not be able to heal him, but I can give him something he's been asking of me. An apology. "I'm sorry for leaving and turning my back on you. I'm sorry you had to go through that alone."

He surprises me by falling to his knees and gripping my hands in his. Tears roll down his cheeks. "Tell me why you did it then. *Please.* For fuck's sake, I need someone to be honest with me for once!"

I sniffle, and my hands shake under his. "I can't. I'm sorry, Gage."

"Oh, come on, Lauren," he begs. "It's been years. Tell me. Whatever it is, it's in the past. We'll get through it."

Is that possible?

It'll make him lose someone else in his life.

My chin dips to my chest as I glance away from him. "I wish I could, but it's not my story to tell."

The skin around his eyes bunches together, and he pulls away. "Are you shitting me? I ripped myself apart and showed you my secrets and scars, and all I ask for in return is your goddamn honesty!"

I want to reach out and console him, but I don't know what his reaction would be. "I'm sorry. This breaks my heart, but I made a promise."

He flinches. "A promise? A promise to whom?"

"That's part of the promise."

"Stop bullshitting me." He brings himself up and snorts, looking at me in disgust. "You took it upon yourself to snoop through my shit before giving me the opportunity to confide in you. Thank you for clearing up where we stand with each other."

"I'm sorry!" I burst out, jumping up from the bed when he turns around to leave. I grab his arm and am surprised when he turns around.

"If you're sorry, tell me why," he hisses.

I don't.

Instead, I kiss him.

My mouth claims his, and I bite his tongue when he attempts to continue his interrogation.

In the back of my mind, I know, when the conversation ends, so will we. He'll leave me, like I did him, at my refusal. He grunts when I push him down on the couch, and he makes another attempt to keep up our discussion when I straddle his hips.

"Lauren," he warns when my mouth meets his again.

I press my finger to his lips, and my voice turns weak. "Please. We can talk about this after you make me feel good."

His erection slides against my core when I rock into him.

"After I make you feel good," I add.

Every move I make feels like I'm walking on eggshells. The chance that Gage could pull away at any second is clear as day, and I'm drawing out everything I can get from him. When tomorrow hits, I know we'll be over.

His arm tightens around my back, and he stands with me in tow. My mind spins with uncertainty.

Is he going to throw me out on my ass already?

His steps are fast and swift as he carries me to the bed and drops me down on it. "It's about time I have you in here again. Maybe I can fuck the truth out of you."

He stands in front of me and undresses while I do the same. There will be no intimate touches this time. No love devotions. It's sex at the wrong time, but in the back of my mind, I'm aware it's sex for the last time.

I hold myself up with my arms, and we're both panting while staring each other down. His face is filled with pain, his work-of-art chest giving away his stressed breathing, and his cock is swollen, creamy pre-cum at its tip.

"Is this how you want me to make you feel good?" he finally asks.

All I can do at this moment is nod.

I scoot up the bed and inhale the scent of him on the sheets as his hard body crawls over mine. A moan escapes me when his member nudges my entrance, and he slides inside me with no warning, sans condom again. His hands search for mine, and he intertwines them, holding them over our heads.

He stills, and his mouth goes to my ear. "Is this how you want to say good-bye because you're too goddamn stubborn?"

I stay quiet and tilt my hips up, a silent beg for more.

He doesn't oblige.

"Tell me," he demands.

"Please, Gage," I cry out.

"Please what? Give you this?"

He keeps his hands in mine and gives me what I asked for.

It's madness.

But so damn good.

"Fucking tell me," he begs.

"More!" I plead.

He lets out a devilish laugh and slams into me harder, my head slightly banging against the headboard. "It seems I'm always giving you more while you give me nothing."

He swiftly pulls out, hauls me up, and throws me on my stomach. In one breath, I'm on my knees, and he's kneeling behind me.

This is breakup sex. Hate sex. *The last time this will happen* sex.

The thought of that hurts, but my twisted soul will take it.

I push my ass up higher while he tortures me before sliding back in. The sound of him slapping my ass echoes through the room, and I don't have to beg for more any longer. He's already giving it.

My body burns with emotions, and my knees feel weak as all my blood races to my core. A whirlwind of eagerness flies through me when he reaches around and plays with my clit to finish me off.

As I come down from my orgasm, my goal is for him to explode inside me. I back up even more and meet his thrusts.

His hands dig into the bottom of my ass. "Fuck! Fuck! Fuck! Yes, take all my cum!"

He goes still, runs his hands up my back, and then collapses next to me. I do the same after I calm my breathing. We're side by side and unsure of what the next move is.

He clears his throat. "Did that convince you enough to tell me?"

"Gage," I croak out, "I told you I can't."

He rolls off the bed and grabs his clothes. "Good-bye for good this time, Lauren."

CHAPTER TWENTY-EIGHT

Lauren

EIGHT DAYS HAVE PASSED without a word from Gage.

They've gone by in a blur.

In Gage's eyes, the solution to our problem is simple. I confess why I broke up with him, he'll digest it and then understand, and then we can work out our problems. He seems to think that, once my truth is out, we'll heal.

He's wrong.

The problem is, if I do what he wants, it'll hurt him more and ruin someone else's life.

He's lost too many people.

I won't let it happen again.

History will repeat itself, and I'll put other people's happiness in front of my own.

After I realized our argument was final, I packed what belongings I had and called my dad to pick me up. I cried the entire ride. He asked if I wanted to talk about it and nodded when I shook my head.

I see the questioning looks from my mom each time I come out of my bedroom, but she doesn't say anything. She was there during my last breakup with Gage.

She knows the symptoms.

Knows when to stay out of it.

All I can think about is what Gage is going through. His losing his son and having no one to comfort him pains me.

I contemplated calling Kyle, but if there's anything I can give Gage now, it's my loyalty to keep his secrets.

To rid my mind of him, I've buried myself in working, searching for a new home, and clashing with my insurance company to cut me a freaking check.

Stella and Hudson's rehearsal dinner is tonight. Their wedding is tomorrow, so I plan to be the most proactive bridesmaid in history. Hopefully, it'll shield me from my thoughts of Gage.

There's nothing better than throwing yourself into a project while healing from a breakup.

Was it a breakup?

We never technically got back together.

We hung out and slept together a few times but never established anything. Never had the *what are we* talk.

Losing Gage this time hurts worse than before, but the first breakup prepared me for living a life without him.

CHAPTER TWENTY-NINE

Gage

MY ATTENTION MOVES from the paperwork sitting on my desk to my office door at the sound of a knock.

I've slept here for the past four nights.

I grew familiar with the excitement of pulling into my driveway, knowing Lauren was in the loft. She's gone now, and the reality of that smacks me in the face every time I pull up.

I could move on and forget about her leaving me. I've come to terms with what happened years ago, but I'll never be satisfied with the unexplained reason of *why* it happened.

Was it something I did?

Did she meet someone else?

Was she no longer in love with me?

Unresolved endings make you question if the late-night conversations, the spilled secrets, the love for you were real. I confessed my demons, opened my chest and bared it all to her, while she gave nothing in return.

The door flies open as soon as I yell, "Come in!"

"You look like hell," Hudson says, shutting the door behind him.

"And you look like a man who enjoyed his bachelor party last night."

Said bachelor party was held at The Down Home Pub. Hudson texted and extended an invite my way, but after my argument with Lauren, I was a no-show.

I respect the dude sitting in the chair across from me. He could've celebrated his last party of singlehood at some expensive club, but he stayed here, true to his roots. It most likely didn't kill him to go home to his fiancée at the end of the night either.

"I assumed you'd be at my wedding after I sent you an invite over a week ago. Your RSVP must've been lost in the mail because, according to my expensive-ass wedding planner, it's nowhere to be found."

"Your sister and I aren't on speaking terms at the moment."

He crosses his arms and legs at the same time and leans back in his chair. "Heard something 'bout that." A sarcastic laugh drops from his throat. "How about you meet her by the swings and fix your problems over fruit snacks?"

If only it were that simple.

"Your sister is … complicated."

"No shit." He sighs and runs his hand through his short beard. "She's not an easy nut to crack, but she's fucking loyal. No one knows what went down between you and her, but I promise you this; she didn't walk away for a bullshit reason. Since she was six, her life plans included you. Something changed her mind. Something serious enough that she'd ruin her life over it."

"That's the problem. She won't tell me."

"Try a different way of convincing her to open up."

"Any tips for a man? She's open with everything but *that*."

"All I've got for you is a good-luck smack on the shoulder and hopes that you'll figure it out." He pushes himself to his feet and extends a paper my way. Another invitation. "Wedding is this weekend if you're free."

———

"I FIGURED YOU'D BE GONE," my dad says when I step into the kitchen.

There was no sleepover in my office last night. My dad made ribs for dinner and insisted on not eating alone. He needed company. I needed company. We devoured our meal and spent the rest of the night watching old action movies.

I knocked down a few beers and convinced myself to sleep in the loft. It was a hell of a lot more comfortable than my office chair. The smell of Lauren on the sheets relaxed me and allowed me to fall asleep.

I snag a glass from a cabinet and fill it up with water. "Why's that?"

"Isn't the Barnes boy's wedding today?"

I chug down the water before answering, "Yes, but I'm not going."

He winces in offense like it's his wedding I'm bailing on. "Why not?"

"Bad idea."

"Something happen between you and Lauren? It sure looked like y'all were rekindling those sparks."

"My love life isn't any of your concern." My attitude borders on rude, but I don't want to talk about her, or where she's at, or what weddings she's attending.

"It's my concern when I want to see my son happy."

"My happiness left long ago, and I refuse to hand over all control to a woman who broke my heart. I'm a broken man, but I'm working on healing, and she's not interested in the same." I scrub my hands over my face in frustration … hurt … something. "I told her about Andy, Pa. And Missy, yet she won't even confess why she left me." A harsh laugh leaves my throat. "It sounds petty, but I'll never get over not knowing what I did wrong for her to end our relationship like she did. It fucked me up, and then losing Andy killed me. The only action I can do to stop losing people I care about is not to put myself in that position any longer."

Fuck. Am I whining?

"I understand, son. You lost the woman you loved and then experienced a loss even greater. Losing a child can be a scary soul-sucker, and you'll never return to being the man you were."

An unfamiliar wave of fear passes over his face, and he grips the edge of the table to stand up. "There's something you should know."

"Yeah?"

"Lauren left you because of me." There's no hesitation in his answer. He was preparing himself for this confession.

I take a step back. "What did you say?"

"I'm the reason she broke up with you."

"What do you mean?"

"You …" He pauses, his voice wavering. "You loved her more than life itself. When she enrolled in school hours away, I knew you'd follow her." His eyes water while he runs his hand down the back of his neck. "I was mourning your mother and terrified of being alone."

"Pa, what did you do?"

Remain calm.

My heart wants to explode from my chest, unleashing all the anger from me. My father's being involved in ruining my love life wasn't the answer I'd been searching for.

His hands shake as he grabs his mug and takes a drink, his Adam's apple bobbing before he sets it back down. "I couldn't lose you, so I went to the diner during one of her shifts and begged her not to let you leave me. I pleaded that she wouldn't take you away."

"You asked her to break up with me?"

Say no. Tell me I heard you wrong.

"She refused, and then I explained my reasoning. She cried and was angry that she had to break someone's heart. Either yours or mine. We went back and forth until I told her I couldn't live without you. That's when she promised she wouldn't take you away from me."

"You asked her to leave to make yourself happy?" I slam my hand against my chest. "What about my happiness, huh? You saw what a mess I was after she left." I'm using all my self-control to reel in my anger. "For years, you've seen me broken over her, and now, you're telling me this? You've had years to do it!"

He experienced the pain of losing my mom. Why would he want me to go through that same hell?

Guilt and hurt are etched along the wrinkles on his face. "I've wanted to tell you for years, but I was so angry with myself. Not only did you leave town and me, but you also lost her for my selfishness."

Don't snap. Keep it together. This is your dad.

"Lauren made me promise to never tell you what I asked of her," he adds. "She's been keeping this secret, so you and I wouldn't lose our relationship. Don't blame her for allowing me to have the only person I have left in this world."

I hold my hand up to stop him from continuing. "I can't do this right now, or I'll end up saying something I've never wanted to say to my father. I have to go."

"Are you going to her?"

"I don't know. I need to get out of here."

He nods, and there's a cold silence as I walk out the door, slamming it shut behind me. I stomp to my truck, kicking gravel, and swing the door open. I sit on the edge of the seat, my feet still outside, and allow my head to fall between my legs, hoping it helps ease the tension running up my neck.

I'm conflicted on whom to be angry with.

She left because he'd asked her to.

She broke my heart, so my father's would stay whole.

Do I hate her or love her for that?

My phone rings, and I debate on answering it. I lift my head and lean back before grabbing the phone from my pocket.

My stomach drops when I see the name flashing on the screen. His check-up calls aren't made until the evening when he's off shift. That means, when I hit the Accept button, my life might fall apart.

"Not a good time, man," I answer.

"There's a chance they found Andy's body," Luke says.

"I'm on my way."

CHAPTER THIRTY

Lauren

"YOU LOOK STUNNING," I tell Stella when she stands to show off her wedding dress to me as well as the other bridesmaids and my mother.

Sure, I saw it months ago when we flew out to LA to meet with her designer, but the wedding-day glow makes it even more breathtaking. It was custom-made to accentuate her curves. The sleeves are lace, the style is fit like a mermaid, and the train is short. It's classy yet casual.

Her dark hair is down in curls with a crystal headband on the crown.

Hudson hit the wife lottery with her, although she says the same about him. Their *coworker with benefits* relationship ended with them getting married. No-commitment promises always end up causing you to fall harder and faster.

No commitment is a way for us to get what we want when we're not strong enough to let our emotions talk. So, you agree to sex with no strings, but everyone knows sex doesn't come without complications.

Hudson and Stella's relationship is ending up in marriage. Willow and Dallas's sex ended up with a baby and a relationship. You penetrate the person in more ways than one.

No matter what anyone says, when you have sex, you give a part of yourself to the other person.

"Thank you," Stella says. "Hudson invited Gage, by the way."

I scrunch my face up. "What? I thought you supported my decision that Gage was no longer a word to be said in my presence."

"To be honest, I hardly know the guy, but Hudson went to his work and asked him to come."

Gage has been Voldemort in the Barnes family since we ended things *again*. I don't want to hear his name. Don't want to think about him. Nothing.

Unfortunately, there's not much I can do to Stella or Hudson today. You can't exactly smack your brother on his wedding day. It'll fuck up his gelled hair.

"Why would he have done that? I told him we weren't on speaking terms. It'd be a major buzzkill for you to walk down the aisle at the sound of our arguing."

She sighs. "He identifies with the situation. Your brother and I had a hard time giving in to each other at first. We're both stubborn. If we had never admitted our wrongs, we wouldn't be here today."

———

THE WEDDING WAS BEAUTIFUL.

Small and intimate in my parents' expansive backyard, which surprised me, given Stella's celebrity roots. The only people present who'd graced the covers of magazines were her castmates and her supermodel sister.

The bride and groom had their first dance, and the bouquet was thrown. And, if you think I went for that thing, you're absolutely wrong.

That doesn't mean I didn't shove Willow to the front of the group and then jump up and down in celebration when she caught it. She and Dallas need to tie the knot.

This family deserves another fairy tale since mine is nothing but *Nightmare on Elm Street*-worthy.

I take another sip of my champagne, hoping it moves me into positive vibes, but something about weddings brings out the PDA craze in couples. All it does is remind me of how much I want to see Gage and smack him with some PDA.

I'm not sure which loss was the worse—the one when I was young and naive or the one when I was old enough to know better but couldn't break another man's heart. His dad's health was deteriorating. My conscience couldn't let me reveal our secret now.

I lick the buttercream frosting off my fork and am washing it down with strawberry champagne when Amos comes barreling toward me, looking frantic and carrying his oxygen tank behind him.

I jump out of my seat and sprint his way, meeting him in front of my parents' house.

"Amos," I say, grabbing his arm to make sure he's stable, "what's going on?"

He bends down at the waist to catch his breath. "You need …" *Gasp.* "He needs …" *Gasp.* "He needs you."

"Gage needs me?"

I've caught the attention of my family, and all eyes are on me. I notice my dad getting up from his table to see what's going on.

"It's Andy," Amos spits out. "Gage came charging into the house and said they … they found Andy's body. He packed a bag, left, and said he'd answer my questions later."

My heart sinks in my chest. "Oh my God. Where's he now?"

"On his way to the airport."

Gage never gave information on what had happened after Missy suffocated Andy, and I never exactly had the chance to ask any further questions.

I help Amos to the front porch and situate him in a chair.

"Do you need a ride?" I rush out. "You can come with me. Let me grab a bag."

I don't think twice before running to my bedroom and throwing clothes into a carry-on. Amos is talking to my parents when I walk out. Their faces are sympathetic. I don't know how much Amos told them, but I can't imagine he would spill the news about Andy without Gage's consent.

"It's not exactly safe for me to fly," Amos says as Hudson and Stella join us on the porch. "I have my truck, a full tank of gas, and am not scared of getting a speeding ticket to take someone there."

I look at my family in torment.

What do I do? Ditch my brother on his wedding day or go track down the man I'm in love with, who's going through something unbearable?

"Go," Hudson says.

"I'll drive you two," my father adds.

"Do you know anything else?" I ask Amos when we get into my dad's truck.

He shakes his head. "He got the call, packed his bags, and left for the airport."

I grab my phone and hit Gage's name. It rings a few times before going straight to voice mail. I smack the glove compartment.

Shit!

I call him again. Voice mail.

This isn't the time to be angry with me, Gage Perry.

"No answer?" Amos asks from the backseat.

I shake my head.

"I told him," Amos says.

I glance back at him. "Told him what?"

He clears his throat as I silently stare at him. "What I asked you to do."

No. Why?

"Amos, you didn't have to do that."

"While I appreciate your word, it was time I did. I robbed

my son of years of happiness, and I needed to own up to my actions. Had I not selfishly asked you to leave him, he would've never moved to Chicago, would've never met Missy, and would've never gone through this hell. Andy might've moved in with a different family and had a mother who wasn't mentally ill. My son wouldn't be bearing these burdens today. He wouldn't be on his way to see his dead son's body had I not asked you to do that. I knew it'd tear him apart, losing you, but I was selfish."

"Amos, none of those things can be blamed on you or Gage."

"I know what it feels like to lose someone you love too early. I was selfish and should be blamed."

CHAPTER THIRTY-ONE

Gage

MY MIND IS RACING.

My flight can't come fast enough.

Minutes feel like hours.

Luke has been regularly updating me, but there hasn't been much information.

A boy's body was found in the lake where Missy's car had been seen earlier on the day of Andy's disappearance, even though she has denied disposing of his body there. Her story changed dozens of times, and it was hard for police to keep up.

My little boy's body had been in that lake for all this time.

I shudder, wishing I could've been the one to go through that pain instead of him. Missy should've saved my little boy and taken me. Killed the person she was angry with, not a little man who was obsessed with Spider-Man and watched too many episodes of *SpongeBob Squarepants.* Man, what I would do to be hanging out on the couch, watching that with him.

Missy left him there to decay in a shitty-ass lake like the heartless bitch she is. She left his body for two fishermen to find early one morning.

Call me a bad dude, but she's a fucking bitch. Period. Point-fucking-blank. Missy is the only woman I'd ever call that name, and she deserves it. She deserves a stronger punishment than prison. I hope what she did haunts her until she takes her last breath.

I'll be present at every appeal her attorney files, fighting for my boy who never got a chance. Andy was my sunshine after Lauren left me in the dark. Those five years I had with him kept me going, woke me up, and made me look forward to the day, and in the end, I was his death.

"Missy's father booked you a private flight," Luke says when I answer his call.

I grit my teeth. "Decline. I want nothing from that motherfucker."

"Take it, bro. No doubt, I wanted to tell him the same and hang up on his ass, but my love for you stopped me. It'll get you here faster, and I know you want that more than anything."

"That's the problem!" My voice rises and breaks at the same time. "I'll never be able to be with him again."

Luke doesn't reply, not trying to push it and giving me plenty of time to calm down. He gets my pain. He knows no words will ever heal my grief. I've been waiting yet dreading this day since Missy admitted to hurting him. Finding him will at least give me the answers that have been killing me.

I went to that lake for weeks, dragging Luke with me, but we never found anything.

There will always be a part of me that knows I could've saved him, should've done more when the signs of Missy's breakdown started to come through, when I realized she hated me for what I couldn't give her.

"The flight leaves in five minutes. I'll text you the info."

I snatch my bags and follow the directions in the text.

Twenty minutes later, I'm boarding a private plan.

CHAPTER THIRTY-TWO

Lauren

"IT'S the only flight to Chicago," I tell Willow over the phone, nearly out of breath from walking around the airport in search of him. "Unless he's hiding out in the restroom, I can't find him." I do another scan of the waiting area. "Should I check in there?"

"If you don't mind seeing random men's cocks pissing in urinals, go right ahead," she answers. "Your brother followed me into the women's restroom there once."

"No details, please. I don't want a conversation that consists of cocks and my brother."

"Do you think Gage might've taken a private jet?"

"A private jet?" I snort. "Gage doesn't have access to those types of luxuries."

"You never know. Let me see what I can do, okay? I have connections with people who can look up flights. I did it for Stella all the time. Call you back."

"Thank you, Willow."

"And, whenever you're ready to talk about it, I'm here."

Willow has been my lifesaver and my new best friend since I lost mine to the cheating-on-Hudson scandal. We've been each other's rock during hard times.

My dad and Amos are on their way home. My mom has been calling for updates every five minutes, and I know she'll be pressing my dad for as many details as she can get.

I'm unsure of where I'll go and what I'll do when I land.

Time for me to figure that out.

Guilt sweeps through me when I go to call Kyle next. I should've called him on my way to the airport, but all I cared about then was getting here. My phone nearly falls from my hand when it rings with an incoming call.

Perfect timing.

"Hey," I answer. "I was about to call you."

"The hell is going on, Lauren?" Kyle shouts. "Gage texted me, asking for time off for an out-of-town emergency and isn't answering his phone. Did something happen between you two? Did you break up with him again?"

"I wish it were that simple," I answer, grabbing my bag and walking down the hallway, away from eavesdropping ears.

"I told you not to make him flee," he grits out. "I lost my best friend once, and I won't let it happen again."

"It's not my fault." I clear my throat. "Did Gage ever tell you about his life in Chicago?"

"The man has been a sealed-up coffin about that shit." His tone lowers. "What do you know?"

I sigh. "It's not my place, but find me any information you can about where he might stay in Chicago. Maybe a friend he still keeps in touch with?"

"Answer me on why he left," he demands.

The severity of the question breaks me down. "Gage had a son who went missing and was assumed to be dead. They found his body today."

"Holy fuck. Give me a few minutes, okay?"

He hangs up, and I walk around the airport, looking for Gage and ignoring the silent and curious looks from people. I'm wearing my bridesmaid dress, sporting an updo, and my cheeks are stained with mascara.

I want to be there for Gage, wrap my arms around him, and absorb slivers of his pain. My job and life are about healing and helping, and it's killing me that the person I most want to heal doesn't want it.

I'll be Gage's backbone while he's crumbling.

I redial his number.

No answer.

I'm grateful when Kyle calls me back and gives me what information he has.

I board the plane, knowing I'll be facing a broken man … if I find him.

CHAPTER THIRTY-THREE

Gage

IT IS no surprise that Missy's parents are waiting for me when I land.

The private jet wasn't an act of sincerity. It was bribery.

I accepted the favor to get to my son faster.

Her parents didn't want Missy to keep Andy. He was dark-skinned, didn't fit into the perfection of their Christmas photos, but they took to him when they realized Missy wasn't breaking. They then made it their mission to scream to the world that their daughter had been such a humanitarian to take an orphaned baby into her home. They didn't make it as known after they found out she was a murderer.

I ignore her parents and stroll straight to Luke, who's waiting for me on the opposite end of the section. I see the dirty looks he's throwing her parents. He despises them as much as I do.

"Thank you for picking me up," I tell him.

His face is sullen, heartbroken. He was Andy's godfather. "I got you." He hugs me—our second one of our entire friendship. The first was after he arrested Missy. "My guest room is cleaned out and ready for you. Let's go."

Missy's mother yells my name at the same time I go to turn

my back to them. She frantically scurries over to us, her husband on her trail, with stress and worry spread over her face like a rash.

Even though the distance is short, she's nearly out of breath when she makes it to me. "Please ... we need to talk."

I bite the side of my lip to inhale the words I want to scream in her face. "Not right now. There's nothing I have to say to you." *Other than you and your family can step the fuck out of my face.*

Missy's mom, Janice, has always been an honest and generous lady, a stay-at-home mother with the full-time job of organizing charity fundraisers. She had my full respect until she defended the woman who'd murdered my child ... her grandchild.

"Five minutes, *please.* That's all I'm asking for. Don't you think we at least deserve that?" she begs.

I toss my bag on the floor in frustration and rub at my temples before replying, "You aren't entitled to shit. When you stop sticking up and fighting for the woman who killed my child, that's when you'll *deserve* my time. I don't owe you or *her* anything. You want my time? My respect? Do the right thing and stand up for Andy. For the love you have for your grandson. Accept that she deserves punishment for what she did."

"I can't stop protecting my child. Nothing she does will ever change the love I have for her in my heart. I don't look at her and see her terrible actions. I look at her and see the scared woman I raised, and I wish I had instilled more strength into her. I look at her and see my heart."

"At least you get to see your child. That luxury got taken from me!"

This is the first time I've listened to Janice's words and taken them to heart. I hear her pain. She raised a daughter who did something horrible, and she's dealing with the guilt of that.

"Gage, let's go, man," Luke says, grabbing my elbow, but I pull out of his hold.

Robert is quiet as he stands next to her. A change from what

I've experienced since the first time I met him. The loudest man in the room isn't used to being powerless.

"She'll never parole," I hiss. "You'll have to kill me before I stop fighting for my son."

"We loved Andy just as much as you did," Robert says.

I snatch my bag from the ground. "Fucking prove it then."

They get my back as I follow Luke out of the airport and to his SUV.

"You've got to calm down, dude. You know how powerful that prick is," he says.

Robert is the mayor of Chicago, and his family litters the political scene.

"He could be the president of the fucking United States, and I wouldn't give a shit. I moved away from this city, so I wouldn't have to look at them, think about them or the hell I went through here." I look out the window. "All I do is think about what happened. How I hadn't stopped it."

"There was nothing you could do."

I ball my hands into fists and hold them against my legs. "I don't know what type of hell I'm walking into." I stare at him with watery eyes. "Tell me what I'm walking into, man."

"You want raw or sugarcoated?"

"Fucking hit me."

"They're running DNA and dental records right now." He stares ahead. "You know, it might not be him. Maybe it's not over yet."

"They found the body in the same lake Missy was seen driving from. You wouldn't have called me and put me through this hell had you not thought it was Andy. You were at the crime scene. You *knew* my son. Tell me, do you think it's him? Tell me what you saw."

He tips his head down and lowers his voice. "The body wasn't … wasn't easily identifiable. It'd been there too long, but from the size, the details, and everything else I know about the situation …" He stops to look away from me. "I'm sorry, buddy, but I think it's him."

"Fuck!" I open the door and release everything in my stomach in the parking garage.

"Let's get you back to my place. I'll talk to everyone involved and provide any information. It'll be too hard for you. I've got this."

I shut the door and use the back of my hand to wipe my mouth. "No, I've got this. I want to know everything, so I can make sure that bitch goes down for what she did. I won't stop fighting for him until I'm fucking dead. She never gave me the chance to say good-bye. Now, I can."

He nods, hands me a fresh water, and we stay silent on the short drive to his house. Luke lives in the same South Side neighborhood he grew up in. A block deemed as the wrong side of town. Even though he has the means to move somewhere safer, he chooses not to.

———

LUKE SOFTLY KNOCKS on the guest room door. "Ready to head to the station? Detective Lewis is working on the case."

Andy is in good hands. Cory Lewis is the best homicide detective in the state and my friend of three years. I have faith he'll help me in every way he can.

"Don't think I'll ever be ready for this," I mutter.

I go to the kitchen and pour a shot of Jack when the doorbell rings.

Luke comes walking into the kitchen. "Someone is at the door for you."

Fuck!

The shot burns down my throat when I take it, and I march into the living room. "Swear to God, if it's the fucking mayor, I'll flip."

"Not the mayor, just the woman in love with you," Lauren says.

CHAPTER THIRTY-FOUR

Lauren

KYLE HAD PULLED through with helpful information by the time I landed. There was no certainty of Gage being at the home of his best friend and coworker in Chicago, but it was all I had to run with on short notice. No one has been able to reach him.

He looks tortured when I step to him. His dark eyes are glassy, his face drained of all color, and his chin is trembling. I wrap my arms around him as a shield of comfort. He shoves his face into my shoulder and pours every emotion onto my skin. I rub his back, using my hand to make small circles while sniffling away my tears.

Even though I never had the fortune to meet Andy, he's in my heart because Gage is in my heart. And, just like that little boy I couldn't save at the hospital, my heart aches that another innocent child was selfishly hurt by someone who was supposed to care for him.

Why?

How?

How could anyone hurt a child, kill a child?

Andy along with so many others were innocent souls taken too soon.

Gage's eyes are bloodshot when he finally pulls away, and silence envelops us while we make eye contact.

Please see the apology in my eyes.

He needs to know that I have his back as he prepares himself to endure days of hell. I have so many questions that I'm scared to ask.

Was it Andy they found? How? Where?

"So, you must be the infamous Lauren?"

My hand flies to my chest when the man steps away from the wall at the corner of the room. I forgot we were in someone else's home. He's tall and tan-skinned with a sleeve of tattoos.

I hug myself into Gage's side and nod. A soothing comfort wraps around me as he pulls me closer to him.

"I've heard so much about you." He holds out his hand. "Luke."

I shake it. "Lauren. Those are all good things you've heard, right?"

He uses the back of his arm to dust away the sweat on his forehead. "I'd be a liar if I said yes. They've all been bad."

No shocker there. It wouldn't be a surprise if Gage convinced the entire city to hate my ass.

I don't look at Gage. He had his reasons for being upset with me.

"Hopefully, you'll make me change my mind about you," Luke says. "I'm getting good vibes from your showing up here, and you have my gratitude for that. I'll give you two time to talk." He nods toward Gage. "Let me know when you're ready to leave."

Luke squeezes Gage's shoulder before walking out of the room.

I pull away and turn to face Gage. "If you have somewhere to be, I don't want to keep you."

Pain closes over Gage's face, and his voice shakes. "I need to go to the station and talk to the detective in charge of the case."

"Oh." The word pops out of my mouth.

Does he want me to leave?

He slides his hands into the pockets of his jeans. "You want to come with me?"

I wipe away my tears. "Of course. I'll be at your side whenever you need me." I point to my outfit. "You mind if I change real quick?"

He shakes his head and shows me to a bedroom down the hallway. I set my bag on the bed next to another one that I assume is Gage's. He lightly kisses my cheek and leaves the room without saying a word. I have so many questions to ask him, but now isn't the time. I change out of my dress into a simple summer dress before going to the restroom to wash my make-up off.

Gage and Luke are waiting for me when I return to the living room, and Gage's hand stays on the base of my back when we follow Luke to his SUV. Gage slides in the backseat next to me, and I grab his clammy hand in mine after we buckle our seatbelts.

"I owe Hudson one hell of a wedding gift for your bailing to come here," Gage says.

I shake my head. "You don't owe him anything. They understand."

"Did you tell them about Andy?"

I swallow. "They know who Andy was, but the details aren't my story to tell."

He blinks. "Kyle?"

"He knows about Andy and helped me find you, but that's it. He needs to hear everything from you."

A stressed breath pulls from his chest. "I have some explaining to do. My dad ... he told me why you broke up with me."

I squeeze his hand. "Let's not talk about that right now, okay? Our problems don't need to be fixed in one day."

My stomach curdles when Luke turns into a back parking lot of what I assume is the station. He slips out of his seat and meets us outside, and we walk in as a team with my hand in Gage's, and Luke's arm swung over his shoulders.

All eyes are on us, and I scan the room to find faces filled with empathy, pain, and fear. These people were coworkers to both him and Missy and also most likely knew Andy. Their hesitation is evident, and a few gain the courage to head our way and hug Gage.

We crowd into the detective's office, and he shuts the door behind us.

I sit down next to Gage, and Luke settles against the wall.

"I wish I had more for you," the detective tells Gage. "The medical examiner told me she'd call the minute the autopsy report was finished. You're my friend, so I promise to pass along all information as soon as it comes, okay? Give me a day, and I'll have more answers for you."

I expect Gage to fight for more information, but to my surprise, he only nods. I'm not sure if he came looking for answers or wanted peace of mind that the body hadn't been identified yet. He wants to know but doesn't. It would answer his questions but set him back.

When someone goes missing, there's still the hope of seeing them again. That faith ends when they're confirmed dead. Your wish turns into dust, and the fear that you'd never hug them again is validated.

I spot a mob of camera crews in front of the station when we leave to head back to Luke's, and it gives me a bad feeling in my chest. It doesn't hit me that the reporters were at the station for Andy's story until we get to Luke's house. News vans and reporters with microphones swarm Luke's front yard when we pull up. They want someone to answer questions about Andy.

That someone most likely being Gage.

Luke parks in the drive and peeks back at us with a distraught look on his face. "Looks like Andy's story went viral."

My attention moves from the crowd to Gage. Every muscle in his body is tense.

"You two going to be okay while I run errands and attempt to ward off these scavengers?" Luke asks.

I peek over at Gage for the answer.

He nods. "We're good. Thanks for everything, man."

Luke unbuckles his seat belt and fishes in his pocket before pulling out a key. "I'll be here for anything you need. I'd suggest going through the back. You know the way."

My heart races as we quickly slide out of the SUV. Our heads stay down, our gaze low, and Gage's hand finds mine as he leads me through the fence to the back door. I hear Luke warning the media scavengers to step off his property at the same time Gage unlocks the door. He bolts the door when we safely make it inside, and his hand is back in mine while I follow him to the bedroom.

I stand in front of him while he sits down on the edge of the bed in exhaustion. He groans and slowly looks up at me in pain when I run my hands through his messy hair.

"I need you, Dyson," is all he says before his hands venture up my summer dress, and he drags my panties to my ankles.

There's no hesitation before I pull my dress over my head, toss it to the floor, and drop to my knees. His lips part when I loosen his belt and pull his pants down. My job tonight is to help him forget about his pain—at least temporarily—and heal the scar tissue over his heart that Missy caused.

His cock springs forth, ready for me, and I draw him into my mouth. His breathing quickens when I pull away to lick him up and down. He grabs the comforter in his fists, and the muscles in his legs tighten as he uses his power to keep them straight.

He's restraining himself.

"Take me how you want," I say around him. "Fuck my face how you want."

My words flip the switch in him. His hand leaves the bed to wrap around my hair, tugging it back, and his dick falls from my lips. He hisses and yanks me back to him, my mouth open, and clenches his hands around my strands.

His hips tilt as he feverishly rams his erection into my mouth, going deeper with each stroke. I let him control my every move, stopping myself from gagging, and I give him what he wants. What he *needs*.

"Fuck, you suck me so good," he says between breaths. "Reach down and play with yourself."

I'm soaked, and my thighs are sticky with my juices when I do as I was told.

"How wet are you for me, Dyson?" he asks in a strained voice.

I stroke my clit one time before pulling away and holding my finger up to him. I'm surprised at how well I'm multitasking. I gasp and nearly fall back when his hand loosens on my hair, so he can lean down and suck my finger.

"So wet," he says. "So delicious."

I cry out at the loss of him when he pulls away again, and then I stare up at him, licking my lips, already missing the taste of his pre-cum.

He pulls his shirt off and pats his lap. "Come here, baby."

I climb on him and moan when his fingernails bite into the skin at my hips.

"Ride me, Dyson. Ride this pain from me."

And that's what I do.

I grip his shoulders while carefully guiding his erection inside me. He doesn't loosen his hold on me as he rocks his hips up to go deeper.

My body quivers as he fills me up, and I set a pace that borders the line of steady and hard. It's rough but intimate.

His large hand wraps around the back of my neck, and he pulls my face down to his. "Did you miss this cock, baby?"

I pull myself up and slam down on him harder. "God, yes, so bad!"

His nose nuzzles mine. "Mmm ... I sure missed your pussy. I've been dreaming about being inside you again." He groans and pumps his hips up. "So fucking good. Bounce on me."

His eyes stay on me as our sweaty bodies move against each other's.

"Take me. Take it all," I moan out, dragging my nails along his back.

"Damn, I love you. I love you so damn much."

My stomach fills with sparks at his admission, and I can't stop myself from responding truthfully, "God, I love you."

His palm finds the roundness of my ass, and he slaps it. His mouth meets mine, and he gives me a different kind of kiss. It's filled with steam and intimacy but also trust and apology.

We ride out our orgasms together, and he holds his hand over my mouth as I scream out my release. I work on leveling my breathing when he brushes my sweaty hair from my face and strokes my cheek.

"Thank you, Dyson," he says, his voice dark and masculine.

He takes me with him while falling on his back and grabs my hand in his, guiding it to his chest. My fingers shake as he slowly drags it to his side, straight to the scar I asked about before.

"This scar … it's from her," he whispers.

I run my finger over the scar again. "Huh?"

"It's from Missy."

I rise up onto my elbows. "She stabbed you?"

He nods. "After she was brought into the station for questioning. No one searched her, given her position at the station and who her family is. When I walked into the interrogation room, she snapped and stabbed me with a knife she had in her pocket."

I bend down and kiss the scar. "I'm sorry she put you through so much hell."

He pulls me into his arms, my chest against his, and his lips hit mine. "You said you love me."

I slap his chest and blush. "So did you."

"There's never been a time I didn't love you."

———

"YOU NEED TO CALL YOUR DAD," I say, turning on my side and nestling myself against Gage's chest.

It's late, and we're cuddled in Luke's guest bedroom after our second round of sex and a much-needed nap. The sound of Gage's phone ringing non-stop is what woke us up.

Reporters and news outlets had managed to get his cell number. He turned it off, gave the detective my number, and asked Luke to keep us updated regularly. He'd have details before anyone. We haven't turned on the TV in fear a story about Andy would pop up.

Gage has been keeping to himself, not bothering to call anyone. I've stayed in contact with his dad, giving him the little updates I have, and everyone in my family tree has texted me. They don't know the details, but they've given me nothing but words of support for Gage.

"The news hit Blue Beech yet?" he asks.

I nod.

"Figured it wouldn't stay quiet for long." He shakes his head. "This is what I was afraid of. I guess money can't cover everything up."

I run my hand over his smooth chest. "Are you … are you going to have a funeral for Andy?"

Is it too early to ask that?

"We had one. An empty casket. In the back of my mind, I thought I'd never find him. I knew what Missy had done. At first, she'd admitted to killing him, but she wouldn't tell us where he was. He deserved a peaceful good-bye." A scoff leaves him. "I'd put a million dollars down that she and her family are pissing themselves at this moment."

"Do you think you'll visit her now?"

"Missy?" He shakes his head with a twisted sneer on his face. "Fuck no. No matter how many times she calls, I'll never visit that piece of trash."

I nod before resting my head on his chest. He's had an exhausting day. Sleep is what he needs because I'm not sure what kind of news will be coming our way tomorrow.

———

I JUMP and drop the water bottle in my hand when a light flips on.

Luke walks into the kitchen, shirtless and wearing only a pair of athletic shorts. "Shit, sorry. I just got back from the gym and didn't think anyone would still be awake."

It takes me a moment to catch my breath. "It's fine. I can't sleep, and not to mention, my work schedule has turned me into an insomniac." My shifts are ever-changing. In the past month alone, I've worked every shift available.

I step out of his way when he walks around the table to the fridge and grabs a bottle for himself.

He opens it before taking a giant gulp and stares my way, as if he's assessing me. "Are you back with him … permanently?"

If I had a single friend, I'd try to set her up with Luke, especially after seeing his six-pack and deep V that disappears underneath his shorts. It's not only his looks he has going for him, but I've also witnessed his character. He's been a good friend to Gage, and he was Gage's backbone when Andy went missing.

"That's my plan," I answer.

"I talked to his dad today. Amos said he's the one who asked you to break up with my boy."

I stare down at my bare feet and silently sip my water. Amos might've admitted to what he asked, but that doesn't stop the guilt from surfacing. I didn't have to agree and go through with it. Leaving Gage was ultimately my choice. I chose his father's happiness over his. I only wish the younger version of me saw it that way. I never thought about what walking away from Gage would do *to Gage*.

"Does Gage know Amos told you?"

"He said something about Amos telling him but I'm not sure how much. I'm nervous about bringing it up right now. He has so much going on and our relationship problems seem so small at the moment."

"You're a loyal one."

I glance back up at him. "What do you mean?"

"You don't throw people under the bus, and you keep your word. You think about people. Shit, from what it sounds like to me, you have a heart of gold."

If only.

"Not everyone would agree with that statement."

"Not everyone knows the real you."

I shuffle my feet. "I grew up in a tight-knit family. My parents taught me to have people's backs."

He nods, giving me a warm smile. "I like that. If only my mom had those same values."

"Bad childhood?"

"Grew up in South Side, Chicago. Dad left my heroin-addicted mom at the word *pregnant*. My grandma took care of me the best she could with the pennies she got from Social Security."

"I'm sorry," I whisper, my tone gentle.

"Don't be. It only made me stronger."

"How did you and Gage meet?"

He scoots out a chair, gestures for me to sit down, and takes the chair across from me when I do. "Funny story. First time I met him was at a bar. We got into some bullshit fight over a pool game and managed to give each other a black eye. And what do you know? I show up to training at the police academy to find him there too. We became friends, graduated from the academy together, and got hired at the same precinct." He chuckles, grinning at the memory. "We call it our fight to brotherhood. Gage was my partner for a short time until The Storm of Missy came riding through. Her daddy dearest donates a courteous chunk of change to the city annually, and she was rewarded with choosing her partner."

"She chose Gage."

"She chose Gage."

I shiver at that revelation. Missy got everything she wanted and still wasn't happy. "I'm glad he had you there for him when his world fell apart."

Luke plays with his bottle. "I was worried when he moved back home. He couldn't bullshit me. Sure, he had good intentions, going back for Amos and to clear his head, but I knew he was ultimately doing it for you. In the back of his mind, his heart, he knew you would be the only person who could heal him. And I fucking prayed you would."

"I'm not so sure about that. The first time I saw him in years, he arrested me."

He raises his brows. "I like that. It'll give you a good story to tell your kids one day."

His response steals my breath, and my heart falters. With all the chaos that has happened since Gage told me about Andy, I've never questioned his outlook on having a family—until now.

"Do you ..." I stutter while searching for the right words. "Do you think he'll want to have kids after *this*?"

Luke doesn't answer until we make eye contact. "That's something you need to talk to him about. He never talked about having children until Missy came along, but then again, he never thought you two would have a second chance."

"Let me guess ..."

The gravelly voice causes me to jump.

Gage steps into the room with sleepy eyes and yawns. "I'm the center of whatever you two are talking about."

"No way," I draw out. "We were talking about best-friend things."

Gage snorts. "You two best friends now?"

"Damn straight," Luke answers. "We're ordering our friendship bracelets tomorrow."

I nod. "They're going to be pink."

"Blue," Luke corrects before standing up. He squeezes my shoulder and then slaps Gage on the back. "I need to hit the shower. Good night."

We both say good night, and Gage waits until he disappears down the hall before falling to his knees in front of me.

"I'm not sure if I thanked you for coming here," he says, grabbing my chin and caressing it with his fingers. "But thank you, Lauren. Thank you for everything—for thinking of my dad, for thinking of Andy, for wanting me even though I was acting selfish."

A tear falls down his cheek and hits my leg.

"I'd follow you anywhere," I say around a sob. "And trust me when I say this, Gage Perry, I will never walk away from you again. Never. You're stuck with me now."

A small glimmer of a smile passes over his lips. "I wouldn't want it any other way."

My lips meet his.

He gets up to grab my hand, and I can't stop myself from smiling at the sight of the scratch marks on his back as he leads me back to bed.

CHAPTER THIRTY-FIVE

Gage

ANDY AMOS PERRY.

My son.

The sweetest and most badass kid I've ever met.

The tiny tot who wrapped his small fist around my heart and held on tighter as he grew up.

The boy who was just confirmed to have been found in the lake.

The phone falls from my hand after Cory breaks the news.

I run to the bathroom.

Vomit.

Slump down against the wall and cry, my knees to my chest.

I wish my life would end.

I didn't fucking protect him. I didn't do my job as a father.

I knew the moment Luke called me and said they'd found a body that it was my boy, but there was that unknown hope that Andy was still out there. Maybe Missy had dropped him off somewhere, like his birth mother had … or maybe she'd given him to someone else in order to hurt me.

Missy is as manipulative as she is beautiful.

It's no surprise when Lauren comes to my side and pulls me

to her. She doesn't flinch at my sobs. All she does is hold me close and let me release my pain.

She'd take it on as her own if she could.

And I'd do the same for her.

Maybe that's when you know your love for someone is real. You'd gladly take every ounce of their pain and lift it onto your shoulders. You'd rather be the one to suffer, the one taking each stab to the heart, than watch them hurt. Loving someone means their pain is your pain, and you're there to carry them when they're down.

Right now, Lauren is ready to carry me wherever I need to go.

———

LAUREN AND LUKE tried to talk me out of coming here, but I can't accept the truth until I see it for myself.

Their love for me is what has them by my side as we walk into the police station.

Cory doesn't want to show me the pictures to identify the body. He suggests Luke do it for me, but I shake my head. It has to be me. I'll regret it as soon as the photo is put on display in front of me. My hands go to the desk to stop myself from falling when Cory shows it to me.

My worst nightmare is now my reality. I've seen plenty of crime scene photos. I knew not to expect his smiling face. But he was my son, and it tears me apart.

My little boy.

Correction: my little boy's body.

The decomposing corpse isn't the boy I played soccer with or the son who wanted to be a cop, just like his daddy, when he grew up.

All I have left of him now are memories.

———

"HEY," Lauren whispers, her voice shy, when I walk into the bedroom with a towel wrapped around my waist, post-shower.

I got in the shower the moment we got back from the station. After seeing those photos and the autopsy report, I was hoping to wash away all the thoughts of how my son had suffered.

It was comforting to have Lauren by my side this time. I went through it alone when Andy went missing. Sure, I had Luke, but there's a difference between a lover and a friend consoling you.

I sit on the edge of the bed. "Can we talk about why you left now and how my dad admitted it was him who had asked you to leave?"

She lifts her hands up, and her brows gather in. "Gage … I can explain."

I stop her from going on. "As much as I want to be angry with you, you thought you were doing the right thing for my father." I let out a heavy sigh. "So, for that, I don't know what I think about it." We've both made mistakes that we regret, and every time I look at Lauren, I see her regret for letting me go.

Her face softens, her eyes watering, and she gives me her back while she moves to the closet. She opens my bag and starts dragging out clothes. My chin trembles when she grabs my hand to help me up and then releases the towel.

"Will you tell me about Andy?" she asks, tossing it to the side.

My shorts are in her hand, and she helps me step into them while I share story after story about the little boy I wish she could've met. I don't stop while she helps me get dressed or when she drags me to the bathroom to comb my hair. She takes care of me while I give her my memories.

———

"I KNOW it's not exactly sane for a woman to suggest her boyfriend talk to his ex-wife, but in this case, I think it might help you heal," Lauren says from across the kitchen table.

Earlier, she gave Luke a grocery list, and he picked up everything we needed for gumbo. I sat in the kitchen and continued my Andy stories while they listened to every word. It felt good to share his memory since I'd hidden every part of him away while I was in Blue Beech.

"Boyfriend?" I ask. "Are we back to that?"

Luke left for work, so it's now the two of us … if you don't count the reporters camping in the front lawn. Most of them bailed after we shut the door in their faces and have retreated to Missy's parents' house.

"I mean … *friend*." She shoves her face into her hands and shakes her head. "Why am I embarrassed? I mean, we've been sleeping together, but what exactly does that mean? I haven't had a boyfriend since you, and come to think of it, we never had *the talk*. We both just knew what we were to the other. Not that I assume we're dating," she continues to ramble. "Let me reword this. It's not exactly sane for a woman to tell her fuck buddy to go talk to his ex-wife."

I lean into the table. "Look at me, Lauren."

She slowly pulls her hands from her face.

"No need to have that talk this time either. You're sure as hell not my *fuck buddy*. You're my girlfriend, the woman I love, my goddamn everything. Let's make that clear right now, okay?"

"Okay," she draws out, a smile playing at her lips. "Glad we got that covered."

"Ditto." My vision starts to go blurry, and my throat feels scratchy as I think about what I'm about to say next. "I think you might be right about the Missy thing."

She flashes me a surprised look.

Even though I can't stand Missy, we need this closure. When she contacts me, it only brings the memories to the surface. It needs to stop. Her name, even the thought of her, is a reminder of what I've lost.

"Thank you for understanding this situation," I tell her.

She stands and circles the table. I grunt when she pulls out my chair and plops down on my lap, wrapping her arms around my neck.

"You're welcome. Give me a call if you need some reinforcement though. I'd love nothing more than to shove my heel into her throat."

"As a man of the law, I'll act like I didn't hear you say that." I lean in to whisper in her ear, "Although I can't say anyone would stop you or arrest you for doing it."

———

IT'S my first and only time visiting her in prison.

A sour taste fills my mouth as I sit in Luke's car and wonder if I'm doing the right thing.

I want to forget about Missy.

After this, she's dead to me.

All evidence against her was circumstantial. She was charged with neglect, child endangerment, involuntary manslaughter, and assault for my stabbing. Her lawyers initially argued, no body, no trial. They claimed there was no cause or time of death, and we had insufficient evidence. Luckily, we had good prosecutors on our side.

They worked with what little evidence they had. They used the voice mails she'd left me. The first one that threatened to hurt Andy and the second that told me I was to blame for what she did to him. She had Googled different methods of suffocation on her phone hours before Andy went missing and none of the endless stories and alibis she told lined up.

Missy fought at first, of course. She claimed the birth mother had kidnapped him but that was disputed after Luke hired someone to identify and track down the woman. She'd been in an inpatient rehab facility at the time. Her second claim was that she had gone to shower, and he was gone when she came back, like Andy had wandered off and started a new life somewhere. In the end, her parents convinced her to take a plea deal. She admitted to suffocating Andy and said she dropped his body in a river close to her house. That river was searched for months and nothing was ever found.

She denied being near the lake where they found his body days ago, even though someone saw her there. I tried so many times to get it searched, but my superiors deemed it unnecessary since there wasn't enough evidence. The real reason was *her parents* didn't find it necessary because they knew there was a chance Missy was lying.

I grab my phone to listen to the voice mail. It's the worst time to do it, but I need to go in there with the right state of mind and fight for Andy.

My head feels like it's spinning, and my body goes cold at the sound of her voice mail. Her words are screamed out around cries.

"GAGE! Gage! You'd better answer my goddamn phone calls, you hear me? I saw them. I saw all the pictures you had saved of that whore. That stupid cunt you love so much who left you. I'm the one who loves you, Gage, not her. Me! I've stood by you and done nothing but try to please you. Me! How could you do this to us? Andy wants his mommy and daddy together with him every night. That's why we have him—to give him a family—and if you can't, then we're wrong for having him … If he can't have that, then he has no family. A boy shouldn't have to live without family … I'll end his hurt for him. I'll let Andy go to heaven where he can have a real family. Say good-bye to us, Gage, since you've decided we aren't worth it. Andy won't be here when you get home. Take that."

. . .

I SHUT my eyes to stop the tears. I'll never forget the day I first heard that voice mail. I was on a fishing trip and never expected Missy would go back to my house in search of more Lauren evidence. We had a key to each other's places for years. She'd started spiraling downhill the past few months. She'd begged me to move in with her, tried to talk me into giving Andy a sibling, and lashed out when I wouldn't take the bait.

I never expected her to hurt him. Me? Sure. But not him. She loved Andy.

Anger can blind love.

I called the station as soon as I got the message and raced to her house.

I was too late.

Even though they found his body, I'm not sure if my visit will change anything with her charges since she took the plea, but I have to try. I also want to hear her admit to what she did and how she'd sent us on a bullshit hunt for his body.

I'm close to throwing up that sour taste when she walks into the cramped room. Being here reminds me of the countless hours I interrogated her until her parents' lawyer stepped in and put a stop to it.

The door opens, and she strolls in with a smile on her face.

"Hey, baby," she greets. Her blonde hair is pulled back into two braids, and bright red lips stand out along her pale features.

There's no denying that Missy is beautiful. She's also sick, and I wish I'd recognized the signs of it before she did what she did.

I inhale a deep breath and run my sweaty hands over my legs. "Hey."

She plops down in the metal seat and inches forward, getting as close to me as possible. I have to stop myself from flinching and pulling away in disgust.

"You're sleeping with her, aren't you?" she spits.

"Who?" I already know the answer to my question.

"That cunt ex of yours." She slams a hand on the table.

"My father hired a PI, Gage. I saw the pictures. She's the same woman who starred in your sacred box of first-love memories." Her tone turns mocking. "You don't forget the woman you despise."

It's becoming more difficult to hold in my anger. "That's what you're concerned about right now? That I'm back with her?"

Tears fall down her cheeks and smear her lipstick. "I gave you so much of myself, Gage! Let you take me any way you wanted, even when I knew she was whom you imagined. I did everything for you—bought you expensive gifts—"

"Which I didn't accept and told you to return them and buy something for Andy," I interrupt.

She tried buying my love with gifts, just like her parents did with her, but it didn't work. You can't buy love from someone who doesn't have it up for sale.

I tap my foot while controlling my anger. "I'm sorry, Missy. I'm sorry I couldn't do enough to make you happy."

Her demeanor changes with my apology. She perks up, and the anger disappears from her face. "You did make me happy, baby! You did. I'm upset with myself that I didn't make you happy. You never acted like I was your world."

Come the fuck on.

The tapping of my foot speeds up, and I wouldn't be surprised if I wore a hole into the floor. "I need you to do me a favor, Missy."

"Anything," she blurts out.

"Admit to what you did. *Please*." My voice breaks. "For Andy. For your family. For *me*."

"Tell me you love me."

I stare at her, blinking. "What?"

"Tell me you love me, and I'll tell you the truth and nothing but the truth."

I grit my teeth. "I love you."

Her fists hit the table. "Say it like you mean it!"

"I love you, Missy, so damn much."

She shuts her eyes and throws her head back. "It sounds so awesome to hear you finally say those words. I knew you loved me. It took you long enough to admit it though."

I don't fucking love her. Bile sweeps up my throat, and I can't wait to brush my teeth for an hour to wash away my words.

"Promise you'll write me," she goes on. "Promise you'll visit me. Some inmates earn conjugal visits. Maybe we can do that."

"Yes, maybe," I lie.

"And you'll leave her?"

"Whatever you want. Just give our son the justice he deserves."

My fake admission gives her hope, and she lets everything out.

I want to die as I digest her confession.

CHAPTER THIRTY-SIX

Lauren

"ARE WE BECOMING BEST FRIENDS?" I ask when I answer Kyle's call.

"Bite me, Satan," he replies. "I'm calling about your arsonist reputation. We found the cause of the fire."

"Please tell me it wasn't a sugar cookie–scented candle from my apartment."

"It was meth."

"Meth! In my apartment?"

The hell?

He chuckles. "No, it never started in your place. Another tenant took up the hobby of cooking it."

Great, so I was living in a meth lab. Cool.

"You're joking."

"Nope, and your creepy-ass landlord is smack dab in the middle of said meth ring. Turns out, phony rich kid has made some dough, selling drugs."

"Can't say it surprises me."

"He has quite the record, including assaulting multiple women. One of his men snitched on him, but we have yet to locate him. You need to be careful until we do. If you see him, call me right away."

Yep. My creep-dar is never wrong.

"I appreciate the heads-up. And can we not mention this to Gage right now?"

"Haven't said a word to him. Don't intend to until shit dies down."

"Thank you."

He blows out a stressed breath. "How's our guy doing?"

I wish I knew the honest answer to that. "He went to see Missy today."

The rational part of me knows this is what he needs even though the irrational half told me to stop him. No matter the outcome, whatever happens with Missy won't be easy. I only hope it clears things up for him. There's no doubt he feels guilt over entrusting Andy in the hands of the woman who killed him.

"Bitch-face, murderer Missy?" he asks.

"The one and only."

"You should've gone with him and beat her ass."

"I think suggesting violence is against the police code of ethics," I say around a laugh. "Although, trust me, there's nothing I would've loved more than that." I'd have been nice about it. Punch her and then, given my professionalism, stitched her up and sent her back to her cell.

"I like you at his side. You've moved yourself up two notches on the devil board."

———

"ANY UPDATES?" I ask Luke, walking into his living room after my shower with a cup of tea in my hand.

At first, I thought being alone with him would be weird, but he's done nothing but make me feel welcome.

No one has heard from or seen Gage.

Willow sent me a link to countless news articles. The media

is having a field day with Andy's story, and Missy was a trending topic on Twitter this morning—#MonsterMissy.

Pictures of them are flooding the internet. Everyone wants justice for Andy, and I'm nervous about how Gage will handle all this attention.

"Sorry," he answers, shaking his head. He snags his beer from the coffee table and falls back against the cushions, stress lining his dark features. "My friend works for the prosecutor's office, and according to him, Missy admitted to everything during her visit with Gage and gave him the answers he had been looking for."

I frown. "As bad as the situation is, I'm glad he got what he had gone there for."

He shakes his head and whistles. "The fucked up part is what Gage had to do to convince her to admit everything."

"What do you mean?" My legs feel weak, and I sink down in a chair before I lose my strength to hold myself up. Whatever is coming isn't good news.

"She insisted he declare his love for her—repeatedly—and that he promise to leave you."

My heart sinks. "What?" I stutter out. "Are ... are you serious?"

He sees the shock and terror on my face. "Lauren, he won't go through with it. He said what he needed to say. I only wanted to give you a heads-up in case you hear it from someone else who's not Gage and who doesn't know the entire story."

"Wow," I draw out.

He wouldn't for real do that, would he?

No way.

"That's the best word to describe it."

"No, I think *fucked up* is better," I say.

He leans forward to tap his beer against my cup. "Looks like we've found a winner."

I rise from my seat and yawn. "I'm going to attempt to get some sleep. Let me know if you hear from him, okay?"

He tilts his head forward. "Of course, and same goes for you. Good night, Lauren."

"Good night."

———

I CAN'T SLEEP.

I've tossed, turned, and checked my phone dozens of times.

Still no word from Gage.

My pulse races when the bedroom door opens, and a silhouette of a body moves through the darkness. I blink, adjusting my eyes, and watch him shed his tee. The moonlight shining through the blinds gives me a glimpse of his chest. He hastily shoves his jeans down and slides into bed, wearing only his boxer briefs.

I flip around to look at him. "Jesus, Gage, where have you been? You had me worried sick."

I sound like my mother.

Is this what it feels like, worrying about someone you love so much that you lose sleep?

He clears his throat, but his voice is still hoarse when he answers, "The lake. I had to apologize." His body shakes when I reach out to touch him and caress his shoulder. "Sorry I've been MIA. I needed time."

"No, I understand," I say.

His skin is warm as I slide my hand from his shoulder to his cheek, wiping away his tears.

I shiver when his hand swoops underneath my T-shirt, and he brushes a thumb against my nipple.

"I love it when you wear my tees," he whispers.

"You've mentioned that once or twice."

I move away to pull it off, but he stops me.

"Leave it. I want to make love to you while you wear nothing but it."

I moan when he rolls on top of me. He pulls my panties and shorts down and slowly slides his cock between my legs.

His lips go to my ear. "I love you."

———

"I'M SORRY. I tried, but no one could take your shift without hitting too much overtime, and you know how the hospital looks at that," Natasha tells me over the phone. "All I could manage was one more day."

"I understand," I say around a sigh. "I appreciate your trying."

I never call in sick. *Never.* Not only am I addicted to my job, but they also need me. Even though it's a small hospital, it stays busy. Normally, I don't have a problem with that, but Gage needs my support. This sucks.

I didn't question him about his meeting with Missy. He has no idea I know what she made him promise. There's no doubt in my mind that Gage loves me and wouldn't walk away from our love. I trust him.

Now, after the hell of a day he's had, I have to break this news to him. I stroll into the bathroom after hanging up and wrap my arms around his waist from behind while he dries off from his shower.

"Bad news," I say, pressing my lips against the damp skin of his back.

"Words I'd be happy to never hear again," he comments, reaching back to give my arm a gentle squeeze.

"No one can cover me at work," I say around a swallow.

His shoulders stiffen. "When do you leave?"

"By tomorrow."

My arms collapse when he turns around to face me, and I lose my breath when he tips my chin up with one finger.

"Mind if I stay a few days?"

"Stay as long as you need."

He cups my chin and brings my lips to his. "I'd better make this day count then."

I smile at his plan but hold my hand out to stop him. "You don't need to worry about entertaining me. You've had a rough few days."

"Spending time with you will help keep my mind off everything."

"Tell me your plan."

"Chicago time with Gage Perry."

"I like the sound of that already."

It is a good idea, and I hate that it's ruined when we walk out the front door. Cameras are in our faces.

"Just ignore them," Gage mutters, grabbing my hand.

I tug on his arm. "Let's go back inside."

"Gage!" a reporter yells. "Did you have anything to do with the disappearance of your son? There have been reports that you knew Missy planned on hurting him!"

I freeze up and clench my fists, holding myself back from smacking the asshole.

My chest aches, and I lose Gage's hold when he darts toward the reporter.

"The fuck did you say?" he screams.

Regret fills the middle-aged man's face. "I, uh …" He pushes his glasses up. "A source told us—off the record, of course—that you were aware that Missy was dangerous."

"Fuck your lying source," Gage snarls. "I loved my son and would've never let Missy near him if she showed one sign of abuse. I came as soon as Missy left the voice mail but was too late." He thrusts his finger in the man's face. "Don't come to me, hoping for a story that will make headlines. The only one you'll receive is that Missy stole my son from me and ruined my life. There's no need for you goddamn scavengers to throw it in my face." He grabs my hand. "Don't fucking follow us."

"Wow," I say as we slip into Luke's SUV.

"This is what I was concerned about," he grits out, his head falling against the steering wheel.

Their cameras follow us as he backs out of the drive and turns down the road.

There's no doubt in my mind, that guy won't be the only reporter we run into today.

"Turn around," I order.

He glances over at me. "What?"

"Turn around. We'll order some deep-dish pizza and watch movies in bed all day."

A portion of the irritation drains from his face. "I like that idea."

CHAPTER THIRTY-SEVEN

Lauren

EXHAUSTION IS MY MIDDLE NAME.

It's early in the morning when I pull into Gage's driveway, and I yawn with each step going up the stairs to the loft before tiredly unlocking the door. I can't wait to eat, take a quick nap, and then see Gage. His flight lands this afternoon, so I plan to catch some sleep and then pick him up with Amos.

We've talked regularly since I came home five days ago, and he's stayed strong. It helps that Luke is there with him, and he has the support from him and his coworkers. They held a memorial for Andy at the lake last night, and I'm sad I had to miss it.

I drop my bag on the table and grab a bottle of water from the fridge at the same time there's a knock on the door. Amos has been visiting me between my shifts and bringing me meals since I've been back. Now that our secret has come out, we've gotten closer.

"It's open!" I call out and snag another bottle for Amos.

"Hello, Lauren."

My hands start to shake as I drop the bottles at the sound of his abrasive voice. I inhale three deep breaths before turning around to face him.

"What are you doing here, Ronnie?"

I pause to take him in. He reeks of alcohol, his button-up shirt is soaked in what looks like more liquor, and his eyes are bloodshot and swollen. One thing Ronnie isn't is in the right frame of mind.

"Have you been following me?" I stupidly accuse.

The evil smirk on his face confirms not only that this is a stupid question, but also that something bad is about to happen. Instead of waiting for his response, I rush over to the knife block and miss my chance at grabbing one when he captures my waist. He swipes the block off the countertop with his free hand, and the sound of knives crashing to the floor masks my groans when he presses against me and shoves my face against the countertop.

I cringe when his wet lips hit my ear and his thick body moves against mine.

"Now, now, tenant," he says mockingly, "why are you making trouble for me? I only wanted to be a good landlord and check that you were okay after the fire."

I bite into my lip to stop myself from crying out and struggle to reach for a candle, anything, to protect myself from him but am stopped when he grabs my arm and pushes it back. A deep pain shoots through me, and I freeze up.

Don't provoke him.

"Ronnie," I say as calmly as I can manage, "I was going for the bottle opener to offer you a beer."

He laughs behind me, and the smell of his breath nearly gives me a contact buzz. "I applaud you for not being as dumb as most women I have to punish, but I'm not falling for your tricks, bitch." He twists my arm against my back, and I buck against him. "Keep doing that, sweetie. It'll only make my dick harder."

I still while taking deep breaths.

"Not so brave now that your little boyfriend isn't with you," he taunts, twisting an arm harder. "You know, no one would've questioned what happened in that apartment had you not been spreading your legs for cop boy."

I stop myself from crying out when he whips me around and pushes me against the counter, my back biting into the rough handle of the drawer. Nausea hits me when he spreads my legs and shifts himself between them.

All I have to do is raise a knee.

It has to be timed perfectly though.

"He was only investigating the fire because you blamed me, Ronnie," I grit out.

He thrusts his hips against mine. "Shouldn't have turned me down."

"Smartest decision I've made in my life."

My response only lights more rage inside him. I have to be smart about this. I nearly gag when I feel his hardness rub against my leg.

"Ronnie, you need to leave before the police come," I warn. "If you go now, no one will hear about this visit, okay?"

He scoffs, "There's a warrant out for my arrest, you dumb cunt. Either way, I'm going to jail." He rolls his hips. "Might as well have some fun before I do."

I try to push him away, but he's stronger than I am. "Please stop. You'll regret this later."

"Trust me, I won't regret this one bit. In fact, I'll relish it forever."

He looks up and meets my gaze for the first time, and I can't stop myself from spitting in his face. I'm a survivor, and I also take no shit. My head slams back against the cabinet when he smacks me across my face, and I taste blood on my lips.

"Now, I'm really going to make you pay," he says, taking a step back to unbuckle his jeans.

I see this as my opportunity and slowly start to lift my knee up, hoping I get a good shot.

We both stop and jump at the sound of Amos's voice.

"Hey, hey, you step away from her right now!" he screams,

stalking into the room, moving as fast as he can with his tank behind him.

Ronnie wipes my spit from his face. "What are you going to do, you old man?"

Amos raises his hand. "I'm going to protect that woman until you kill me. Do you hear me?" He holds his phone up. "I also hit the emergency button on my phone, and the police will be here any minute."

Ronnie steps away from me and kicks Amos's oxygen tank. I grab the candle I was going for and bust it over his head at the same time he punches Amos in the face. Ronnie falls. This is what some might call my stupid moment, but I disagree. Instead of making sure Ronnie is down, I rush over to Amos's side as blood pours from his nose.

The front door slamming catches my attention, and I rush down the stairs to catch Ronnie, but his expensive sports car is already flying down the street.

I run back into the loft with disappointment and situate Amos on the couch and hold a towel to his nose.

"What the fuck happened here?" Kyle shouts minutes later, appearing in the doorway. "Amos called with an emergency."

"Ronnie decided to pay me a visit," I say, biting back tears.

"Oh, fuck me!" Kyle yells. "That dumb junkie!"

"Can we not tell Gage about this?" I ask Amos, standing up.

His glassy eyes meet mine. "Last time we made a pact like that, you two didn't talk to each other for nearly a decade."

"When it rains, it fucking pours," I cry out.

CHAPTER THIRTY-EIGHT

Gage

I HIT Lauren's name while making my way through the airport.

The call goes straight to voice mail.

Seconds later, Kyle's name flashes across my phone screen.

"Hey, man," I answer.

We've briefly talked since I flew to Chicago. I want to tell him everything in person.

"I have something to tell you, but promise you won't freak out," he says with caution.

The fuck kind of statement is that?

"Depends on what it is."

"There was a situation."

"What do you mean, situation?" I've had enough *situations* to last a lifetime.

His breathing is heavy on the other end. "Ronnie ... he, uh ..."

"The landlord?"

"The landlord."

"What about the fucking landlord?" The volume of my voice grants me looks from people passing by.

"The building fire was caused by him cooking drugs there."

How the fuck is that a situation for me?

I'm happy it gives us the answer we were looking for and that people will stop giving Lauren a hard time.

"Good. Lauren won't be blamed for that fire now."

"Too late. Ronnie blamed her for his getting busted and paid her a visit at your place."

My breathing falters, and I stop in place. "The fuck did you just say?"

"He came to the loft and assaulted her. Thankfully, your dad walked in and fought him off. They're both a little banged up, but everyone is fine."

"And the landlord? Is he in custody?"

"Not yet, but we're on it. Everything is fine. We'll get him. I promise."

"Asshole touched my girl and my father, so no, everything is not fucking fine." My jaw clenches. "And why am I just now hearing this?"

"It happened only a few hours ago, and you were on a plane."

I speed-walk through the airport. "I'm going to fucking kill him."

"Not smart to say, given you're surrounded by people."

I raise my voice. "I. Am. Going. To. Kill. That. Motherfucker."

"Point taken."

"Where is she?" I snag my bag from the baggage claim, throw it over my shoulder, and sprint out of the building.

"Her parents'. We offered to take her and your dad to the hospital, but Lauren fixed herself and your dad up, and they're okay."

"I'll be there as soon as I can."

I hang up on him and start looking for an open cab.

A blue truck swerves into the pedestrian lane and stops next to me.

"Get in," Kyle yells through the open window.

I shut the door behind me and meet his stare. "Motherfucker will pay for this."

———

THE RIDE to town feels like it takes ages, and I jump out of Kyle's truck as soon as we pull in front of Lauren's parents' house. I race through the front door to find Lauren and her family in the living room, and two fellow officers are standing in the hallway that leads to the kitchen.

I rush over to Lauren and take her face in my hand, holding it back and inspecting it, searching for any marks. "Are you okay, baby?"

Her cheek is bruised, her lips swollen, but other than that, she's in one piece.

Thank God.

The landlord won't be blessed with the same destiny when I get my hands on him.

Her brown eyes water as she stares up at me and nods. "I'm fine. Just a little shaky, is all."

Typical, strong-willed Lauren.

My lips smack into hers before I take another scan of the room. "My dad?"

"He's in the bathroom," Lauren's dad says, standing up from the couch.

Lauren's father, John, has his legs planted wide when he stands and loosens his collar. Rory, Lauren's mom, is next to her with wet eyes.

Kyle moves away from the corner of the room and smacks John on the back. "We'll get the dude. I promise you that, sir."

"The fucker will pay for it. *I can promise you that*," I bite out, not caring about my language in front of them.

Typically, I'm a respectful dude but not when a man has hurt two people I'd die for.

Lauren's lips tremble, and she winces, like it pains her.

"We have guys out looking for him. You don't need to worry about this," Kyle tells me.

I help Lauren when she struggles to get up, and she wraps her hand around my arm.

"Let them deal with Ronnie, okay?" she says. "Please don't go after him."

"I'll never stop stressing over someone hurting my family."

He will pay, and he will pay at my hands.

She sighs and nods. It's not an agreement. It's a promise that we'll be having this conversation in private at a later time.

I kiss her cheek when my dad walks in, and I march across the room to pull him into a hug.

"Thank you," I say before doing the same inspection I did with Lauren.

As with Lauren, I can tell he's been roughed up, but he's okay. Physically at least.

We stayed in contact when I was in Chicago but haven't broached his admission that he was the one to ask Lauren to break up with me. That conversation won't be held tonight either. It will happen, but causing more chaos than we have going on isn't smart, and as pissed as I am, I can't get angry with him.

Who knows how much time we'll have to work out our problems?

We'll talk, but there will be no grudges held.

We stay at Lauren's until it grows dark, and Kyle drives us home. We don't go to the loft. It's part of an open investigation. Plus, I might snap if I see the evidence of the destruction Ronnie caused. I pace in the kitchen, and Lauren makes herself and my dad each a bowl of ice cream before they walk me through what happened with Ronnie.

Later, I do another inspection of her while we shower. My nails bite into my knuckles as I eye the bruises on the backs of her thighs and back. I help her dry off, and we sleep in my old bedroom.

Ronnie will go down for this.

————

"YOU SURE YOU don't want to stay home?"

I'm spread out on the floor next to Lauren in my childhood bedroom. The twin-size bed we started the night in proved not to be big enough for the both of us. After I rolled off twice, I moved to the floor. Lauren joined me after waking up to an empty bed. We ended up snuggling in a build-a-fort made of blankets and pillows.

"I'm positive I don't," she answers. "You know we're short-staffed."

"They'll understand if you explain to them that you were assaulted."

Not that she would tell them.

I know I've lost when she gets up and starts to rummage through the overnight bag she packed from her parents. "They'd absolutely understand, but sitting around, thinking about the suit-wearing creep putting his hands on me, isn't what I want to do today. Work will rid my thoughts of him."

We both shudder at the thought of Ronnie.

I lift myself up onto my elbows. "Then, let me take you."

She shakes her head and leans down to kiss my lips. "I'll be fine, babe."

I grab her elbow and pull her back down next to me. "The lunatic who assaulted you is on the loose."

I already feel like a piece-of-shit boyfriend for not being there to protect her the first time. It can't happen again.

The final decision is made during breakfast. News to me, Lauren arranged for my father to volunteer at the hospital when she worked. He'll assist people with directions and be with her if she needs anything.

My goal today is tracking Ronnie down.

———

I'VE BEEN STALKING Ronnie's recent transactions and GPS locations from his phone records since I walked into the station. He has multiple rental properties, and I plan to visit each one. If he's not there, I'll question the tenants.

My time is saved when I spot his most recent location is fifteen minutes out of Blue Beech.

Appreciate your making it easy for me, dumbass.

I stop by Kyle's office before leaving for my manhunt and knock on his door. "I need to run a quick errand. Be back in an hour."

He stands and snags his wallet from the desk. "I'm coming with you. I need some fresh air."

"Nah, I'm good." I hold my hand up to stop him. "It's a dry-cleaning pickup for Lauren. Nothing fun."

His lips press into a thin line. "Sorry, partner, but you're on the clock, which means, I'm by your side during every move you make. I'll maybe even follow you to the urinals today."

I turn around and walk away without saying another word, and he follows me to the cruiser.

Not another word leaves him until he's buckling his seat belt. "I know you got a hit on Ronnie's whereabouts."

Kyle can't be dragged into my shit. I can't have him losing his job if trouble arises with Ronnie. I'll be the only one facing the consequences of my actions. I need to find a way to blow him off and pray to God that Ronnie doesn't change locations before I do.

"You don't know shit," I mutter, failing to meet his gaze as I shove the key into the ignition.

"I beg to differ, liar face. Let me and the guys handle him, and I'll keep you updated. I fucking swear it, Gage. You're not in a sane state of mind to be handling this. I can't risk your doing something stupid, like killing the predator asshole."

"He'd deserve it," I grit out.

"Good point." He snags the keys before I can stop him. "Promise me you won't leave any marks on the dude, okay? Give me your word, and I'm your wingman."

"Can't do that, brother. I'm sorry."

"There goes that idea. Hopefully, Sierra will know how to cover up any bruises with all the makeup she has." He throws the keys into my lap. "Let's find this asshole."

———

RONNIE'S shiny red BMW is parked in the driveway of the rental.

The idiot couldn't even hide out from the cops right.

Even better, the front door is unlocked.

Guy might as well have left us a breadcrumb trail.

The entire ride, I attempted to talk Kyle out of coming with me, but there was no changing my best friend's mind. He has my back, no matter what, and the way he loosened his collar when we parked down the street told me he shared the same hatred toward Ronnie not only assaulting my family, but other women as well.

I don't see Ronnie as a threat, but my gun is still in my hand. And Kyle takes the same precaution. I carefully open the door, and he follows me in. It's quiet, and the place reeks of alcohol, drugs, and piss. The living room is clear. So is the kitchen … with the exception of the meth lab set up inside.

Kyle glances back at me with a glare and shakes his head, mouthing, *Piece of shit*, before we hang a left down the hall. With the amount of drugs, I'd expect to see more people here, protecting the supply.

Dumbest drug dealer in history.

We find him passed out, naked, in a bedroom that has the door torn off the hinges with a woman next to him in the same position.

Disgust spirals through me.

Did he drug her? Rape her? Is she here by choice?

Dirty needles and more drugs litter the nightstand. I stalk around the bed and watch him sleeping soundly with not a care in the world after he nearly destroyed my girl's and my father's lives. That seems to be the problem with so many people. They don't think of the impact their actions have on other people.

My anger takes over, and before I can stop myself, I snatch him from the bed. He grunts, and the wall shakes when his naked body slams against it. It's a sight I wish I could bleach from my eyes. My hand immediately goes to his throat before he even has the chance to open his eyes.

"Good morning, motherfucker," I say, spitting in his face.

He opens his mouth to talk back, but my grip is too tight. I get a rush of satisfaction at the sight of his face turning red. My eyes stay on him until his bedmate screams and covers herself with the sheet.

"Don't worry," Kyle assures her, stepping further into the room. "We won't hurt you."

Her attention flickers from him to the array of drugs in the room. She's worried about being busted for possession.

Ronnie no longer looks like the man I met at the apartment. His cheeks are sunken in. His pupils are dilated, and his body is frail. The drugs have taken the best of him. Not saying his best was much.

"Gage," Kyle finally warns at the realization that Ronnie is on the verge of passing out at my hands.

Ronnie grabs his throat while trying to catch his breath when I release him, and you'd think he'd be smart enough to keep his mouth shut.

His words only prove further that he's the dumbest motherfucker in the room.

"I see you're here about your cunt of a girlfriend," he says, spitting at my feet.

I respond by swinging my fist back and punching him in the

face. He staggers back against the wall, but that doesn't stop his mouth from talking. Asshole must not value his life.

"Did she tell you how hard I rubbed my big dick against her?" he taunts. "She said it felt better than yours."

I grab him by the hair and throw him down on his knees. My gun goes straight to his temple while I grit my teeth and try to talk myself down from blowing his brains out. The chick screams while Kyle rushes to my side.

"Okay, that's enough!" Kyle cries out.

I'm conflicted about my next move. The gun stays in its place, biting into Ronnie's head, and the anger inside me can't dim enough to convince me to pull back.

I can't shoot him.

I'd lose everything.

It's also not who I am.

I'm not a killer.

"Goddamn it," I hiss when Kyle slowly takes the gun from me.

Seconds later, a deep pain thrums through my head when the naked junkie chick strikes me in the side of the face with a candlestick.

CHAPTER THIRTY-NINE

Lauren

"BARNES, your hunk of a police boyfriend is here," Jay announces, throwing open the break-room door and waking me up from my nap. A conflicted look flickers across his face.

I rub at my tired eyes. It was nice, being in Gage's arms last night, but our pillow fort was far from comfortable. "Huh?"

Am I still dreaming?

"Gage is here," he clarifies.

I jump up from the couch. "To visit me?"

He had a full shift at work today, so for him to be here this early means something is up.

"Nope. He's in the ER."

"The hell?" I shove past him and run down the hallway, my heart on fire.

Jay stays behind me while relaying information. "From what it looked like, he got himself into an altercation. There's blood but no broken limbs or trauma."

Of course he did.

"Even though he's fine," Jay goes on, "he's insisting you're his nurse. Word is, he and your landlord threw blows at each other." He pats my back. "He's waiting for you in Lavender."

I stop to look at him. "Lavender? We never send patients there."

Lavender is a room the size of a closet that wasn't given a second chance during the hospital's latest remodel. It got its name because everything—the walls, the decor—is a dingy purple. The overstock supplies are stored in there, and we only use it as a last resort, so I'm confused on why he's in there. We've been slow today and nowhere near crowded.

"Your man isn't in much need of medical attention, to be honest. Therefore, he was sent to Lavender." He shoves the iPad we keep our charts on into my hands. "I'll give you some time, and I won't come in until you call me and tell me it's safe."

"It's safe?" I repeat.

He elbows me. "In case he needs you to *care for him*."

I slap his arm. "I'm at freaking work, Jay! Not at some porn shoot!"

He walks away, laughing, and I run down the hallway to Lavender. I swing the door open to find Gage in a gown, sitting in a chair, holding a piece of gauze to the side of his face. His cheek is caked with blood, and his lip is cut. Other than that, he seems to be untouched.

A sense of déjà vu rams into me from the last time he came into the hospital.

"Jesus, stitches again?" I hiss, storming into the room. "What the hell happened?"

My question is dumb because I already know. There's no doubt in my mind that Gage hunted down Ronnie today. I could see the fury in his face when he left this morning but didn't think it'd end up with him in the hospital.

"Ronnie's junkie girlfriend thanked me for taking her sleazy boyfriend away by smacking me with a candlestick," he says.

"Are you nuts?" I screech. "Ronnie is a dangerous drug dealer. You could've been killed."

"But I wasn't. The fucker is weak sauce, Dyson. No one is scared of him. Hell, I had him pinned against the wall, and he didn't do shit. It was his fuckmate who took matters into her own hands." He stands and grabs me around the waist, no pain in his eyes. "Trust me, he looks worse than I do."

He pushes into me, and I shiver at the feel of his erection brushing against my scrubs.

"I came here for some TLC, Nurse Barnes."

I wrap my arms around his neck and laugh. "Oh, really?"

A smile tilts at his lips. "I told you my favorite porn was patient and nurse."

"That porn dream will have to wait unless you want to get off while I give you stitches."

He nuzzles my neck. "The stitches can wait."

My blood runs hot when I look down and see the length of his manhood under the thin gown.

"Right now, I have something else I want you to heal."

I expel a long breath. "I can get fired for this, you know?"

I untie the back of the gown, revealing his throbbing cock, before dropping to my knees. I'm not sure who's more turned on —him or me.

Gage's fingers wrap around my ponytail. "Jay said he'd give us plenty of time for you to make me feel better."

His dick twitches when I wrap my fingers around it and start stroking him.

"I'm so going to hell for this."

I grunt when I'm picked up and tossed on the ancient medical bed. He strips off my scrubs and climbs over me.

"If this is what brings you there, I'll be right by your side."

I take a good look at his wound while he tilts my hips up and places his erection between my legs. "I do need to examine your wound and most likely give you stitches."

"Examine something else first."

With one swift motion, he's inside me, and the bed creaks with our every movement.

CHAPTER FORTY

Gage

"ARE YOU GAGE?"

I lose my breath upon looking up from Andy's grave and seeing the woman standing next to me.

A single rose is in her hand while a tear runs down her cheek. She's a skinny thing, barely any meat to her bones, and her hair is pulled back into a sloppy ponytail.

I know who she is, but I'll let her do the introducing.

I stand up and wipe the dirt off the knees of my jeans. "Yes?"

"I'm Darla Long … Andy's birth mother."

Darla Long is a mother to four other children who were put in the system. She has had six drug overdoses, has been admitted into three different rehab facilities over the course of ten years, and has a record a mile long, full of shoplifting, solicitation, and possession charges.

As much as I should hate this woman for abandoning Andy, I can't.

I can't because, just like her, I let him down.

She shoves her feet against the grass. "I'm sure you hate me for what I did. I was young, an addict, and his father kicked me out on the streets when he found out I was pregnant. Another homeless woman told me that my baby would be safe if I dropped him off at the station. I stood in the shadows when you picked my baby up and rescued him. I watched him from afar while you gave him a better life than I ever could."

"Yet I failed him." I scrub my hands over my face and sigh.

Pain strikes across her face. "We all failed him."

She's right.

She did. I did. Missy did. The system did.

Why is there no better way to protect our children?

"I want to thank you," she goes on.

Her words are like a smack in the face.

"For what?"

"For giving my son love for the time he was here. He had someone who put him first, who fed him and gave him a warm and comfortable home." Fresh tears stream down her cheeks now. "I wish I could've met him before he went to heaven."

My neck goes stiff, and my gaze turns watery. "I'm sorry you were never given that opportunity."

Anger surfaces over the hurt. "And, that woman, I hate her. As much as I want to be angry with you, I can't because I see your heart, and I know it was with Andy every day you had him. It's still there. I want to thank you for trying to save my son when others, myself included, didn't give a damn about him."

I nod, choking back a sob, and open my arms.

She doesn't hesitate before hugging me.

I'VE RECEIVED three letters from Missy since my visit, and each one has been thrown in the trash, unopened. The media attention has died off after no one was willing to give interviews, even for the vast amount of money they were throwing out for exclusive stories.

They brought more charges onto Missy after her admission to me at the prison, but she took a plea again and it never went to trial. Last night, Luke sent me a report, claiming Missy was diagnosed with bipolar disorder, and she was finally seeking treatment for it. Who knows how long she's been suffering with it? But, with her parents' need to keep a clean appearance, I'm sure it's been for years. With her new diagnosis, she wants an appeal now that she is in the right state of mind.

That's the shitty thing about mental illness.

People are afraid to ask for help.

They're ashamed, afraid to be the brunt of a joke, and they feel weak. Not a day will go by that I'll forgive Missy, but the state of her mental awareness casts understanding in me.

I say my last good-bye to Andy's gravestone as the sun starts to set behind it.

CHAPTER FORTY-ONE

Lauren

"SOMETHING SMELLS GOOD," Gage sings out after walking into the loft. He starts to dance by the stove. "And my girl is making gumbo!"

Our initial plan was to buy a house, but we delayed the house-hunting in exchange for staying in the loft. Amos enjoys having us around, and we like his company just as much. It took time for Gage to fully forgive his father for what he'd asked me to do so many years ago, but they're working on strengthening their relationship.

Life is more relaxing when there are no secrets.

It took us a week after Ronnie's assault before we managed to walk into the loft without wanting to puke, but eventually, we put that in the back of our minds. Ronnie is locked up, and more women have come forward with claims that he assaulted them.

From what Gage says, the bastard will be spending a good chunk of his life in jail for the assaults and the apparent drug ring he had going on … in my old apartment building.

I jump off the couch and snap my fingers to stop Gage from taking a bite from the pot. We finally broke down and bought a new couch … *after* breaking our cherished, memory-holding one during a night of drunken sex. I still miss that ugly-ass thing though.

I swat his hand away when I reach him. "Don't you dare touch that! It's for dinner tonight."

Gage frowns and drops the spoon. "Anyone ever tell you that you're no fun, Dyson?"

I smack his stomach. "You didn't say that last night, and I doubt you'll be saying it when we get back from dinner with my family."

He pulls me into him and wraps his arms around me. "I love it when you play dirty."

Amos bursts into the loft without knocking. "You two ready to go? I have a bet with Hudson on the game, and you know how much I hate losing money."

Gage is in charge of holding the gumbo as we walk down the steps and get into his truck. Our monthly family dinners have expanded. Amos along with Gage are always invited. Kyle has also been known to make a few appearances. He claims it's because my mom makes great food, but we all know he likes me more than he puts on. I've graduated from the Satan nickname.

This dinner is important to us tonight.

I move around in my seat, unable to get comfortable, as excitement thrums through me.

Gage leans in before starting the truck. "How long are we waiting before we break the news?" he asks.

"As it's looking right now, about ten seconds," I answer.

————

I'M GOING to chicken out. I'm going to chicken out.

My breathing catches in my throat when I stand up and look at everyone sitting at the long outdoor table in my parents' backyard. Gage and I didn't have a plan on *when* we were breaking the news, but he said he'd wait until I made the first move.

All eyes go to me. My mom sets her drink down, and my dad drops the spoon in his hand. I feel like the main character in a movie who's about to announce a life-changing event.

Granted, I am making an announcement about a life-changing event.

I look down and glare at Gage, who's still in his chair next to me. I flick the top of his head, and he tosses his napkin on the table before standing up and clearing his throat.

There's a beaming smile on his face that hasn't left since we got the news. I nod, giving him the go-ahead, wanting him to have this moment.

He throws his hands up. "We're having a baby!"

The celebrations occur, and my family is already making bets on whether we'll have a boy or girl. All I want is a healthy baby and to be the best mother I can be. I have no doubt that Gage will fulfill the perfect father role. The light on his face when the doctor confirmed the nineteen tests we'd taken were for sure positive was something I wished I could take a picture of and keep forever.

I had held back from asking Gage if he wanted to have children. It was a sensitive topic I wasn't sure how to approach. Luckily, he came to me after *cumming* in me. He helped clean me up and then asked me what I thought about going off birth control and starting a family. Even though he asked it so casually, I knew it meant so much for him to say those words. I had no hesitation in answering him with a yes, but I questioned if he was sure. He nodded, took my hand, and we went to the bathroom together to toss my pills in the trash.

This is his second chance.

Our second chance.

As the evening turns into dawn, Amos is at our side, telling everyone good-bye. He wraps his arms around me and Gage and grins. "You *three* ready to go home?"

EPILOGUE

Gage

I GRIN as I stare at the screen.

It's our first ultrasound. I don't think either one of us managed to get a minute of sleep last night. We spent our time throwing out possible baby names and talking about nursery paint colors, and we discussed whether the baby would look more like her or me.

Lauren's face shines as she squeezes my hand, her focus on the screen as well. "Our first view of our little one."

"I can't wait to meet him or her."

We hold our breath and nod when the tech asks if we want to know the sex.

We nod.

It's a girl.

We're having a princess.

The tech consumes our attention while she shows us our daughter. She has an adorable face with my nose even though Lauren disputes that you can't see any facial features yet.

The photo stays in my hand the entire ride back to our new home. It pained us to leave the loft, but there wasn't enough room for our growing family. We're only minutes away from my dad if he needs anything. The ultrasound photo gets put into a frame, and we settle it between a picture of Lauren and me and one of Andy after his first soccer game.

I've begun dealing with my guilt over losing Andy. The pain of being unable to stop his death will always be there, but it's less frequent now. He's my son whom I lost too soon, a little man who crawled into my life and made it brighter each day. I hope I did the same for him during the small amount of time he had here.

I grab his photo and relax on the couch while wiping a single tear as I stare at my first child. He would've been a kick-ass big brother. Our little girl would have screamed at him for helping me warn off boyfriends, and I could've shown him Blue Beech. His smile would've lit our small town up.

Lauren plops down next to me, and I rub her growing stomach before placing the photo of him on top of it.

"This is your big bro," I whisper, leaning down so that my mouth is at her bellybutton, hoping our girl can understand every word even though it's doubtful. "I'll tell you all about him when you get older. He would've loved you so much."

Lauren strokes my hair as a sob leaves her throat.

She visited Andy's grave with me last month. We bought hot dogs at his favorite stand at the Navy Pier and took them to his place of peace, making sure we had an extra one for him. I now have to live off the good memories, so the bad ones don't pull me back into the darkness.

"Our little girl will be happy, knowing Andy is watching over her like a guardian angel," Lauren whispers.

"He'll be the best damn big brother ever," I muster out.

I kiss her stomach one last time before falling to my knees. The small box has been lodged in my pocket all day after I asked John for his blessing. I exhale while looking up into her curious eyes. Since I asked my dad for my mother's ring, I've been debating on whether to make it a private or public proposal. My mind wasn't made up until this very moment.

She says *yes*.

Giving someone a second chance is oftentimes frowned upon.

Sometimes a second chance isn't an option, but we were lucky enough to realize we're stronger together.

We're no longer exes.

We're going to be husband and wife.

We're going to be parents.

We're going to be happy.

ALSO BY CHARITY FERRELL

BLUE BEECH SERIES

(each book can be read as a standalone)

Just A Fling

Just One Night

Just Exes

Just Neighbors

Just Roommates

Just Friends

TWISTED FOX SERIES

Stirred

Shaken

Straight Up

Chaser

Last Round

STANDALONES

Bad For You

Beneath Our Faults

Pop Rock

Pretty and Reckless

Revive Me

Wild Thoughts

RISKY DUET

Risky

Worth The Risk

ACKNOWLEDGMENTS

I'm terrible at writing these things. I never want to forget anyone. If I have, I'm sorry.

Thank you to my other half, per usual, for supporting me. You help when I doubt myself, plotting issues, and never care about my lack of cooking skills. Thank you for understanding how much time and attention goes into my books.

Thank you to the editors that are the bomb.com: Jovana and Bex.

Thank you to the marketing pros: Give Me Books and Collen with Itsy Bitsy Book Bits.

Thank you to my readers—you are the real MVPS. You have given me so much happiness—I can't even explain it. There are so many books out there, and you picked mine up and used your valuable time to read it.

Thank you to my Reader Group, the ARC readers, and those who have taken their time to leave a review for any of my books.

All of you are so appreciated.

ABOUT THE AUTHOR

Charity Ferrell is a Wall Street Journal and USA Today bestselling author. She resides in Indianapolis, Indiana with her boyfriend and two fur babies. Her passion is writing about broken people finding love while adding a dash of humor and heartbreak. Angst is her happy place.

When she's not writing, she's on a Starbucks run, shopping online, or spending time with her family.

www.charityferrell.com

Made in United States
North Haven, CT
21 August 2022

22982558R00168